"Jesse, promise me you will never do that again..."

Jesse cupped Emily's shoulder. "Do what?"

"Face down three men."

"Emily, I can't promise you that. It's my job."

"To die protecting others?"

He nodded.

"So you can prove you're a good man?"

Her words cut him. "I vowed to honor the law and protect my fellow man, and I intend to live up to my vow."

He heard the hard tone of his voice but couldn't help it. Seemed she wasn't all that different than the other young ladies he'd tried to court who either hated his profession or, even more strongly, hated his background. What had made him think she might be? Only his misguided dreams.

Not that he was courting her or had even considered it.

After all, who courted a woman who didn't know who she was?

Linda Ford lives on a ranch in Alberta, Canada, near enough to the Rocky Mountains that she can enjoy them on a daily basis. She and her husband raised fourteen children—four homemade, ten adopted. She currently shares her home and life with her husband, a grown son, a live-in paraplegic client and a continual (and welcome) stream of kids, kids-in-law, grandkids and assorted friends and relatives.

Books by Linda Ford

Love Inspired Historical

Big Sky Country

Montana Cowboy Daddy
Montana Cowboy Family
Montana Cowboy's Baby
Montana Bride by Christmas
Montana Groom of Convenience
Montana Lawman Rescuer

Montana Cowboys

The Cowboy's Ready-Made Family
The Cowboy's Baby Bond
The Cowboy's City Girl

Christmas in Eden Valley

A Daddy for Christmas
A Baby for Christmas
A Home for Christmas

Lone Star Cowboy League: Multiple Blessings

The Rancher's Surprise Triplets

Journey West

Wagon Train Reunion

Visit the Author Profile page at Harlequin.com for more titles.

LINDA FORD

Montana Lawman Rescuer

HARLEQUIN® LOVE INSPIRED® HISTORICAL

Recycling programs for this product may not exist in your area.

ISBN-13: 978-1-335-36963-5

Montana Lawman Rescuer

This edition published by arrangement with Love Inspired Books.

www.Harlequin.com

Printed in U.S.A.

What time I am afraid, I will trust in thee.
—*Psalms* 56:3

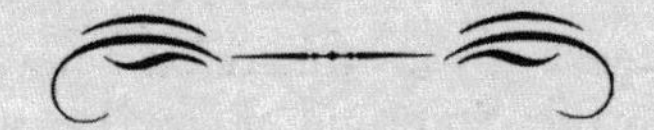

For a special young lady, my granddaughter, Jordyn, on her graduation. You have grown more beautiful with every birthday. Your spirit is strong and beautiful, too. May you follow the path God has set before you as you embark on a new chapter of your life. So proud of you. Love you.

Chapter One

Bella Creek, Montana, summer 1891

What was she doing sitting on the ground, her head throbbing? She slowly turned to take in her surroundings. The stagecoach lay on its side, one wheel broken in half.

"Ma'am?"

Blinking away the pain behind her eyes, she turned toward the voice. A man with dark brown hair and dark brown eyes faced her from a few feet away. A gray cowboy hat had been pushed back, allowing her to see his strong features clearly. He hunkered down on his haunches, his look gentle and patient, making her feel safe even though he was a stranger and she in an awkward position. Or perhaps it was the silver star on his chest that made her feel safe.

"Do you recall what happened? Who did this?" His voice eased through her thoughts.

"There were three men chasing us. They yelled at the driver to stop and shot at him. Then we went over the edge of the cliff." Her voice wobbled as she recalled the terror.

"I'm sorry to question you when you're injured, but if you can tell me anything about the men, it would help."

She pressed her hands to her face, drew in a deep breath and let her mind fill with the terrifying pictures of the robbery and accident. "Three of them, like I said. With their faces covered." She squinted. "One man wore a pair of boots with silver tips."

"Very good. That will be useful in identifying them."

She screwed up her face. "I wish I could remember more." She grimaced.

"Take it easy. You and the boy are okay."

At the man's words, she shifted her gaze slowly and painfully to her other side.

"Mikey?" Poor little boy looked terrified. As well he should. She shuddered as she recalled the horror of that chase, the gunshots making her wince and the scream that tore from her throat when the stagecoach started to tumble. Her heart went to the child and she held out her hand.

With a muffled cry he scuttled to her side and pressed tight to her.

"Ma'am?"

She lifted her gaze to the man waiting patiently.

"I'm the sheriff, Jesse Hill. I'll see that you get safely to your destination."

She squinted as she tried to recall the details of her trip. Obviously she'd been going somewhere to be on the stage, but at the moment, she couldn't recall her plans.

The sheriff kept his steady gaze on her. "What's your name?"

"Emily—" There had to be more to it than that. Emily what? But she couldn't remember.

"Emily?" His voice, deep and kind, prodded her for more information.

"It's…it's…" Despite the pain the movement brought, she shook her head. "I can't remember. I don't know my last name." Panic clawed at her throat. She scrambled to her feet and swayed. "Oh, my head." She pressed her palms to her temples, felt a lump on the right side and moaned.

Sheriff Jesse Hill had also risen and he caught her elbow. "Steady, now. You're hurt. Why don't you sit down again until you feel better?"

"I can't." She clung to his hand to keep from falling and breathed deeply to still the rolling of her stomach. "I must find my belongings. They'll have my name on them."

"Miss Emily, everything is gone." His words drained the strength from her.

"Gone." She sank to the ground and stared at Mikey. How did she know the little boy's name? Who was he?

"Is this your son?" The sheriff squatted down beside her. "The two of you were the only passengers on the stagecoach."

She looked at the little boy, his blue eyes wide with shock, his blond hair tousled. She shook her head, and then turned back to the sheriff. "I don't remember." The words whispered from her as if she couldn't bear to hear them aloud. Surely she would know if she had a child. If she was married. She looked at her hand.

No ring. She squinted. No depression to indicate she'd recently worn one.

The sheriff spoke to Mikey. "What's your name, son?"

Mikey patted his tummy. "I Mikey."

"Do you have another name?" The sheriff spoke softly.

Emily could hardly breathe as she waited for the child to reply, hoping the information would enable her to remember something…anything.

"I Mikey."

She pressed her lips together and blinked back disappointment.

Sheriff Hill chuckled. "Hi, Mikey. Pleased to meet you. How old are you?"

He held up two fingers. "'Most…" He struggled to get a third finger up bringing a chuckle from Emily. The sound ended on a groan as her head protested the sound.

Knowing how any sudden movement increased the pain in her head and brought a twinge of nausea, she slowly turned her gaze back to the sheriff. "Mr. Hill, I can't remember who I am or where I'm going." She would not cry but tears stung her eyes. A sob caught in the back of her throat.

Mikey sensed her distress. Or perhaps only felt his own and again pressed to her side. "Mem…mem… mem…" he chanted.

Was he saying his name? Hers? Or did he mean mama?

Mikey stuck a thumb in his mouth. Somehow, Emily found comfort in watching him suck it.

"Calm down, Miss Emily. You'll be okay in a few minutes."

His assurance drove back the sense of panic. "Of course. My head hurts. As soon as it's better, I'll be better." *Please, Lord Jesus, let it be so.* And soon. Not knowing who she was or where she belonged left her fighting to make her lungs work.

The sheriff patted her arm. "You'll be just fine. At least you are safe and in one piece."

"Not quite."

He eyed her carefully. "How's that? Are you injured elsewhere?"

She smiled though her lips quivered. "I seem to be missing some of my memories."

He looked sympathetic, or at least, she hoped that was what she saw. "I'm sure they'll return once the shock has worn off."

A wagon rumbled down the slope toward the scene of the wreck.

Sheriff Hill pushed to his feet. "I sent for help and here it is. I'll take you to town and we'll sort out things." He offered her a hand up.

She placed her fingers in his strong grip. And then couldn't let go. He was the only thing between her and an abyss of darkness. She shivered.

Perhaps he understood, for he held her tightly. Or more likely, he was only making sure she didn't fall.

"Come along, little fella." He scooped Mikey into his other arm.

Mikey giggled. "'Kay." He patted the man's cheek. "Nice."

"Thanks. Good of you to think so." The sheriff's droll response brought a smile to Emily's lips.

"Not used to being told you're nice?" It felt good to be able to tease a little, despite the seriousness of the situation.

"Get told it all the time," he said with a shrug. "But not often by a little boy who has just met me. He must be a good judge of character." He slid her a look that he no doubt meant to be serious but he couldn't hide the teasing light in his eyes.

She laughed, ignoring the way the sound brought pain to her head. "Aren't all children good judges of character? Accepting us for who we truly are?" The question stirred a thought, as if it meant more to her than simply an observation. She stared inward at the teasing memory, willing it to open the door to who she was. But it flitted away.

The sheriff guided her toward the wagon. Two men jumped down, carrying dark blankets.

She turned to follow their journey. They bent over a body, covered it with one of the blankets, hoisted it up and moved it to the wagon, where they put it in the back.

Emily's legs shook. The sheriff had lifted Mikey up to the seat and turned back to Emily in time to see her fold.

He caught her before she hit the ground and swept her into his arms.

She clung to his firm shoulders. "Those poor men." The driver and the shotgun rider were both dead. She and the boy were alive, but she didn't remember her name. Or a destination. It was too much and she wept.

His arms tightened around her. "It's okay." He didn't seem in the least flustered by her emotions. "I'll take you to see the doctor. He'll be able to fix you up."

"I hope so." Her words were interspersed with sobs. "But what if he can't?" She couldn't hold back the wail but she quickly choked it off. "'What time I am afraid, I will trust in thee. In God I have put my trust; I will not fear.'" The scripture verse had never meant more to her. Not even when…

But she couldn't remember.

"Psalm Fifty-six," the sheriff said. "Hang on to those thoughts."

"Thank you, sheriff. Did anyone tell you that you have an encouraging way about you?"

"Sure, my grandmother says it all the time." He smiled at her, his face so close to hers she could see the dark shadow of his whiskers, the smile lines about his eyes and something in his gaze that filled her with courage. "And seeing as I have no choice but to use your name, you best use mine and call me Jesse."

"Thank you, Jesse." She meant for more than the use of his name.

He lifted her to the wagon seat. "My pleasure."

She closed her eyes as another body was placed in the wagon box. Then the two men climbed into the back. Jesse sat beside her on the seat and flicked the reins. She pulled Mikey to her knees, finding comfort in the warmth of his small body.

"Where are we going?" she asked.

"Bella Creek, Montana. Does that name ring a bell?"

She rolled the name—Bella Creek—round and round in her head. "Nothing. Not even the faintest chime." Montana. That would be why she saw mountains nearby. Why was she here?

He grinned at her. "Maybe someone is waiting for you."

"Wouldn't that be nice?" Except she didn't feel any sense of looking forward to joining anyone. She grabbed Jesse's arm and hung on like a drowning woman to a life buoy. "But what if there isn't? Where will I go?"

"Now, don't you worry. If no one is meeting you, then I will take you to my grandmother. You can stay there until we sort things out." His smile was gentle, promising to keep her safe. Was it the star on his chest that made her feel that way? Or the fact he had rescued her? Or was it the plain and simple fear that she was alone without any knowledge of who she was?

Jesse Hill had known something was amiss when the stagecoach was more than an hour late. Hoping he'd find it broken down, he'd gone looking. When he saw the wrecked coach at the bottom of an incline, he had approached with caution. It might well have been a simple accident, but having been a sheriff for four of his twenty-five years and having worked with the sheriff before him since he was twelve, he knew better than to ride mindlessly toward such a scene.

First he'd seen the bodies of two men. He had recognized the driver and his partner.

Nerves twitching at evidence that a crime had been committed, he'd studied the stagecoach, waiting for someone to make a sound should there be anyone hiding. A movement to the right had jerked his gaze in that direction and he'd seen a child sitting on the ground.

And then he'd seen the woman.

She'd clutched at her head and moaned.

He'd hunkered down before her, spoken to her.

Her eyes had jerked toward him and she'd blinked as if trying to bring him into focus. Dark blue eyes. Golden-blond hair matted with dirt. He'd guessed her to be in her twenties, though he was not a good judge of young women. She wore a navy skirt and blue flowered shirtwaist, now streaked with dirt and torn at the elbow.

He had waited for her to sort out her thoughts and then asked her name.

He'd wanted to soothe her when she couldn't remember. And now she clung to his arm like she was afraid to let go. The little boy snuggled against her as if he knew he was safe in her arms. That alone convinced him she was a good woman.

Was the boy her son? Why else would he be traveling with her? And where was she going with him?

"I will help you figure out who you are." They approached Bella Creek. "First, I'll take you to the doctor so he can examine both of you."

He pulled to a halt before the doctor's house. "You wait there until I help you." He had visions of her trying to climb down on her own and getting dizzy. Perhaps incurring another blow to her head. He gave the two men with him instructions to take the bodies to the undertaker. "Then check and see if anyone is waiting for the stagecoach."

He ran around to take Mikey and set him on the ground, then he reached up to lift Emily down. She was of medium height and weighed hardly a thing. Though he might be feeling just a bit protective of her.

He took Mikey by one hand and Emily by the other and led them into the doctor's office.

Doc Baker looked up, saw the condition of Emily's clothes and bounded to his feet. "What do we have here?"

"They were passengers on the stagecoach. It's been robbed. I found it at the bottom of Knotley's Hill."

"The driver and his friend?"

He led Emily to the nearest chair and she sank to it with a groan before he answered the doc. "They're in the back of the wagon."

Doc nodded, understanding his meaning. "I'm sorry."

Jesse drew the doctor a few steps away. "This is Emily and Mikey. Emily can't remember anything but her first name."

Doc nodded. "I'll examine her." He turned his attention to his patients. "Shall I look at the youngster first?" Doc didn't expect an answer. "How about you sit up here, young man?" He patted the examining table.

"'Kay." Mikey scrambled up and sat facing the doctor, his eyes revealing wariness.

"I'm not going to hurt you." Doc ran his hands along the boy's body as he spoke. "Can you tell me what happened?"

Mikey rattled off an explanation that was mostly unintelligible. Between the odd word Jesse understood and the way Mikey waved his arms, Jesse understood bad guys had chased them. They shot guns and then they flew through the air. "Owie." He pulled up his trousers to show a scraped knee.

Doc examined it carefully. “I think it needs a cleaning and a dressing. What do you think?”

Mikey nodded. “’Kay.”

Doc poured water into a basin and gently cleaned the wound, then covered it with a wide swath of bandaging. “How’s that?”

Mikey nodded. “Good.”

Jesse watched Emily as she kept her attention on Mikey and the doctor. A tender smile curved her lips. This boy seemed to hold a special place in her heart.

Doc helped Mikey from the table. “Now let’s look at the young lady. Jesse, would you take Mikey into the waiting room? I’ll call you when I’m done.”

Jesse held his hand out to the boy. Mikey hesitated.

“It’s okay,” Emily said. “Go along with the nice man.”

Mikey nodded and obediently took Jesse’s hand.

Jesse paused at the door and looked back at her. She sat on the edge of the table, much as Mikey had, and looked every bit as apprehensive. Jesse wanted to offer her some kind of assurance. But before he could speak, she looked in his direction, correctly read his concern and smiled.

“I’m okay. Don’t worry.”

Ironic that she felt she had to reassure him when he had wanted to reassure her.

He pulled the door shut behind him. *Father in heaven, help her remember who she is.* This woman deserved to be with those who loved her. Parents. A brother or a sister. An aunt or an uncle. Perhaps even a husband, though she wore no wedding ring.

Did that mean she was unmarried?

Perhaps she'd be able to tell him after the doctor did his examination.

Jesse sat down.

Mikey pulled a children's book from the nearby table and handed it to Jesse. "Read me." He waited for Jesse to take him on his knee.

Jesse lifted him up and turned the pages of a brightly colored book. "Ball. Cat. Dog. Apple." He read the words and pointed out the pictures without paying attention as he tipped his head toward the door, listening to the murmur of voices.

Mikey repeated each word.

The outer door squeaked and young Clarence poked his head in. Clarence often helped Jesse. "Didn't see anyone waiting for the stagecoach. Asked at the store and at the hotel."

"Thanks." Why was no one waiting for her? What had brought her to town?

He jerked toward the inner door as it opened.

"Mikey, can you read the book by yourself while I talk to the sheriff?" the doctor asked.

"'Kay."

Jesse rose, transferred the boy to the chair, settled him with the book, then followed the doctor into the examining room. "Is she alright?" he asked.

Doc Baker nodded. "A concussion is the only injury I found. It's responsible for her loss of memory."

Emily looked ready to cry and Jesse went to her side. He didn't reach for her hand. He had no right. But she took his and squeezed with a strength that surprised him.

"What if I don't remember?" Her voice shook with tension.

"Now don't you worry, miss. You've been in an accident. You've banged your head. Your memory will return in its own good time. Don't push it or fret. That only interferes with healing."

Her grip tightened. Jesse squeezed back.

"What's going to happen to me? To him?" She nodded toward the room where Mikey waited. "If he's my son, wouldn't I remember? But if he's not, then why do I have him with me?"

Doc patted her hand. "You aren't wearing a wedding ring so I would think you are unmarried. As to who Mikey is to you…well there could be any number of explanations. Perhaps he's a nephew or the child of a friend you planned to meet."

Jesse could have informed the doctor that he didn't sound at all convincing.

"But what are we to do?" Emily wailed.

"I'll take you home to my grandmother." Jesse had already told her that, but perhaps she hadn't thought he meant it. Or had she forgotten that, too?

"There you go." Doc stepped back, his job done. "Mrs. Whitley will take good care of you. As will Jesse." Doc gave Jesse a look that informed him he better do so.

"I sure will." It was all he could do not to wrap his arm about her shoulders and hold her tight. Her situation made him feel protective. "It's my job."

He helped Emily to her feet. In the waiting room, he scooped Mikey into one arm. As they stepped outside, he offered his elbow to Emily and she clung to it. Whether out of fear of her unknown future or out of lingering dizziness, he couldn't say. In either case, he meant to make sure she was okay before he let her out of his sight.

She shivered and he pulled her tighter to his side. Then he realized she shivered from cold, not concern. Dark, rain-filled clouds scudded across the sky.

If he didn't get back to the stagecoach before the rain came, any trail the thieves had left would be washed away.

But he couldn't go until he had Emily and Mikey in his grandmother's care.

The wind picked up in velocity. The sky darkened. He hurried them toward home. He reached the gate and nudged it open.

Emily held back, studying the house.

He followed the direction of her troubled gaze. "The house is twelve years old. It was built when old Mr. Marshall started Bella Creek so people wouldn't have to live in the rough mining town of Wolf Hollow if they didn't want to." His home was two stories. Four bedrooms upstairs. The main floor had a room used for Grandmother's seamstress business, as well as a welcoming kitchen and a cozy living room. At least, that's how he viewed them.

"Come on. I'll introduce you to my grandmother." He put Mikey down and held out his hand to invite her to join him.

She held back. "She doesn't know me." Her eyes came to him. "I don't know me. Maybe I'm someone you wouldn't want to know. Maybe I've done something wrong."

"Have you?" Maybe the direct approach would unlock her memories.

She held his gaze for a moment, then her eyes darkened. "I—I think—" She shook her head.

"Remember what the doctor said. Don't try too hard."

She nodded, relief clearing her eyes.

Was it possible she did have a checkered past? Was she running from someone or something?

It was his duty to find out who she was, and if her past involved breaking the law, he would deal with that according to his sworn duty. He would not be fooled by her innocent looks.

Chapter Two

Emily reluctantly allowed Jesse to draw her toward the house. He'd asked if she'd done something wrong. The question had triggered a response in her brain—one that made her stomach clench. She swayed a little with dizziness, grateful that Jesse held her arm so she wouldn't fall.

She tried not to think of all the things she might be guilty of, but it made her head pound. "Jesse, wait." She pulled him back.

Jesse faced her, his expression so kind that she couldn't swallow. "Everything is going to be okay."

"I don't know that. Just as I don't know who I am or what I've done. I don't even know who Mikey is. My son? A friend's son?" A word hovered in the back of her mind. A word that described Mikey. She almost captured it, but then it slipped away. The wind stung her eyes and made her shudder. Not knowing was the worst feeling in the world.

"Emily, I know you're frightened. Remember the verse you quoted? 'What time I am afraid, I will trust in thee.' Do you believe it?"

She didn't have to think to nod a yes.

"That says to me you are a child of God."

She nodded again. "I belong to Him. Have since I was a child." How did she know that and yet couldn't recall her name or her relationship to Mikey?

"God will not abandon you now. Do you believe that?" His gaze held hers, full of assurance and faith.

"I do." She sucked in air until her lungs would hold no more. "I'm ready." She gripped his hand with all her strength as he led the way up the path to the front door of a welcoming-looking house. He opened the door and called, "Gram, I got company for you."

A dog barked from somewhere inside.

Mikey pressed to Emily's legs. He vibrated and she squeezed his shoulder. "We're going to be just fine, Mikey." The doctor had assured her that her memory would return, though he couldn't guess as to when. In its own good time, he'd said. Be patient, he'd warned. Not that she saw she had much choice.

They stepped through a tiny entryway with oval-shaped glass in both the outer and inner door. The beveled edges of the glass would refract the light and make rainbow colors on the floors and walls that children would admire.

She gave the room a sweeping glance, hoping something would trigger her mind into remembering. The front room in which they stood was welcoming. A dark green couch had a knitted afghan in variegated greens on one arm, and an overstuffed armchair sat on either side of the couch. A yellow canary sang in a cage close to a window.

Mikey noticed it and pointed. "Bir, bir."

"Bird. That's right," she murmured as she continued her study. One big window overlooked the street, another on the far wall revealed a wide-branched tree with a garden table and two wrought-iron chairs beneath its leafy arches. A fine place to sit and read or sew. A fireplace, a full bookcase and a china cupboard of knickknacks all combined to make the room warm and welcoming.

But nothing triggered a sudden remembrance of who she was.

Three doors led from the room. One revealed a set of stairs, the second gave a glimpse of a kitchen. The third flew open and a small, older woman flew out, a little brown dog that looked to be part Chihuahua barking at her heels.

"Muffin, be quiet," the woman ordered, and the dog immediately settled down. "Company. What a pleasant surprise. Do come in. I prefer to serve tea in the kitchen." She hesitated. "But if you prefer the living room, that is fine with me."

Jesse chuckled. "Gram, I'd like you to meet Emily and Mikey. Emily, Mikey, this is my grandmother, Mrs. Whitley."

"Pleased to meet you." Emily offered her hand.

The petite woman had twinkling brown eyes and white hair in a loose bun. Something about the spry lady brought a smile to Emily's lips.

Mrs. Whitley took Emily's hand between her own. "It's my pleasure, for sure." She touched Mikey on the head and dropped her hand again before Mikey could respond. She shifted her gaze to Jesse. "Bring your guests to the kitchen, then you can tell me what's going on."

"Yes, ma'am."

The note of fondness in his voice eased the strain gripping Emily's heart. She knew that Jesse was the sheriff and this lady was his grandmother. From their short interaction, she knew nothing more except they were genuinely fond of and respected each other. It was enough to know she would be safe here until her memory returned.

They made their way to the kitchen.

She studied this room as carefully as she had the other. A worn, wooden table sat by big windows that gave a view of the backyard with a garden in its full glory, a row of raspberry bushes along the fence and flowers blooming in a riot of reds and pinks and white in wide rows. Vegetable plants were visible beyond the flowers.

Another window over the kitchen sink looked out on the side yard and the same leafy tree as she'd seen from the living room. There were also generous cupboards and a polished stove.

Emily held back a frustrated sigh that, although she knew the name of everything in the room and what its use was, nothing triggered her memory.

Mrs. Whitley bustled about preparing tea. She served milk and cookies to Mikey and waved Emily to a chair. Jesse sat beside her.

In a low voice he explained about the stagecoach robbery and accident.

Emily shuddered.

"I'm sorry. I know this is difficult for you." He patted her arm.

Mrs. Whitley touched her arm on the other side. "You must feel all out of place, not knowing who you are, but not to worry, my dear. You'll soon be right as rain in June. You're welcome to stay here as long as you need." She shifted her attention to Mikey and brushed his hair off his forehead. "It will be nice to have a little man around again. It's been some time since Jesse here was small." The glance she gave Jesse revealed a wealth of love and affection.

Emily turned from watching them to study Mikey. She felt a fondness for him that soothed her, but shouldn't she know if he was her son? She couldn't imagine forgetting a child she'd carried for nine months.

She didn't realize how long she'd been looking at the boy, nor how worried she'd become, until Jesse touched her shoulder. She jolted as if he'd awakened her from a dream. If only he had.

"Don't fret. Remember what the doctor said."

"I know. Don't push it."

"Grandma, Emily, I hate to rush out but I must get back to the stagecoach and look for clues before it rains."

"You go do what you need to," Mrs. Whitley said. "We'll be just fine. Won't we?" She directed her question to Emily as Jesse waited at the kitchen doorway, preparing to leave the house.

Emily murmured, "Of course," though she felt like nothing in her world was fine at the moment. Except, she amended, that she was sitting at a table with a kindly grandmother. She'd been rescued by a kind, handsome man whom she felt she could trust. After all, he was the sheriff and his grandmother adored him.

Was that enough basis for trust? A dark cloud hovered at the back of her mind making her feel guilty.

What had she done? Had she been involved in the planning of the robbery in some way? Surely not. And yet that dark cloud of suspicion lingered just out of reach. Why would she feel this sting of guilt unless she had done something wrong?

"Would you like to see your bedroom?" Mrs. Whitley's question sent a shudder across Emily's shoulders.

How long had she been staring into space, searching her mind? She jerked her attention to the woman, pushing back the wave of dizziness the movement gave her. "It's most generous of you to take in a pair of strangers, especially when you know nothing about us."

The woman chuckled softly. "I suppose I know as much about you at the moment as you know about yourself, but we aren't going to worry about that. Your memory will return when it's time and we'll be patient because, my dear, these things are in the hands of a loving, caring God."

Tears sprang to Emily's eyes. She blinked them back. "I know it's so. Thank you for reminding me." She held out a hand to Mikey and they followed Mrs. Whitley out of the room. Her head hurt with the movement but taking her mind to other things was preferable to sitting and fretting.

"You've seen the living room. I hope you will make yourself at home. There are books to read if you care to. This is my pet canary, Dickie." She tapped one of the wires of the cage. "Dickie, say hello to our guests."

The bird made a clicking sound followed by a chirp.

"Good boy."

Mrs. Whitley led them up the stairs. "The first

room is Jesse's. He often has to be up at odd hours taking care of things."

Emily caught a glimpse as they passed the door and saw a room much like her first impression of Jesse—masculine—with a quilt made in dark browns and greens covering the bed, a heavy wardrobe with the door closed and a table beside the bed on which rested a Bible and a lamp. Seeing evidence of the man's faith increased her courage.

"The room across the hall is mine." Mrs. Whitley paused before the open door.

It was decorated with a frilly lace bed skirt, lacy curtains, a white crocheted spread, pictures of flowers and a shelf full of dainty china. Emily chuckled. "His room is so masculine. Yours quite the opposite."

Mrs. Whitley gave her a cheery smile. "You'd wonder how such different people could live together in complete harmony, and yet we do." She led the way to the end of the hall where two more doors stood across from each other. She opened the one on the left. It was a tidy little room with a double bed covered in a crazy patchwork quilt, a dresser and a table, and on the table was a Bible. The window, Emily knew, would look out on that leafy tree. It would be a pleasant place to spend the night. And then? Hopefully her memory would have returned and she could get on with her plans. Whatever they were.

"You can put your things in here." Mrs. Whitley pressed her fingers to her mouth. Her eyes widened. "Oh, my dear. I am so sorry. You have no belongings. Now I wonder what use a woman's and a child's luggage would be to three robbers." Jesse had told his grandmother the details of the robbery. Mrs. Whitley patted Emily's arm. "Never mind. Jesse might find some of your things. If not, we'll soon have you fixed up. I'd offer you something of mine but I'm afraid it would be too small. The people of Bella Creek are kind and generous, though, especially the Marshalls." As she talked she opened the fourth door into a room similar to the one she'd shown Emily. "Mikey can sleep in here. Would you like that, young man?"

Mikey stood in the doorway, studied the room a moment then turned to face the women. "Mem, mem, mem, mem."

"What is he saying?" Mrs. Whitley asked.

"I don't know. Perhaps he's asking for his mama." Emily knelt to face Mikey. "Honey, I don't know what you mean."

He nodded and stuck his thumb in his mouth. His wide blue eyes studied her.

She got the feeling she had disappointed him. But she had no idea why. She rose. "We'll be very comfortable. Thank you."

Mrs. Whitley nodded. "If you need anything, just let me know."

Emily knew the woman couldn't give her what she needed the most—answers about who she was.

"Now, come along and I'll show you my favorite room of the house." They followed her back down the stairs and across the living room to the door from which she had burst not long ago.

Emily followed her into a room full of fabric and a large table on which Mrs. Whitley had been cutting out a garment. An open cupboard held various colored threads and several pincushions. In the corner stood a dress form. Emily circled the room, touching several things. "This feels familiar."

"Good. Feel free to explore. It might help you remember."

Emily lifted a big pair of cutting shears, balancing them in one hand and then the other. She had handled a pair like this. She could see herself sewing a seam, feel the pride she took in her tiny, even stitches. But nothing more would come and she set the scissors aside with a sigh.

"Anything?" Mrs. Whitley asked.

"I'm afraid not."

"Well, not to worry." She turned to Mikey. "I think I might have a few toys around. Would you like to help me find them?"

Mikey smiled. "'Kay."

Emily followed them from the room, pausing at the doorway to look back. The sense of familiarity lingered, but nothing more came.

Mrs. Whitley opened a cupboard that revealed a space under the stairs. "Look at that. A whole box of toys." She pulled the box toward them. "Mikey, have a look and see if there is anything you'd like to play with."

The boy knelt and took out a ball, a collection of farm animals, several books and a little wagon. He soon played happily.

Emily looked about, at a loss as to what she should do. "Were you making something?" She nodded toward the sewing room.

"I am making several dresses for a Mrs. Abernathy. She's in the family way and none of her clothes fit. Would you like to see what I'm doing?"

"Yes, please." Emily moved Mikey and the toys closer to the door where she could watch him. As she straightened, the room tipped sideways. She sank to the floor, clutching her head in her hands.

Mrs. Whitley rushed to her side. "Forgive me. What was I thinking to drag you all over the house? Jesse will be unhappy with me." She tsked. "Can you make it to the sofa?"

Emily struggled to her feet, clinging to the older woman's hand. Mrs. Whitley wasn't a big woman, but she put her arm about Emily's waist and guided her to the couch with every bit as much strength as Emily had felt in Mrs. Whitley's grandson.

Emily practically fell to the couch and leaned her head against the back. The room continued to circle and sway.

Mikey followed them and leaned against Emily's knees.

She wanted to reassure him, but opening her eyes churned her stomach.

"Lie down and rest." Mrs. Whitley placed a pillow beneath her head and pulled the green afghan over her. "Would a cold cloth to your forehead help?" She rushed away to get such before Emily could answer and placed it on her forehead.

"Thank you." The coolness soothed her head.

"Just rest. We'll be quiet. Won't we, Mikey?"

Emily listened to them slip away to the kitchen. Their voices came from a dark tunnel. *Lord Jesus, please make my dizziness go away and bring back my memory.*

The canary sang as she lay there. She might have slept if it had been possible to relax, but she lay stiff as a board, fearing the slightest motion. She willed herself to remember her past, but her mind was full of dark tunnels that led nowhere.

Jesse paused at the door to take off his wet slicker and hang it on the nearby hook. It had stopped raining, but not before he'd gotten a good soaking. The downpour had made it impossible for him to track the criminals. He would go back later and examine every inch of the ground.

He shook water from his hat and hung it next to the slicker. He kicked off his wet boots and left them on the porch, then he stepped into the house. His heart crashed against his ribs at the sight of Emily, motionless on the couch. He hurried forward. Had she…? Was she…?

The blanket over her rose a bit and he gasped a shot of air.

She wasn't dead. But she didn't look very well, either. Although her eyes were closed, tension fanned out from the corners of them.

He slipped closer. "Emily?"

Her eyes flew open and she winced.

"Are you okay?"

"My head hurts." She sat up, closing her eyes for a moment then opening them to study him. "Tell me you found the culprits and have them locked up."

"The rain made it impossible to track them. However, I found something." He returned to the door and picked up the damaged and stained satchel. He pulled a stool close and set it there.

"Does this look familiar?" he asked.

"It's a satchel."

"Have a closer look at it."

"Is it mine?" Her voice trembled.

"Look inside."

She did so and removed a water-damaged Bible and a packet of hairpins. She ran her fingers along the inside. "That's all? Was there nothing else? My clothes? Something to indicate who I am?" She had a desperate look in her eyes.

He did his best to sound more encouraged than he felt. "This is all I found." He'd searched the stagecoach and a wide circle around it, but apart from trampled grass and the imprint of an oddly shaped horseshoe, he'd found nothing. If he ever saw a hoofprint with that contour, he'd know what its rider had been up to the first week of July. "I can't think why they took personal belongings."

A sharp object—likely a knife—had damaged the satchel. He guessed the robbers did not want any reminder of God in their possession and had tossed aside the Bible and satchel. Nothing else remained of the stagecoach's contents or the belongings of its two occupants.

"May I?" She asked permission to open the Bible.

"Yes, of course." He'd hoped for eagerness and recognition, but she showed neither.

She opened the book and read the name inscribed on the flyleaf. "Emily Smith." She looked at Jesse. "Is this me?"

"I hoped it was and that it would bring back your memory." He rubbed his neck. "I didn't find the men responsible for your accident, nor any proof of your identity." He'd failed and was disappointed with himself.

She slowly turned the pages. "Maybe something in here will tell me who I am." Many of the pages were stuck together from being wet and she carefully pulled them apart. Two were thick and refused to separate. "It feels as if there is something between these. But I don't want to tear the paper. I can't bring myself to purposely damage the Bible."

He sensed tears and frustration close to the surface and gently took the Bible from her. "Let me try." Jesse could not get the pages apart. "There's certainly something there. Maybe steam will work." He headed for the kitchen.

"I'm coming." She moved cautiously, swayed a little.

He stopped, caught her arm and guided her into the kitchen where Mikey played with some of his old toys and Gram stirred a pot on the stove.

Gram saw Emily. "Should you be up? You look pale." She gave Jesse a sorrowful look. "I should have insisted she rest. Instead, I dragged her around the house showing her every room."

"I'm fine, though I don't mind sitting." Emily sank into the nearest chair.

Jesse showed Gram the Bible and explained his plan to separate the pages.

"It's worth a try." Gram pulled the kettle forward to the hottest part of the stove and they waited for it to boil.

"Okay, here goes." He steamed the edges of the pages until they softened then slowly pulled them apart. "It looks like a letter." He handed it to Emily.

She stared at the folded paper and drew in her lips.

He sat across the corner from her. “Isn’t it better to know?”

“Maybe.” Fear, hope and caution threaded through her voice. “Or maybe I’ll regret what I discover.” She laughed, a mirthless sound. “Of course, we have no idea if this is even mine.”

He squeezed her hands. “There’s one way to find out. Open the letter.”

With trembling fingers she unfolded the page and read it aloud.

> Dear Abigail and John.
> The bearer of this note is Miss Emily Smith. I have entrusted her with the special task of bringing to you Michael, also known as Mikey. When you asked me regarding adoption I knew he was perfect for you even though he isn’t an infant. He’s affectionate, easygoing and a real joy. Please accept him as your own. It might help him settle if you allowed Miss Emily to stay with you a few days.
>
> I am looking forward to a letter from you expressing your delight at the child I have chosen for you.
> My sincerest regards,
> Your Aunt Hilda

She stared at the letter. “So, I’m Emily Smith?”

“It would seem so.”

She lifted her face, her blue eyes darkened with despair. “But who is Emily Smith?”

He didn’t have an answer for her.

Chapter Three

Emily looked down at her clothes and grimaced. "What am I going to do?"

He knew she meant more than her missing clothes. Her loss of memory mattered far more, but he couldn't do anything about that. However, he could do something about the other.

"Don't worry. I'll find something. I'll go ask the preacher's wife to help." He ignored her protest as he headed for the door.

His grandmother waved him away. "I'll keep an eye on her. Little Mikey is content to play with the toys."

Jesse shifted direction and knelt in front of the boy, recalling how lost he'd felt when his mother left him. Mikey was with strangers and a woman who didn't remember him. It had to be frightening. He patted Mikey's head.

Mikey looked at him solemnly.

"You're a good little boy," Jesse said.

"'Kay." Mikey studied him a moment. "Mem, mem, mem."

Jesse wondered if the boy meant to say Emily or was he asking for his mama.

He nodded. "'Kay."

His answer seemed to satisfy the boy, who returned to the toys. Jesse left the house and headed toward the church and the manse that stood next door to it. It hadn't rained as hard in town as it had at the robbery site, which was unfortunate for his search efforts. He said hello to Evan, the preacher's four-year-old son who played in the yard with his dog, and then knocked on the door.

Annie opened and greeted him. "Hi, Jesse."

Annie's maiden name was Marshall. Jesse had been best friends with her brother, Conner, for more years than he cared to count. Annie was like a sister to him. Funny to think that all three of her brothers were now married and she had married the preacher.

"I have a favor to ask."

"Come on in and tell me what it is."

He followed her into the kitchen, accepted a cup of coffee and helped himself to the cookies she offered. Hugh came from his adjoining office.

"Good, you're both here. Saves me having to tell the story twice." He explained about the stagecoach robbery and finding Emily with no memory and young Mikey who couldn't tell them anything.

"All their belongings are gone. I hoped—"

"Say no more. I'll gather up enough for her and the boy. How big is she?"

"She comes to about here." He indicated his shoulder. "She's slender. Too big for anything of Gram's, too small for yours."

Annie studied Jesse intently a moment.

He couldn't help but wonder what was going on in her busy mind.

"How old is she?"

"Annie, how would I know? She can't remember."

"Give it your best guess. I need to know what sort of clothes she'd like to wear."

"I'd say she was about your age." Annie had recently turned twenty. "Give or take a year or two." He tried to think what else he could tell Annie that might be of help. "She's wearing a blue top like yours and a dark skirt. Just ordinary clothes."

Again Annie's study of him lasted a heartbeat longer than was comfortable. What did she think she saw or understood?

She nodded as if she'd made up her mind about something. "And the boy?"

"Says he's almost—" He held up three fingers as had Mikey. "Smaller than Evan. It must be an awful feeling not to remember who you are."

Annie leaned closer, her eyes sparkling. "Maybe this is an answer to my prayers."

He sat back and stared at her. "You prayed the stagecoach would be robbed?" He shifted his gaze to Hugh. "Did you know this?"

Hugh squeezed Annie's hand, giving her an adoring look. "I think you better explain things."

Annie brought her gaze back to Jesse. "Of course I didn't pray that, silly. I've been praying a young woman would come into your life."

Jesse stared at her. "You can't mean—she might be married for all we know." He recalled her worry about having done something wrong. "You haven't even seen her and yet you—" He shook his head, stunned at her words. “We don’t know who she is and she can’t remember. She might be hiding, for all we know.”

“I think who she is when she can’t remember is who she really is. No masks. Nothing to hide. Just the real Emily. Perhaps more real than the person she is when she can remember all the things that have happened to her.”

He stared at her. Could she be right? “It makes no difference in any case. My job is to apprehend the robbers and take care of Emily and Mikey until we can see them safely to their destination. I have no other interest in them. And I can’t think why you’d suggest otherwise. You know how I feel about women.”

She dismissed his protest with a wave of her hand. “A good woman would change your mind, but I understand you have reason not to trust them.”

He tried not to sputter. The trouble was, she knew too much about him. But her judgment was way off. “Your grandfather is the matchmaker in your family. One is quite enough, don’t you think?”

She laughed. “I’m sure he’ll do his share. But never mind. Perhaps I am being premature.”

“Perhaps?”

“I’ll come and see for myself what kind of woman she is.”

“Now, wait a minute.”

“I need to see both of them to know what size clothing they need.”

“I thought I told you enough.” He didn’t want her coming over. As soon as she saw Emily she would decide she was more than suitable. After all, she was a beautiful woman and, if the way she treated Mikey was any indication, a kind one, too.

But who was she? The question had to be answered before any of them could make a judgment about her.

Emily tried to tell herself she wasn't anxious for Jesse to return. But she would be lying. Yes, she hoped he would bring her something to wear besides her soiled shirtwaist and skirt. But even if he brought back nothing, she found his presence steadying. And why shouldn't she? He was the sheriff. His job meant she was safe with him and he would do everything he could do to help her.

She sat at the table peeling potatoes for the evening meal. At first, Mrs. Whitley had refused her help but Emily insisted. "There's no point in sitting about trying to remember who I am. Far better to be busy."

The older woman had agreed, on the condition that Emily sit to work. "Jesse would have my hide if anything happened while he's gone. That boy takes his responsibilities very seriously." She looked out the window and waved as someone passed in the alley, then continued. "You might even say he is overly conscientious. Now, I don't mean just about doing his job, but about life in general. He has impossibly high expectations of others so he is often disappointed." She gave a sad shake of her head.

Emily didn't know if she meant the words as a warning, but Emily took them that way. What if she had committed a crime or contributed to one? Why else would she have such a worry? And if she had, Jesse would be...well, not disappointed because he had no reason to trust her or have expectations of her.

She'd already wondered aloud in his presence if she might be guilty of something.

But what could she have done? She tried to think of holding a gun and using it for evil, but it didn't feel as though she knew how to shoot a gun, let alone use it to harm someone.

The outer door clicked. She heard Jesse murmur something as he stepped inside.

Muffin, who had been sitting on the floor watching Mikey play, barked then whined and bounded for the door.

A female voice greeted the dog.

Jesse had a sweetheart? Well, of course he did. Emily just hadn't considered it.

He stepped into the kitchen with a tall woman at his side. A stunningly beautiful woman with blue eyes to rival a clear sky and hair the color of the sun.

Emily sat very still, feeling mousy in contrast.

"Hello, Gram. How are you?"

"Hello, Annie."

Jesse turned Annie to face Emily. "Emily, this is my good friend, Annie Arness. She's the preacher's wife. She's promised to find you something to wear, and Mikey, too. Mikey, say hello to Mrs. Arness."

"'Lo." Muffin had returned to his side and Mikey clutched at the dog's back.

"I'm pleased to meet you," Emily said. Annie was married to the preacher?

"Likewise." Annie turned to Jesse. "You didn't tell me she was beautiful."

Jesse gave the woman a look so full of warning it surprised Emily that she didn't lose her smile. Instead, she chuckled. "I'll behave myself. Don't worry."

"You better."

Emily recalled his grandmother's words about him having high expectations of others and wondered if Annie had disappointed him.

Annie turned her attention back to Emily. "I am sorry to hear of your misfortune, and both my husband and I will pray you regain your memory quickly." She clapped her hands together. "In the meantime, I'll take care of finding you some fresh clothing. Jesse, where's my bag?"

Jesse held forth a valise and Annie took it from him.

"I brought a few of Evan's things that are too small for him." She pulled out two pairs of overalls, three little shirts, nightwear, socks and other necessities. "I think they'll fit Mikey okay. Unfortunately, I didn't have anything handy that would be your size. Jesse said you were taller than Gram, here, and shorter than me."

Emily's head began to hurt at the rapid delivery of Annie's words.

Jesse caught Annie's arm. "Emily needs to rest."

"Oh, I'm sorry. I'll return with a few things." She slipped away.

Emily called her thanks then closed her eyes. She heard the chair next to hers being pulled out. A warm hand touched her elbow.

"Are you okay?"

She opened her eyes and looked into Jesse's concerned face. She would have nodded but knew the movement would hurt, so she whispered, "I'm as good as can be expected, I suppose."

He chuckled. “The doc would be proud of your answer.”

She grinned, already feeling better.

Mrs. Whitley moved a pot on the stove. The scraping sound reminded Emily she had offered to help prepare supper.

“I need to finish peeling the potatoes.” Emily picked up the knife to resume her task. She felt Jesse’s study and paused to look at him. “What?”

“Nothing.” He jerked his gaze to the basin of potato peelings.

Mrs. Whitley chuckled. “He’s pretending he hadn’t noticed that you are, indeed, beautiful.”

Heat stole up Emily’s neck and stalled at her cheeks. “I’m a mess, and I know it. My clothes are grubby and no doubt my hair is untidy. I can’t remember who I am.” A sob choked off the last of her words and she clamped her lips together. She would not cry. It made her look weak and needy.

“Everything will be okay.” Jesse sounded so reassuring she allowed herself to believe him. Any minute she would wake up and remember exactly who she was and where she was going.

She pushed aside the swirling darkness her thoughts caused, finished peeling the potatoes and handed the pot to Mrs. Whitley.

The older woman thanked her. “Jesse, why don’t you take Emily and Mikey outside? Sitting in the sun will do them both good. A change of scenery might help her feel better. Take Muffin with you, too. She needs to go out for a bit.”

“Good idea.”

Emily wondered if they'd had the same thought as she…something outside might trigger her memory.

The dog had already rushed to the door at the mention of her name. Jesse reached out a hand to invite Mikey along. He waited at the door for her to join them.

Emily got to her feet, pleased that she felt no dizziness, and went to his side. He took her hand. He might have done so to make sure she didn't fall. She might have let him for the very same reason or it might be she found courage and strength in the way he held her as he led her to a bench by the side of the house. She hadn't been able to see it from the windows. Nor had she seen the little shed at the end of the wide stoop.

He sat beside her.

Mikey chased Muffin across the small patch of grass, giggling with joyful abandon.

She took in the flowers against the weathered picket fence, the shade-providing trees, the vegetable garden and the bushes, and relaxed with a sigh. "Everything about this place is serene. Your grandmother has a special touch."

"My gram is a special person."

"I can see that. So…you live with your grandmother?"

Jesse startled at her question. People didn't often ask him about why he lived with Gram. Those he considered friends knew. But he didn't mind telling her. In fact, with her eyes closed, he found it easy to talk of his past. "I was told that my pa died when I was two, and that Ma couldn't deal with it and started to wander. She left me with Gram. That was before we moved to Bella Creek. We saw Ma maybe two or three times a year. And then we didn't. I was eleven when we learned she had died." And when he'd learned the truth about his parentage.

"How sad for you. I'm sorry. I can't imagine how I would react to such news."

He chuckled in a self-mocking way. "I got angry. I wondered why I couldn't be enough reason for her to stay around. And I don't refer to her death."

Emily said nothing, but he sensed her waiting and he continued.

"I always believed she had died in an accident, but one of the bigger boys—a bully—told me she died in a house for soiled doves. At first, I thought that was a place for unhappy women, but that misconception was soon cleared up for me. Turns out she didn't even know who my father was." He thought of that troubled time in his past. "I thank God that someone cared enough to set me on the right path."

"Your grandmother?" She studied him, her eyes shadowed with pain.

"You should be resting, not listening to my personal history."

Her eyelids fluttered closed. "Who knows what will make my memory return? Besides, your voice eases my headache. Please continue."

"Very well." He returned to their conversation. "My grandmother was doing her best with me, but was on a losing track until Grandfather Marshall came to visit. His wife had been Gram's best friend. He saw how things were going with me and suggested she move to Bella Creek. Said there was need for a good seamstress. But he knew I needed a change of scenery…a chance to direct my energies in a positive direction."

"It seems to have worked. Right?"

Another mocking laugh. "Not at first. The then-sheriff found me setting a fire behind the hotel. He led me to the jail. I thought he was going to lock me up, but instead he gave me a job cleaning his office and running errands. He spoke slowly and carefully. And I listened." Jesse lowered his voice to imitate Sheriff Good's way of speaking. "He said things like, 'Every decision you make takes you down a road. Make sure you choose a road you want to be on at the end.' 'A man is only as good as his word.' 'When it comes to right and wrong, there is no compromise.' 'Avoid all appearance of evil.'"

He leaned back. Thinking of Sheriff Good always filled him with pleasure. "He was a fine man."

He had taught Jesse to be proud of himself, and he still was. His smile turned downward. Not all people valued him as he'd like. Four years ago, Agnes Breckenridge had moved to town with her family and she'd made it obvious she liked him. They courted. But when he mentioned marriage, she'd demurred. Said she wanted more than the small town of Bella Creek could offer. He'd said he would go elsewhere if she desired it.

Knowing he must be honest about who he was, and uncertain what she'd heard around town, he had told her the circumstances of his birth. That's when he learned that she wanted a man with more than he could offer. Not a man who didn't know his father's identity. She left town to return to an old beau and abandoned him to nurse his pain. His experience with women after that had been equally unsuccessful.

He knew he wasn't enough of a man for any woman to love, despite his grandmother's insistence that he was a fine man. He hadn't been enough reason for his ma to stick around and he hadn't been enough for Agnes.

He had no intention of risking his heart again and likely again being rejected. No, sir. He would stick to what he knew he could do well—be a sheriff.

He brought his thoughts back to the present. "Gram has put up with me all these years." He gave a mocking chuckle. Seems she was the only one willing to do so.

"I'm only guessing, but I think that might have been more a pleasure than a hardship."

Her response eased some of the strain from him and he grinned at her. "I've been trying to make up for the misery I put her through for a few years."

She looked deep into his eyes, searching for something. He wished he knew what she sought and could provide it.

She sat back with a sigh.

"You remembered something?"

"Only a feeling."

"Tell me about it. Talking might help."

"It might." She remained silent a moment as if collecting her thoughts. "I remember looking into someone's face, searching for something. I feel like I didn't find what I looked for. But that's all there is. No name. No face. Nothing." Her breathing came too fast. She pressed her hand to her eyes.

Jesse squeezed her shoulder. "Don't try so hard.

Let your memory come back when it's time. It might take a day or two. You know, until that bump goes away." He brushed the side of her head.

She filled her lungs slowly and leaned back. "I'll try to relax." She glanced about the yard. "The flowers are beautiful."

"Gram likes to grow enough to take bouquets to the church every Sunday."

Emily inhaled deeply. "I smell sweet peas." She closed her eyes. "I see myself with my arms full of the flower. I'm happy and laughing."

She broke off and he waited, wondering if this was the beginning of her memory returning, but she shook her head.

"I can't see anything more."

"Stay here. I'll get you some raspberries." He strode toward the bushes. The flowers had triggered a flash of remembrance. Perhaps raspberries would do the same. If not, she could at least enjoy the sweetness of them.

Emily watched Jesse cross the yard, moving like a man with no worries, no hurries. She knew that couldn't be true. Especially as a robbery had been committed, two men murdered and he had in his care a woman who couldn't tell him anything about herself.

He cupped his hand and filled it, then returned to her side and offered the raspberries to her.

"Thanks." What a kind, generous man. She took one and sniffed it, finding the scent familiar and full of pleasant memories. "My grandmother had a big raspberry patch. She let us kids pick the berries and eat them." She popped the berries into her mouth one by one and let the taste explode in her mouth.

He sat quietly at her side, perhaps letting her remember and talk.

She finished the fruit. "I don't recall anything more. Not where she lived nor how many children I shared the experience with." How could her mind be so stubborn?

"Let it be." He stretched his legs out before him. "I might wish I could forget a few things, but I'd want to choose which they were."

"Like what?"

"Being a rebellious young man, as I told you. Knowing what kind of life my mother lived. So sad. It's hard to forgive her."

Emily jerked to her feet and took three steps. Her lungs had forgotten how to work.

Jesse hurried to her side. "What's wrong?"

"I don't know but something you said made me feel—" She couldn't say what she felt. "I'm afraid of who I might be."

He turned her to face him and kept his hands on her shoulders. "Emily, I don't know who you are or what you've done, but I can't imagine it's anything you should be afraid of."

She shook her head, ignoring the pain the movement brought. "But you don't know. I don't know."

He led her back to the bench and waited for her to sit, then sat beside her and took her hands. "Emily, let me pray for you."

She turned her palms into his and held on tight. "I'd like that." She bowed her head.

"Father God, You know the beginning from the

end. You know everything there is to know about Emily. Bring those memories back to her and help her to be calm and patient until You do." A moment of silence surrounded them. Birds sang overhead. Leaves rustled. The scent of flowers filled the air. And sweet, blessed peace filled her soul.

"Amen," he said.

She slowly brought her gaze to his. "Thank you. I will trust and not fear."

"Good to hear." He slipped away and returned with a handful of sweet peas in pink, purple and white. "Enjoy one of the many of God's gifts to you."

She took the flowers and buried her nose in them. "Thank you. God's gifts? I think having you and your grandmother take me in is one of them." She lowered her gaze lest he think her too bold.

Bold? The word hammered inside her head. Had she been too bold in the past? *I will trust and not fear.* She dismissed the thought. In God's time all things would be brought to her memory.

She hoped God's time would be sooner rather than later.

Chapter Four

Jesse watched Emily inhale the scent of the flowers. Several times she had mentioned concern about a checkered past. He didn't know if it indicated that she'd had one or if it was simply a fear born of not knowing. Perhaps he would ask Dr. Baker his opinion. But not now. He sat back, content to enjoy Emily's pleasure in the flowers and Mikey's play as he and the old dog romped about on the lawn. He wouldn't have thought Muffin had that much energy left in her.

He used to do the same with Muffin, only he would have been much older. Someone had left Muffin at Marshall's Mercantile as a pup and Gram had brought her home. The playful dog had provided Jesse with many hours of fun and unconditional affection. Nice that Mikey found the same.

Poor boy. Jesse needed to find the couple who were going to adopt him and see if he could discover who Aunt Hilda was. Hopefully that would give Mikey a home and Emily her past.

He picked up a bit of wood and joined Mikey and Muffin. He tossed the wood. "Fetch."

Muffin raced after it and brought it back.

Jesse gave the wood to Mikey. "You throw it for her."

The toss landed three feet in front of the boy and Muffin brought it back to him.

Mikey bounced up and down, squealing in excitement. He threw the wood again. "Go." He giggled so hard that he fell to the ground.

Emily joined Jesse. "He's sure having fun."

Jesse pulled her hand around his elbow, telling himself it was to make sure she didn't have a dizzy spell. But it was more than that. He wanted to keep her close, protect her.

How foolish could he be? He knew nothing about this woman. Her name but not her past. Not whether she was married, though he'd again studied her ring finger and seen no evidence of any recent wearing of a ring. Unless she was like his mother. She certainly didn't look the part. Not that it mattered. He was only doing his job as a sheriff.

The door opened and Annie rushed out, bearing a shopping basket full of clothes. "I believe I have everything you'll need for a day or two." She set the basket on the stoop and proceeded to pull out three outfits for Emily's inspection. A brown skirt, a navy one and two shirtwaists—one white, the other pink—and a dress that seemed a little fancier. There were more things, but she didn't reveal them. Jesse guessed they were of a personal nature.

"Aunt Mary had them tucked away," Annie said. "She's put on some weight and couldn't wear them."

That would explain the slight mothball smell. Annie's aunt Mary and uncle George ran the Marshall's Mercantile store.

Emily touched the garments. She looked troubled.

He moved a step closer, waiting for her to explain what bothered her.

"Thank you," she said to Annie. "I'm grateful for your help. I just wish..." She fluttered a hand. "I feel like such a nuisance."

"Even if you had your memory, it wouldn't change that your belongings are missing." Jesse touched her elbow as he spoke, relieved when her clouded expression cleared.

"It's strange that they would take everything," Annie said. "What use would they have for a woman's or a child's things? Well, unless one of them was, indeed, married with a child. Or was it sheer meanness?"

"I aim to find out the reason for what they've done, and I will find them and bring them to justice."

Emily grew thoughtful. "I fear I am keeping you from pursuing them. Please don't let me stand in your way."

"I won't." Except she was. He could have continued his search this afternoon, but when he found the satchel he had brought it back to town hoping it would stimulate her memory. He couldn't deny he felt overly protective of Emily, given her situation. But then, keeping her safe and connecting her to her friends and family was also part of his job.

Annie folded the items back into the basket. "I need to get back to my family, but don't hesitate to let me know if I can help in any way." She patted Emily's arm. "You can find me in the manse behind the church. Just turn left when you leave this house and go until you reach the church. We live right beside it. Jesse's office is straight across the street."

"Thank you again," Emily murmured.

Annie hesitated, as if wanting to say more. Instead she looked at Jesse. "Take good care of her. And if you need anything, you know where to find me." She called goodbye to Mikey and left.

Emily twisted her hands together.

He caught them and stilled them. "You're worrying again. I know it can't be easy." He feared she might overtax her brain and get dizzy. "Let's sit again."

"I can't. I need to move."

So they walked to the back gate. There she stopped.

If he talked, it might help her to quit fretting about her loss of memory. "Annie is like a sister to me. She's a Marshall. Grandfather Marshall is responsible for the existence of Bella Creek. When the mining town to the northwest of here sprang up, it was…and still is…a rough place. Grandfather decided it wasn't suitable for decent folk. He has two sons—one is George, who runs the Marshall's Mercantile store. If you need anything, put it on my bill there. I'll explain the circumstances to him."

She turned, a protest forming.

He resisted the urge to tuck a wayward strand of hair behind her ear. She hadn't looked in a mirror or she would have noted the dust marring her face and how untidy her hair was. He was half tempted to pull out his handkerchief and wipe her cheeks but didn't want to frighten her. "Now don't fret. Things will work out soon enough. I'm sure of it. I was telling you about the Marshalls. Bud is Grandfather's other son. He is one of the owners of the Marshall Five Ranch about five miles west of town. He has four children. You've met Annie. She has three brothers, all tall, blond and blue-eyed, like she is. Dawson, Conner and Logan. Conner has been my best friend for a long time."

Seeing that she listened, her own troubles momentarily forgotten, he continued to tell about the Marshall family—how all four of them had married in the past year. "There was a fire in town a year and a half ago. Took out a whole block of buildings. They've all been rebuilt." He told of how the Marshalls had been responsible for bringing in a new teacher and doctor. "You met him. Doc Baker." He related how the community had worked together in making a fair successful in order to purchase a bell for the church. "It can also be used to alert the citizens to an emergency, like a fire."

She chuckled. "Sounds to me like this should have been called Marshallville."

He laughed. "In a way, it was. Bella is Grandmother Marshall's name."

"She must be pleased."

"She passed away years ago."

Emily grew thoughtful. She looked untroubled so he stayed quiet. After a few minutes, she sighed. "It all sounds so…idyllic, peaceful. As if nothing would ever go wrong here."

"There's been a stagecoach robbery and a double murder, so I wouldn't say it has been trouble-free."

His arms were crossed and she rested her hand on his forearm. "I'm keeping you from your task of finding those men. Please don't feel you need to watch over me." She lowered her head, making it impossible for him to see her eyes. "Though I confess I find a great deal of comfort and encouragement in your presence."

Her words made him feel as if he mattered. It was nice to be valued by someone for a reason other than the star on his chest.

He clamped his teeth together. Was he forgetting all those lessons of how worthless he was—to his mother, to Agnes, to half a dozen other young women who had wandered in and out of his life? But he sensed her need for reassurance and could not deny it. "Emily, you can count on me to see you through this."

She tipped her head back. Her gaze held his. He felt her search deep into his soul. She smiled. "I know, and I thank you."

His breath eased out. How could she have such ready trust in him? She didn't know who he was, apart from the sheriff.

Be cautious, he warned himself.

Could he trust her? He knew his answer should be no. But like Annie said, Emily without a memory was likely the real Emily, and he found her sweet and pure.

He must do all he could to find out who she was.

"I hate to leave you, but I need to send some letters to inquire where you got on the stage and perhaps learn who Aunt Hilda, Abigail and John are." It was too late to send messages back along the line today, but he could get letters ready and start asking questions.

"I'll be fine. I'll sit and rest while Mikey plays." She returned to the bench and appeared to be relaxed.

"I'll be back as soon as I've taken care of business."

The best thing he could do for Emily at the moment was help her get Mikey to his adoptive parents. This Abigail and John would be waiting for their child. More than that, they would know who Aunt Hilda was and where Emily had come from. Once he knew that, he would be able to find Emily's family.

"No need to rush on my account." She smiled.

He really needed to leave, but he hesitated to do so. It took a great deal of effort to force his steps to the house. "Gram, I have to go. Keep an eye on that pair, would you?"

She chuckled. "Do you really need to ask?"

"Thanks." He left via the front door.

Jesse strode down Mineral Street, checking on each store. He completed his circuit then went to Marshall's Mercantile. His jaw muscles hurt and he realized he'd chomped down on his teeth way too hard and forced himself to relax. Someone had threatened his town. Whoever was responsible for the robbery and murder, for bringing harm to a young woman and little boy, would be found and captured. Jesse Hill would see to it.

He entered the store and let his eyes adjust to the interior dimness. He circled the inside of the store as George waited on a customer. The displays were familiar to Jesse, so he took little notice of the goods, though he paused to look at the women's wear and wondered if something in the array would spark Emily's memory.

The customer left with his arms full. George turned to Jesse. George Marshall saw almost everyone in the area or passing through because they soon learned his store was well stocked and could supply their needs.

"Howdy, Jesse. Find those robbers yet?"

"Not yet, I'm afraid." He explained Mikey and Emily at the house and Emily's loss of memory, though George had by now likely heard a dozen different versions of the details concerning the pair Jesse brought in.

"Could she at least give a description of the men responsible?"

"Pretty sketchy one. They covered their faces, so she is unable to describe what they look like."

"Didn't find anything at the site to tell you who they are?"

"One of the horses had an odd-shaped horseshoe that will help identify the robbers. The rain made it impossible to follow their tracks." He leaned on the counter. "Any strangers around recently? Someone who might have been checking out the stagecoach schedule? Or someone waiting for an arrival?"

"There was a stranger in town today buying supplies. Said he was joining his partner at Wolf Hollow."

"Sounds innocent enough. Did you happen to notice anything odd about his boots?"

George laughed. "Don't often have cause to notice a man's feet. Why?"

"Emily said the one thing she saw was that one of the robbers had silver-tipped boots."

"Well, I'll sure be keeping my eye open for that and will let you know."

"Have you heard of a couple by the name of Abigail and John?"

"What's their last name?"

"'Fraid I don't know." Jesse told about the letter.

George stroked his chin. "There was an Abigail

and John Newman who lived north of Wolf Hollow. They came in once or twice. I remember because she would always go to the selection of baby items and look so longingly at them that I wondered if she had lost a baby."

"I'll plan on heading out to Wolf Hollow tomorrow and look around." It was the perfect place for riffraff to hide. He had two things to look for—a horse with an odd-shaped shoe and a man with silver-tipped boots. And a third—a couple by the name of Newman.

George chuckled. "How do you plan to find an Aunt Hilda?"

"Now, that is going to be more difficult, I think. An aunt who sends a boy for adoption." That fact alone gave him a few clues. "She could work in an orphanage or be a preacher's wife who helps orphans find homes."

"Or a lawyer's wife. Or she could simply be acting as agent for her niece or nephew and their spouse."

"I simply don't have enough information to go on. All I can do is send letters down the line to the various sheriffs with the few facts I have and hope someone, somewhere can connect the dots." He said goodbye to George and stepped into the street.

He went to his office and penned half a dozen letters, all saying the same thing, then took the sealed envelopes to George to send out on the next stagecoach.

There was nothing more he could do until morning.

Nothing more to prevent him from returning to the house to see if Emily had remembered anything.

Mrs. Whitley called from the back door. "Supper is ready. Come and get it while it's hot."

Emily jerked around. What had she been thinking, to waste time sitting on the garden bench when she should be helping? She rushed to the woman, her haste bringing on a bout of dizziness. She paused and sucked in air. "Forgive me for not helping you more."

Mrs. Whitley chuckled. "It seems to me you need to remember that you have been in a serious accident and need to be resting."

"But I don't want to take advantage of your kindness."

"You need to be gentle with yourself." The older woman studied her with kindly eyes. "Too often young people like you are hard on themselves. If only I could make every one of you see that you need to slow down and enjoy the present."

Emily laughed softly. "I think I have no choice but to do so at the moment, seeing as I have no past and no future."

Jesse came in from the other room. She hadn't heard him return. He squeezed her shoulder. "Whatever your past, your present and your future, it is safe in God's hands."

Mrs. Whitley patted Emily's arm. "I couldn't have said it better myself." She whistled for the dog. Mikey laughed as he trotted after the animal.

"Did you find out anything?" Emily asked Jesse.

"George Marshall says there's a couple by the name of Abigail and John Newman north of Wolf Hollow. I'll go out tomorrow and see if I can locate them."

Her heart clung to her ribs. "I'll come along, if I may. If it's them, then—" She glanced toward Mikey. He would be joining his new parents.

And what would become of her? Would she stay, as

the Hilda who wrote the letter suggested? Or would they prefer she leave them to adjust on their own?

She didn't know what to expect and tears threatened. She would not cry and she forced her attention to the table covered with a red-and-green checkered tablecloth and set with four places of white china. Emily studied the table. Was there something familiar about it? Or was she only hoping for a reminder of any sort? A clear vase held a bouquet of flowers, among them sweet peas, their aroma subtly filling the air.

Jesse pointed her toward a basin of hot water and she helped Mikey wash up, and then washed and dried her own hands and face. A small mirror above the cupboard revealed how disheveled her hair was. She smoothed it back with her hands. Bits of dirt and grass fell to her shoulders.

"I am truly a mess." She would like nothing better than a bath. Mikey needed one, also. But she couldn't ask her hosts to go to the trouble of filling a tub for her. Perhaps she could do it herself. The pain in the side of her head reminded her she wouldn't be able to. She'd have to be content to be safe in a kind home.

She returned to the table and sat on the chair Mrs. Whitley indicated. Mikey sat at her left. Jesse dropped into the chair across from her, and his grandmother sat at the head of the table to Emily's right.

"Jesse, would you ask the blessing?" his grandmother said.

Jesse bowed his head. "Dear heavenly Father, we are grateful for so many things. For the lives of Emily and Mikey spared in the accident." His voice deepened.

Emily stole a glance from under her eyelids,

amazed to see the man's throat work as if his emotions had grown too strong to bear. Did it really matter that much to him? Why would it, other than he was a kind and caring man?

She closed her eyes as he continued. "Help Emily's memory to return. Help me find the men and bring them to justice. Thank you for the sunshine and the rain, for the good times and the bad times, and for the bounty we are about to enjoy. Amen."

"Amen," Mrs. Whitley echoed.

Emily kept her head lowered a moment longer. For good times and bad times? Could she thank God for both? This would surely qualify as a bad time. She wasn't about to rejoice about losing her memory. But she would trust God to bring it back. For that she would be glad.

She took the bowl of mashed potatoes Mrs. Whitley passed, served herself and helped Mikey. Stewed meat in rich gravy, baby carrots fresh from the garden and sweet lettuce, also from the garden, followed. She enjoyed a taste of each.

"Mrs. Whitley, this is excellent. Thank you."

"It's ordinary fare. But thank you and please, would you call me Gram? I think it would be so much easier for you."

"Thank you, Gram."

"The young man, as well." She reached for Mikey's hand. "Would you like to call me Gram?"

His eyes widened. "My Gram?"

"Yes, I can be your gram if you like."

"'Kay." He gave a heartwarming smile then returned to enjoying his meal.

As they ate, both Gram and Jesse told her more

about the town and the area. She suspected they hoped something they said would help her remember, but nothing came to her.

As soon as they finished, Gram brought them each a bowl of fresh raspberries with cream so thick they had to spoon it out of the bowl. Again, the raspberries made her remember a time of laughter and joy and an older woman. She closed her eyes and tried to get a clearer picture of the person she knew to be her grandmother. All that came was a merry laugh and a big red apron with generous pockets.

She opened her eyes to find Jesse and Gram watching her. Jesse's eyes asked a silent question and she shook her head. "I hear laughter, but that is all."

He held her gaze, his eyes full of encouragement. "It's nice to know your first memories are of happy times in your life. I hope the rest of your memories are as happy and sweet when they come."

She caught her bottom lip between her teeth to hold back a protest. When she could speak without giving away her fear, she said, "Seems too much to think I wouldn't have my share of good and bad."

"Every life needs both sunshine and rain. Just like my flowers out there," Gram said.

"Described that way, I will try and be happy about both." At the moment, she'd be glad to simply get her memory back.

But despite having said that, a shiver crossed her shoulders. There were times, she knew, that the bad could be so awful it was more like a destructive hailstorm than a nourishing rain.

Jesse must have read her thoughts, because he leaned forward. "Emily."

She turned to him, immediately finding strength in his steady brown eyes.

"'I will trust and not fear.'"

She nodded. "I have to keep reminding myself."

"I'll remind you as often as I think you need it."

"Me, too," Gram said.

"Mem, mem, mem, mem," Mikey added and the adults all laughed.

When the meal was over, Jesse got to his feet. "I hate to leave you." He spoke directly to Emily. "But I must make my rounds of the town. People need to know I am doing that part of my job."

She rose, as well. "Of course. There is no need to worry about me. I'll be fine."

His smile was gentle. "I'll be back shortly, unless there is trouble, which I don't expect."

She listened to his departing footsteps and the closing of the door then pulled her thoughts back to the kitchen. After all, she didn't need his presence to feel safe.

Except she did. He had become her lifeline.

She dismissed the idea. At the moment she had no past and no future, but she had the present and she would face it without fear.

"I'll help with dishes."

Gram looked ready to refuse then nodded. "I expect it's easier if you keep busy. You can wash. That way you won't have to move around too much."

As Emily scrubbed the dishes, she tried to think how she could manage a bath for Mikey and herself without asking for another favor from these kind people. But the dishes were done, the floor swept and the kitchen clean, and still she could think of no way.

Mikey had been playing with the toys, Muffin at his side. He rubbed his eyes and whined.

"He's getting tired," Emily said. "I need to get him ready for bed."

"Of course. What do you need?"

"Would you mind if I heated enough water to give him a little bath?"

The door opened and closed, and Jesse entered in time to hear her request. "You will do no such thing. Sit down and amuse the little guy while I take care of the water."

She opened her mouth to protest then sat. Fatigue had set in. "I take it the town was quiet."

"Quiet as church. Good thing, too. Or you would be trying to deal with kettles of hot water."

Gram snorted. "Do you really think I would have allowed that?"

Jesse seemed to remember his grandmother was in the room and chuckled. "I don't suppose you would, but now I'm here and I'll take care of it." He gave Emily a stern look. "All of it."

She didn't know what he meant, but she was too weary to care.

"I'd like to spend a bit more time in my sewing room, so I'll leave you two to manage." Gram left the kitchen and soon could be heard singing softly in the other room.

Jesse put water on to heat then went outside and returned with a square washtub. He soon had several inches of warm water in it.

Emily lifted Mikey to her lap, kissed the top of his head and removed his dirty clothes.

With a giggle, he escaped her arms and ran across the room.

Emily was about to chase him when Jesse crossed the room in long strides and scooped the little boy into his arms.

"You little rascal. You come back here." He tickled Mikey.

Jolly, belly-rolling chuckles indicated the boy's enjoyment.

Emily laughed too. "He has the best laugh."

Jesse grinned at her. "Just hearing it makes the world a better place." He headed for the tub and Emily hurried to join him.

She fully intended to take care of washing Mikey, but Jesse knelt by the tub, too. Their arms brushed.

He looked at her, something warm and sweet in his eyes.

She jerked her gaze to the little boy. She understood what was going on. Lost, without memory, she clung to the man who had saved her. He made her feel safe. But it meant nothing.

Jesse grabbed the bar of soap while Emily sorted out her thoughts. He lathered up the boy and rinsed him off. All the while, Mikey chattered away and splashed.

Emily wiped water from her face and stole a look at Jesse. Liquid dripped from his chin. The front of his shirt was dark with water. He turned his head to wipe his face on his shoulder and looked straight into her eyes. He grinned. "Happy child. Wet adults. Is this the usual mix?"

"I think so." She held his gaze and caught her breath. Her answer had come swiftly and surely, as if she was speaking from experience. But no memory came. "I'll wash his hair." She bent Mikey backward and scrubbed the dirt from his head.

"You certainly know how to handle him."

She lifted him from the tub and wrapped a towel about him. "I suppose it indicates something. I just wish I knew what." She stared at the tub of water and remembered laughter and joy. She had bathed a child in a tub like this.

She sat back on her heels. "I remember bathing children." Her eyes refused to blink as she looked at Jesse. Was it possible Mikey was hers? A sob caught in her throat. How could she forget her own flesh and blood? Not to mention a husband. She looked at her ring finger. Bare. She rubbed it. Could not remember ever wearing a ring. Perhaps she'd never married. That made Mikey…

Pain tore through her insides. Who was she?

Jesse caught her around her shoulders. She leaned into his damp shirtfront.

"You're tired and overthinking all this. I think a good night's sleep might be what you need."

Mikey patted her cheeks. "Mem, mem, mem."

She realized they were nose to nose, both leaning on Jesse's chest. At some point, he had taken Mikey from her and she hadn't even noticed. The realization made the dark hole inside her expand and she shuddered.

Jesse tightened his arm about her and sat her up. "I'll dress this little man then help you."

She wasn't sure what sort of help he meant to offer, but as he put Mikey into a nightshirt, she scrubbed the little boy's garments in the bath water and rinsed them. She was about to take them outside and hang them on the line when Jesse took them from her. "You take it easy while I do this."

He led her to a chair, put Mikey on her knee and headed outside with the wet laundry.

She sang a lullaby to Mikey, the tune coming from a distant memory. Was it one her mother had sung to her? And she'd sung to other babies? Like Jesse said, she was trying too hard.

Mikey relaxed against her; his breathing deepened.

Jesse returned, smiled at the little guy asleep on her lap and carried the tub out to dispose of the water.

There went any hope of getting her own bath.

She lifted her chin. Tomorrow she would go with Jesse to turn Mikey over to the Newmans. They would know who she was.

She stiffened inside. What if she didn't care for what she learned? She sucked in a deep breath. She would face whatever the future held with as much strength as she could muster.

Chapter Five

Jesse smiled as he hung the small garments on the line. What a pleasure he'd had bathing and dressing the little guy. Seeing him asleep on Emily's lap, his blond hair damp from his bath, filled Jesse's heart with yearning. He blamed the Marshalls for that feeling. They'd all married and ended up with ready-made families, their happiness evident to all.

Jesse did not plan to seek the same. But he had a job to do, taking care of Emily and Mikey until he could see her safely to the Newmans. He would go out there tomorrow and locate the family. He'd take her along because, as she said, when he found the Newmans they would be expecting Mikey, though it bothered him to think they lived close to the rough mining town. He planned to look around Wolf Hollow for a man with silver-tipped boots, but he wouldn't do that until Emily and Mikey were turned over to the Newmans and safely settled.

He should be happy for them that they had found the family expecting them, but it would be hard to leave Emily in the care of strangers when she didn't remember who she was. Of course, they might know her. Perhaps seeing them would trigger her memory.

While he thought about the situation, he worked. Perhaps he was being too bold in thinking Emily would enjoy a bath, but he doubted it. He had built Gram a little outdoor washhouse at the corner of her home. It was a place she could do the laundry in the warm months and also enjoy a leisurely bath in total privacy.

He returned to the kitchen. "Let me take him upstairs and tuck him into his bed." He edged his arms around the boy. The three of them formed a triangle of bodies. He wanted to pull her into his arms and hold her tight. Assure her he would take care of her. But he didn't have the right and he avoided looking directly at Emily, too aware of the wayward direction of his thoughts. He straightened, breaking contact with her arms.

Mikey snuffled but didn't waken.

Emily pushed to her feet. "I better make sure he'll be okay."

"I can handle this. I prepared a bath for you." By the heat in his cheeks, he knew his ruddy complexion had darkened. Would she be offended by his offer?

Her eyes widened. "Really? You did that for me?"

"I thought you'd enjoy it."

Her breath came out in a whoosh. "You have no idea how much I longed for one. But how did you know?" She brushed her hand over her hair. "I guess it's self-evident."

If his arms hadn't been full he would have caught her hands and assured her he had only been thinking of her comfort.

She looked about, a question in her eyes.

He grinned, enjoying her confusion. "Did you notice the little shed at the side of the house?"

She nodded, her gaze clinging to his, full of expectation. "Yes?"

If only he could answer all her questions as easily as he answered this one. "You'll find a tub full of water awaiting you."

"Thank you." She caught up the basket of clothing Annie had left and scurried away.

He chuckled softly, then took Mikey upstairs and put him into bed. He pulled a chair close and sat watching the boy sleep. The little guy sucked his thumb and snuggled into the covers.

As he waited to make sure Mikey would stay asleep, he prayed for this pair he had rescued and wisdom for himself. Something about their precarious state triggered a protective yearning in the depths of his heart. He recognized the dangers of letting his heart rule his head. But perhaps his concern was justified, even if his duties as the sheriff didn't require he help this pair. He knew what it was like to feel lost, abandoned, wondering if anyone cared. Except he'd always had Gram and he added thanks to his prayers.

Mikey didn't stir, so Jesse returned downstairs. Gram stepped from her workroom.

"How are they?"

He tipped his head toward the ceiling. "Little guy is asleep. Emily is out in the washhouse."

"Oh, good. I wanted to offer her a bath but didn't know if she would think I was commenting on her condition."

The sound of the back door opening warned of Emily's return. She wore a red plaid robe and matching slippers. Her hair hung down her back, now dark as new leather gloves. Her cheeks were pink. Her eyes seemed bluer, as if darkened by the evening dusk.

She kept her gaze lowered.

He understood she must feel awkward. "Mikey didn't even stir when I put him into bed."

She nodded. "I would have emptied the tub but I wasn't sure what you wanted done with the water."

Gram chuckled. "Jesse has it set to drain to my garden. All he does is pull the plug and the water runs out through a hose. Not that we're lazy, you understand."

It was a joke between them and Jesse added his usual comment. "I prefer to think of it as efficient."

Emily grinned at them. "It sounds smart to me. Now if you don't mind, I think I'll go up to bed."

"Of course," Gram said. "You must be very tired."

"I am." She hoisted the basket of clothes, slipped past Jesse and climbed the stairs.

He stood immobile. Was she going to be okay?

Would she have her memory back when she woke tomorrow morning?

"I'm going to make another round," he told Gram and went out to the dusky street. He sauntered toward the center of town, his eyes and ears alert for any sign of unusual behavior.

A horse galloped past, almost running him down.

Jesse jumped out of the way and reached for his pistol. If the rider was set on mischief Jesse would soon persuade him to change his mind, though he would use words before he used his gun.

But the horse skidded to a halt before Dr. Baker's house and the rider leapt off. "Doc, Doc."

Jesse broke into a trot. Sounded like trouble. He might be needed. *Please, don't let it be a death.* It was the hardest thing he had to do as a sheriff—take care of bodies and let loved ones know.

The man pounded on the door. "Doc."

Dr. Baker opened the door. "What is it?"

"My boy is having trouble breathing. We done everything we can think to do."

Jesse recognized Jed Wallace from down by the river. He had a passel of young ones.

"Let me get my bag."

"I'll get your horse," Jesse called, and he jogged around to the back to saddle the horse Doc kept close by.

The others joined him and Doc swung into the saddle.

Jesse caught the distraught man's elbow. "I pray your boy will be okay."

"Thanks, sheriff." He mounted and rode away.

Jesse finished his rounds. Everything quiet. A peaceful, safe little town, just as Grandfather Marshall had planned. Except for three men who had robbed the stagecoach, killed the driver and shotgun rider, and left Emily injured. She was alive, and for that he was grateful. Perhaps by morning she'd remember who she was.

Would she be someone's wife? Would she have a family, as she had wondered?

He finished his rounds and, satisfied all was well, he returned home. Gram had gone to bed, leaving a lamp burning low to welcome him. He slipped off his boots and tiptoed upstairs, careful to miss the squeaky third step. At the top, he paused. When he heard no sounds of distress, he relaxed and went to his room.

But sleep did not come as quickly as usual. He strained to hear any unfamiliar noise. After a few minutes, he admitted he heard nothing to cause concern and fell asleep. He couldn't say how much later it was when the creak of his door opening jerked him fully awake. He reached for his gun belt hung over the post of his headrail.

Faint moonlight revealed the gaping door. He saw no one.

A snuffling sound said there was someone there.

He lowered his gaze. A very small person stood in the opening. "Mikey? Are you scared?"

"I is."

Jesse sat up. "Come here, boy."

Mikey ran across the floor and threw himself into Jesse's arms. His little heart pounded hard enough that Jesse could feel it.

He held the boy tight until he calmed. Now what? He rather doubted Mikey would go back to his own bed.

"I seep you."

He wanted to sleep with Jesse. Jesse had no problem with that, but what if Emily checked on the boy in the night and found him missing?

Mikey scrambled from Jesse's arms and crawled under the covers.

Jesse chuckled. "Seems the decision has been made." He normally slept with the door open, the better to hear any disturbance but had closed it because of his guests. Now he decided to leave it ajar. He'd hear

Emily if she got up to look for Mikey and be able to call out and reassure her the boy was safe and sound.

He settled back in bed, a little body crowded to his back. It was a pleasant sensation, even if Mikey did squirm around and noisily suck his thumb.

Tomorrow he'd take Emily and Mikey to the Newman family.

It wasn't as if he wanted to keep them. The only reason either of them had turned to him for comfort was because he was the sheriff and provided a sense of safety. Otherwise, there would be nothing about him they'd notice.

Hadn't he learned well enough that as simply Jesse Hill—not Sheriff Hill—he was of no value to most people?

Chapter Six

Emily wakened as the pink dawn touched the inside of the bedroom. She stretched. "Ow." A bruise on the side of her head stilled her movements. Every part of her body hurt like someone had used a carpet beater on her. The ceiling seemed whiter than she remembered. The picture on the wall at the end of the bed was new. She looked at the quilt on her bed. Was it new, as well?

She jerked upright. This wasn't her room.

She groaned. "I remember what happened." She'd been in an accident. A robbery. That's what had caused the bump on her head. She sprang to the floor. Where was Mikey? She grabbed the robe someone had lent her and rushed across the hall.

The bed was empty.

Panic clawed at her throat and she groaned.

"Emily?" The voice came from across the hall.

"If you're looking for Mikey, he's with me."

Pressing a hand to her throat, she rushed back into the room where she'd awakened, closed the door and sank to the edge of the bed. She was Emily. But Emily who? She rocked back and forth, willing her brain to clear, but nothing more came. Her memory had not returned.

She went to the window and looked out at the leafy willow tree, reviewing everything she could recall. She was with the sheriff, Jesse Hill, and Gram. She knew she was safe with them, but she couldn't still the fear that intermingled with her frustration. She recalled one more thing. She was to deliver Mikey to the Newman family today.

There was nothing to be gained by staring out the window, and she chose a pink shirtwaist and brown skirt from the basket of clothes and quickly dressed. She used the comb and brush that had been part of the basket's contents along with hairpins and a Bible. She brushed her hair and rolled it into a loose bun then examined herself in the mirror on the bureau. It would do.

Her hands clasped together, she paused at the closed door. She might not be able to remember her name, but she remembered yesterday and how she had clung to Jesse. Perhaps it was understandable, given what she'd been through, but it would not continue. He didn't need to be associated with the likes of her.

She stood motionless. *The likes of her?* Why did that thought come to mind? Was she a bad person? Someone decent people should avoid? But if that was the case, why was Mikey with her? Would someone entrust a child to her if she wasn't a decent person? If only she could find answers to her many questions.

Sucking in courage, she opened the door and stepped into the hall.

Jesse strode out of his room, Mikey perched in one arm and grinning at her over Jesse's shoulder.

Her eyes stung. Mikey looked like he had found home. It was all Emily could do not to rush into the circle of Jesse's other arm. Everything else was gone but the strength radiating from this man.

Mikey saw her. "Mem, mem, mem," he babbled.

Jesse faced her. "I hope you slept well."

"Yes, thank you."

His eyes held a question.

She shook her head. "Nothing."

"I'm sorry." He reached out and took her hand. "It will come."

"Maybe no one cares where I am." She tried and failed to keep the tremor from her voice.

He pulled her close. "That simply doesn't make sense. Someone is out there waiting for you to return from your errand with Mikey, expecting a letter from you to say you have arrived safely. I'm sure the Newmans will be able to help us."

They descended the stairs into the kitchen, where Gram stirred a fry pan of potatoes. A pot of coffee filled the air with a delicious aroma.

Mikey saw Muffin and demanded to be put down. The dog and boy greeted each other with squirmy hugs.

"Do you drink coffee?" Jesse asked.

"I believe I do, and if I don't, I'm about to start."

He kissed Gram on the cheek. They exchanged a glance and Jesse shook his head.

Emily knew he'd informed her that Emily's memory had not returned.

He poured them each a cup of the hot liquid. They sat at the table, which Gram had already set.

"I'm feeling much better today." She had no idea when Jesse would begin the trip to the Newmans.

Gram carried the potatoes, bacon and eggs to the table and sat at her place. "I enjoy having company."

Emily nodded, not knowing what else she could do to help.

"Come to breakfast, Mikey," Jesse called.

The boy climbed up beside the man, gazing at him with wide-eyed adoration.

Gram chuckled. "Seems someone has laid a claim to you." She moved the little boy's plate across the table so Mikey could sit by Jesse.

Looking at the pair of them, seeing the mutual admiration, filled Emily with such emptiness she wondered she didn't collapse like a lifeless paper doll.

Jesse looked at her, his gaze steady.

She shamelessly clung to his look, feeling much like Mikey. *Keep me safe.*

He nodded as if understanding…as if giving his promise.

He bowed his head and asked the blessing on the food and added a desire for Emily to remember who she was.

She silently agreed, ignoring the tremor that raced across her shoulders. She surely couldn't be a bad person. That dark fear was only from not knowing.

After they finished breakfast, Jesse reached back to the cupboard behind him and got a Bible. "We always read a portion before we begin our day."

"I like that."

"We are reading from John's gospel, chapter fourteen. ‘Peace I leave with you, my peace I give unto you: not as the world giveth, give I unto you. Let not your heart be troubled, neither let it be afraid.’” He stopped and met Emily’s gaze. “I believe that is a word you need today. Don’t let your circumstances trouble you.”

Tears escaped without forewarning. “Excuse me,” she managed and hurried from the room. But where could she go? She stopped before the window in the living room, and stared at the table and chairs beneath the tree. If only she could find the sort of peace the view offered. She would not find it in her circumstances. Only in trusting God’s word. But it was so hard.

The canary sang cheerfully, as if to point out that he was confined to a cage and yet he could sing.

Yes, she realized, it could be so much worse.

She sucked in a deep breath and slowly released it along with her worries and fears.

Jesse touched her shoulder and she was glad she had found a safe resting place for her heart before he came to her.

“What’s wrong?”

She smiled at him. “Momentary panic, I suppose, but then I realized how well God has taken care of me by having a good, noble man find me. A man who trusts God.”

He looked surprised. “I’m just doing my job.”

She was only a job to him? She had no reason to be hurt.

His eyes grew serious. “I don’t know much about you but enough to know you are a caring person and someone is frantically looking for you. Maybe not yet, but as soon as you fail to show up when expected."

"I suppose that might be so. Thank you for making me feel better."

"I'm off to Wolf Hollow this morning as soon as I make my rounds." He hesitated, as if wondering if she still meant to accompany him.

Part of her wished to stay here where she felt safe, but only by facing what lay ahead could she hope to learn the truth about herself.

"I want to come."

Jesse made a circuit of the town. He stopped at several homes to check on the occupants—an older woman who lived alone, an elderly couple who were getting frail and often needed someone to take out ashes or get water for them. He visited a home where the children had recently been sick. The mother said they were on the mend and she didn't need him to fetch the doctor or get anything from the store.

Things were quiet in Bella Creek and should anything arise, Clarence could deal with it. He was only looking for excuses to delay leaving town with Emily and Mikey. He wasn't in any hurry to deliver them to the Newman family. But she was no doubt anxious to get on the way.

He got a wagon from the livery barn and drove to the house. For a moment, he sat holding the slack reins in his hands. He could not, in all honesty, delay any longer and he jumped down and went indoors.

Emily stood in the middle of the room, a bonnet on her head and a valise at her heels. Mikey sat on the floor and hugged Muffin.

Emily pulled in her lips. “I’ve told him several times that he’s going to meet his new mama and papa, but either he didn’t comprehend or he didn’t want any more changes.”

Jesse suspected the latter.

Gram watched from nearby, her eyes glistening with unshed tears and a hankie twisted in her hands. “I won’t cry. I don’t want to upset the boy. But I hate to see you go.”

Jesse thought part of Gram’s emotion was due to the fact she didn’t know what lay ahead for them and wished she could keep them here safe and sound. Feelings not unlike Jesse’s. He caught up the bag filled with their few possessions. “Who’s ready to go for a ride?”

Mikey clung to Muffin. “Doggie go?”

Jesse squatted before him. “Muffin has to stay with Gram.”

Mikey’s arms tightened around Muffin’s neck enough that Jesse feared for the dog.

Gram hurried into the kitchen and brought out a basket. “Mikey, there are cookies in here to eat on your trip.”

Mikey looked from the offered treat to the dog and slowly released Muffin. He stood. His fists were curled and his jaw set.

Jesse looked at Emily, and saw she, too, fought her emotions. If only he could change things for all of them, but the boy was spoken for and Emily needed to find out who she was. He took Mikey’s hand and the picnic basket and settled them in the wagon before going back to get their bags.

Gram wrapped Emily in her arms. “I wish you

nothing but the best. However, if things don't work out, you are always welcome here."

Emily sniffed. "Thank you for everything." She clung to Gram a second longer then headed for the door without glancing back.

Gram caught Jesse's arm. "Make sure they are okay before you leave them."

"I will." He hurried to help Emily to the seat, stowed their things and climbed up beside her. He sat motionless, unable to bring himself to flick the reins. If she spoke one word of doubt he would leave them both with Gram and go explain to the Newmans there'd been a change of plans.

She glanced his direction, then away again and said nothing. Her wishes were plain to see.

"Giddyap." The wheels turned slowly at first. He could halt the wagon in an instant. But no one uttered a word. He glanced at Mikey. The boy's bottom lip trembled. Jesse looked at Emily. She stared straight ahead, her jaw set hard, her hands clenched so tight her knuckles were like white marbles.

The town fell behind them and the open road lay ahead. It would take several hours to reach the place George had described. How would he endure watching Mikey and Emily in such misery for the length of the trip?

"I wonder if there's a little boy who would like to help drive the wagon?" he asked.

Mikey jerked toward him, his eyes wide with surprise. "Me?"

"Yup. You're the best boy for the job." Jesse pulled Mikey to his knees and cupped the little hands in one of his.

Mikey took his task very seriously and spoke orders to the horses. Of course, neither the adults nor the horses understood a word.

Jesse shifted closer to Emily. "If you're not happy with the situation you can change your mind."

"I know. But I wouldn't leave Mikey on his own until he's settled."

He'd meant Mikey as well as Emily, but he didn't say that. "I wouldn't want you to miss the beauty of the drive because you're worried."

"Who says I'm worried?"

He wrapped his arm about her stiff shoulders. "You are so tense I could rest a board across here, and the muscles in your cheeks are twitching."

She relaxed her shoulders and gave a smile that was almost a grimace. "All gone. See."

He chuckled. "Good. Now look about you. See the mountain peaks. Some people like them best with snowcaps. I like them this time of year, all blue and moody."

She looked at him. "Why Jesse Hill. I think you might be a poet."

Thankfully his dark skin would hide his blush.

She touched his cheeks. "Too much sun?" Her innocent tone did not fool him. His skin had given away his embarrassment. She smiled and shifted her attention to the mountains. "'As the mountains are round about Jerusalem, so the LORD is round about his people from henceforth even forever.'" She slowly faced him. "The Lord is with us. He will guide and protect."

He nodded. He knew it and wanted her to find comfort in also believing, but sometimes it was hard to let the Lord run things when they seemed to be going a direction he didn't care for.

She continued. "I have been praying to regain my memory, and this is the only thing I have that provides direction."

What could he say? He wanted her to get her memory back. Wanted her to learn her past and who she was. The trouble was, even in such a short time, he had grown to like who she was in the present. He knew she might forget him when her memory returned.

He should be used to being forgotten after all the times his mother seemed to have done so. And then Agnes. And the other girls whom he had not allowed himself to grow fond of. Which, he freely admitted, might explain why they had so readily moved on to other beaus.

They stopped at a little stream for the picnic Gram had prepared. He spread a gray woolen blanket for them to sit on, though Mikey wasn't interested in sitting. He ran. He paused to turn over rocks and study the beetles scurrying away. He ran some more, skidding to a halt to look at the leaves overhead. He saw a crow's nest. A raucous cawing protested the intrusion and Mikey jumped up and down in glee.

Jesse and Emily sat on the blanket, laughing at Mikey's antics.

The boy turned to them and said, "Bird." His face worked. "Gram, bird." With a cry, he threw himself into Emily's arms.

Tears welled up in her eyes as she soothed the child. "Gram's bird will be singing a little song right about now. Do you know what he's singing?"

Mikey stopped crying. He puckered his lips as if to whistle but the sounds he made came from his throat. Yet they were surprisingly like Dickie's birdsong.

Both Jesse and Emily burst out laughing.

Emily hugged Mikey. "That's exactly right."

Jesse turned his attention to opening the picnic basket and putting out the food, not wanting them to see how he struggled to control his emotions. He was reluctant to let Mikey and Emily go to strangers even though he and Gram were also strangers to them.

"Gram outdid herself. There's fried chicken, buns, baby carrots and peas in their pods." He continued to bring out items. "Savory little biscuits." Little biscuits made with spicy sausage meat. She normally made them only at Christmas. He blinked furiously at the sign of her concern for this unfortunate pair. Perhaps she was lonely for more family than Jesse provided.

"I eat," Mikey said and plunked down on the blanket.

"As soon as I say grace." Jesse bowed his head.

"Jesse?" Emily whispered when he didn't say anything. "Are you okay?"

"Fine." He took her hand and reached for Mikey's. He wished they could stay like this forever. It wasn't possible. It had been a long time since he'd allowed himself to admit how much he wanted to be seen as worthy of a woman's affections. However, his mother's occupation had marked him. He was a man with no known father. The lack left part of him missing. All the more reason for him to do his best to help Emily regain her memory.

"Father God," he prayed. "Thank You for the beauty of the world, for the joy of friends, the enthusiasm of children and food to sustain us. Grant us a safe journey and provide Emily the information she needs. In Jesus' name. Amen."

Emily smiled. "That was lovely. Like a blessing."

"I wish nothing less than for your life to be blessed in every way." Mikey practically drooled in anticipation and Jesse handed him a piece of chicken.

They enjoyed the picnic, finishing up with a selection of cookies.

"Gram wanted to be sure we didn't go hungry," Emily said as she packed away the leftovers.

Mikey had taken to running again. Not going anywhere. Just running.

"Let him enjoy himself," Jesse said, in no hurry to leave this spot. "He must get tired sitting in the wagon. Perhaps you'd like to move around, too, before we resume our trip."

"Good idea."

He scrambled to his feet and held his hand out to help her, keeping hold of it once she was upright. Mikey had headed toward a pile of rocks a few yards from where they'd eaten and they followed him. He climbed on the rocks and waved his arms.

Jesse saw a patch of blue flowers hiding in the grass and guided Emily toward them.

"Bluebells. I love them." She knelt and lifted each shy head. She sat back on her heels, a look of peace upon her face.

He squatted beside her, wanting to share the moment.

She turned to him, her eyes a luminous blue as if they'd captured the color of the sky and the flowers.

"What a good reminder. God tends each little flower. How much more will He take care of me?"

For the first time, he realized how uncertain she was about this trip and what she would discover. He cupped her chin with his hand and quoted a verse from the passage where Jesus had taught about the flowers of the field. "'Take therefore no thought for the morrow: for the morrow shall take thought for the things of itself.'" He meant it to encourage her, but it was an equally good reminder to him.

He plucked one stem of the bluebells and handed it to her, knowing he would never again see the delicate flower without remembering this moment. If only he had time to get to know her better. Normally he guarded his heart from such emotions, but her state of mind had brought out a protectiveness in him that was reluctant to let go.

They got to their feet and faced each other.

A cloud drifted over the sun and a cool breeze teased their skin.

She shivered and her eyes darkened.

"Are you cold?" He'd welcomed the breeze to relieve the heat.

"Cold? No." Her gaze went past him, darted from place to place. Tension caught at the corners of her mouth. She made nervous motions with her fingers as if chasing something away.

He wanted to hold her, still her frantic movements, but she seemed unaware of him and he feared to startle her, perhaps sending her into a panic.

"There's a storm coming. I should have noticed. I shouldn't be here. I can't stay." Her eyes were glazed as she stared into the clouded sky.

He was almost certain she relived something from her past and he could no longer stand back and leave her struggling alone. He caught her by the shoulders, cautiously gauging her reaction. “Emily, it’s okay.”

He knew from the way she shivered that it wasn’t. Had she regained her memory? If so, would she remember where she was and who he was? But, more importantly at the moment, was her memory troublesome?

Emily clung shamelessly to Jesse as the fear ebbed. It was something from her past, but what? And why did the approaching storm frighten her? Why did she feel she had to run away? Why had regret and distress darkened her thoughts? What had she done that was so wrong?

“You’re okay. You’re safe. I would never let anything harm you.” His words quenched the nameless uncertainty, filling her with assurance.

“I’m fine now.” Not quite fine enough to stand on her own two feet, though.

He leaned back to look into her face. “Do you remember who I am?”

She smiled. “Of course. You’re my rescuer, Sheriff Jesse Hill.”

Relief filled his eyes. “I thought you had remembered your past. Doc warned me you might forget what happened from the time after your accident until the moment you get your memory back.” His smile was lopsided.

“He told me the same thing.” Why must she have only one or the other?

Mikey’s scream tore her from Jesse’s arms and she

raced toward the boy, who lay on the ground by the pile of rocks.

He sat up and held his arms out to her.

"Oh, Mikey." He'd fallen on a sharp rock and cut his forehead, and it bled profusely.

Jesse was at her side, taking out his handkerchief to wipe away the blood. "It's not deep."

"Thank goodness." She took Mikey in her arms and hurried back to the wagon. "I shouldn't be here. I shouldn't have stayed." Why did she use those words? It wasn't what she meant and yet they seemed stuck in her head. "I'm supposed to be taking care of him. Now he will go to his new home with a cut on his forehead. I shouldn't—" She stopped herself before she could say anything more because the words did not fit the situation and yet she couldn't get past them.

Jesse helped her to the wagon seat. "It was an accident. He's an active little boy. His new parents will love him even with a cut on his head. Or they aren't worthy of him."

His words did little to comfort her. And it wasn't just because Mikey had had a fall.

It was the thoughts that continued to echo in her head.

It was also the knowledge that she would soon say goodbye to Jesse and start over again. He and Gram were the only people she knew at the moment, and the thought of leaving them left her floundering.

It was also the fear of what she'd learn when she found out who she was. Telling herself she had nothing to fear did not help.

"They'll love him when they see him," she said in answer to Jesse's comment.

"Yes, they will."

She looked ahead, facing her future. She had to move on as Emily Smith…someone she didn't remember and someone with something in her past that frightened her.

Jesse gathered up the blanket and the picnic basket, stowed them in the back of the wagon and they were on their way again.

Mikey sat on her knees and fell asleep. She let the warm sun and the steady creak of the wagon and clomp of the horses' hooves lull her into a drowsy state.

Her head slumped forward and she jerked awake. "How much farther?"

"We're getting close, according to the directions George gave me. Mr. Newman said they were near the fork where one road went west over the mountains and the other continued north toward the British Territories. George remembered it clearly because Mr. Newman said Oregon lay to the west and he'd heard good things about Oregon. Look, there's a fork now. I expect that's the one he meant."

Jesse reined in the horses, and Emily sat up and looked about. "There's no house here."

"There's a trail to the right. It probably leads to a homestead. We'll ask there."

The trail was two ruts the width of the wagon wheels. They'd gone a short distance when she made out a house, a barn and a few outbuildings. Smoke came from the chimney. As they drew closer, she made out three horses, a cow in the pasture and chickens running free.

Her heart clenched. Her chest hurt. She didn't remember reaching for Jesse's hand but she squeezed it rather hard.

She and Mikey were about to start a new chapter in their lives.

The chickens scattered as the wagon entered the yard. Jesse pulled to a halt. "Hello, the house," he called.

A woman opened the door. The first thing Emily noticed was the baby in her arms and the toddler at her side. She'd expected Mrs. Newman to be childless. Why else would she be seeking to adopt?

A man stepped out of the barn. "Howdy, strangers. What can I do for you?"

"Are you the Newmans?" Jesse said.

"'Fraid not," the man said.

"You know of anyone hereabouts with that name?"

The man scratched his head. "Well, now. This here place used to belong to John Newman. He and his wife sold it to us. They be the folks you're looking for?"

"That's the people," Jesse said. "Mind telling me where they went?"

"Sure thing. They packed up and headed for Oregon. Said they was meeting some other folks to make the journey. That's about all I can tell you, except they said to send any correspondence that came for them to Oregon City. Hope it weren't important what you wanted them for."

Emily could hardly swallow. One hand clung to Jesse, the other clutched Mikey tight. Of all the things she thought this trip would bring to pass, news of the Newmans moving away had never entered her head.

"Thanks for your help." Jesse touched the brim of his hat and reined the horses in a circle. Not until they were several yards down the trail did either of them speak.

"What now?" he asked.

"I simply don't know. I'm no closer to knowing who I am. Mikey is without a family and—" She couldn't finish.

They reached the road and he turned back in the direction from which they'd come.

"I'll take you back to Bella Creek and you can send a letter to them."

"How long before they get there, do you suppose?"

"I can't rightly say, but I suppose a month more or less, depending on circumstances."

"They might be there already. I'll write as soon as we get back. But—"

"But how are you going to get him to them now they are in Oregon?"

She nodded. "I can't see them making the return journey this year. They'd end up crossing the mountain passes after the snows came." She couldn't send Mikey with strangers making the journey. She couldn't think what she should do.

"You can only do what is humanly possible. The results are in God's hands."

"I know." She sounded as uncertain as she felt. "I counted on this leading me to my past so I could learn who I am."

"Don't despair. God will provide another way."

She didn't answer. It felt to her like all possible avenues led nowhere.

They rattled along on the trail back to Bella Creek.

Mikey squirmed and fussed. She gave him a drink

of water. He continued to squirm. She put him by her feet but he wasn't happy.

"He's tired of being confined. We'll stop over there and take a break." Jesse turned off the road toward a little clump of trees. "It's a good thing Gram was so generous with the food," he said as they shared the last of the picnic lunch. Mikey was the only one unaffected by the results of their trip and ran around with abandon.

Emily couldn't sit still, couldn't stand still, and paced from the wagon to the trees and back again.

Jesse leaned against the wagon box and watched her. "I wish I could help."

"I need to know who I am." She turned and made another circuit.

Perhaps understanding that her inner turmoil was too great for her to be able to relax, he left her to pace and went to Mikey, chasing him and making him laugh.

The sound of such abandoned joy stilled her worries. Things would work out. She just had to trust and wait.

The rest of the return trip passed in relative peace. She filled her senses with the beauty of her surroundings, the pleasure of the little boy on her knees and the steady presence of Jesse at her side.

They reached Bella Creek and drove toward Gram's house.

Jesse set Mikey on the ground and helped Emily alight. She clung to his arm as they went to the door and stepped into the house.

Muffin nearly turned inside out in excitement at

the sight of the little boy, and Mikey fell to his knees and hugged the dog.

Gram came from the sewing room. “What’s all this fuss?”

Emily rushed into Gram’s arms and burst into tears.

Gram led her to the kitchen, leaving Mikey playing with the dog. “Now, tell me what happened.”

Seeing Emily was unable to speak, Jesse explained. “So she is no closer to knowing who she is.”

Gram patted Emily’s back. “Both you and Mikey are safe and that’s what matters. I confess I am very glad you’re back. I was worried about how you’d do if your memory didn’t return.”

Emily swallowed her last sob and stepped away from the warm, welcoming arms. “Thank you, and I’m sorry for being such a baby.”

“Nonsense. I spent a few hours weeping while you were gone. Now I think we could all use a cup of tea and some cookies.”

Jesse pressed a hand to her shoulder. “You have a home here as long as you need it.”

She sniffed. “I am overwhelmed by your kindness.” It was tempting to forget trying to learn about her past and simply settle down in this town and start over.

But she couldn’t. At any time her memory could return, or someone would appear who knew who she was, and what ever of good or bad her past held would be revealed.

Unable to dismiss the dark shadow that hovered over her, she shivered.

Chapter Seven

They ate early, as was their custom, so Jesse could make his rounds about town and Gram could go to bed whenever she wanted to.

As soon as they were done with supper, he pushed back. "Gram, I'm going to take Emily and Mikey for a walk."

"Excellent." Gram turned to Emily. "Now, don't you fuss about helping with the dishes. I can manage quite fine. You run along and enjoy yourselves."

Emily demurred a moment. Jesse thought she might refuse, but then she nodded. "Thank you. You are most generous."

Gram leaned over Emily giving her a hug about her shoulders. "It's a pleasure to have your company." She straightened and nodded at Jesse. "You take good care of the both of them."

"Yes, ma'am." He did his best to sound as if she had scolded him even though he had every intention of keeping them safe.

Emily chuckled. "I can see she raised you right."

He was at Gram's side. "She surely did." He kissed her soft cheek.

"Oh, go away with you." Gram tried to sound annoyed but her pleasure at his compliment brought a pleased look to her eyes.

"Mikey come?" The little boy bounced on the balls of his feet.

"Yes, Mikey can come." Jesse reached for his hand, pleased that the boy was so trusting of him. It made him feel tall and strong and refreshed his intention of taking care of both of them until their future was decided.

When they reached the sidewalk, Mikey dropped Jesse's hand to bend and examine a ladybug. Jesse pulled Emily's arm around his elbow. He was not letting this young woman out of his sight. Not until someone came to claim her. "I sent messages back along the line. Someone sold you a ticket. They'll know something about you, if only where you bought the ticket."

"It will take time to hear back."

"In the meantime, you are safe here."

She stiffened.

Why had he used the word safe? It wasn't what he meant. But he decided to let it go, lest anything he say only make her more worried about her circumstances.

"How are you feeling?" He expected she would be stiff and sore after her accident, but that wasn't all he meant. He wondered how she felt about being back in Bella Creek.

"I have bruises all over but nothing serious."

"Do you want to see the doctor again? He said

your bruises weren't of any concern, but maybe he can check the bump on your head."

She slowed to face him. "Do you think he could help me remember?"

Maybe he shouldn't have said anything. He only thought the doctor might offer some suggestions. Perhaps look again at the lump on her head.

Her shoulders drooped. "He can't help my memory return, can he?"

"He said it would come back. Be patient." He thought of the evening ahead of them, wondered how he could help her.

He didn't have to guard his heart because this was a temporary situation.

Would she even remember him once her memory returned?

Emily was glad when Jesse dropped the subject of visiting the doctor. She would gladly seek medical help if there was any hope of it fixing her memory. But they had both heard the doctor. Her memory would return in its own good time.

Jesse seemed in no hurry as they walked down the street. Emily understood that he was letting her take in the sights and sounds of the town, hoping something would make her remember. She inhaled the lingering heat of the day, laden with the scent of suppers cooking. The sound of wagons and horses trotting along a street out of sight warned her of activity in that direction.

"Howdy, sheriff." A woman with a baby in her arms called from the yard they passed.

"How are you, Mrs. Beech? How's the little one?"

"Good. Good. You have a new friend?"

Emily understood he had no choice but to introduce her and Mikey, but she wished they could have avoided it.

They exchanged greetings then moved on. Mikey barely slowed enough to say hi to the woman. Everything on the ground grabbed his attention.

"Meeting that woman made you uncomfortable?" Jesse said.

"It's awkward to be introduced when I don't know who I am."

"But perhaps someone will arrive who recognizes you."

"So long as it's someone kind."

Their slow pace allowed him time to study her. She tried not to wonder what he looked for and what he saw.

"Are you worried about the robbers?" he asked. "I know everyone around here. I'll know if a stranger rides in. Until then, relax and trust me."

She held his gaze. It was easy to trust him. Even if he hadn't been the sheriff, there was something about him that made her instinctively think she was safe with him.

But then what did she know? She didn't even know her own name. Perhaps her trust was misplaced just like it had been when—

She caught her breath and held on to the thought. Had she trusted someone who had proven false? But who and what? She shook her head.

Jesse spoke. "What is it?"

"I don't know. But I feel like I almost remembered

something and it wasn't a happy memory." She explained what she felt.

"I'm sorry someone was like that." He watched her a moment. "I understand how hurtful it can be. My mother was my first experience in discovering you can't always count on people. Then there was a girl I let myself grow fond of. Agnes Breckenridge." He shrugged as if it didn't matter, but she sensed a deep hurt. She listened carefully for him to say what he'd learned. Whatever he said would be something she should pay attention to.

"Let's just say she taught me a valuable lesson and it's that you can't count on people. I learned to trust people only if they can prove to be one hundred percent reliable. Accept no excuses or half-truths."

She managed to hide her shiver. He'd left no doubt about how he would look at her if she learned she had a disturbing past. She must keep her distance from him, keep her heart from turning toward him, and she pulled her arm from his and put six inches between them.

He quirked an eyebrow but she wouldn't try and explain.

The hoofbeats of an approaching horse jerked her gaze to the street. A man was riding toward them. Who was he? Did he know her? Did he pose a danger?

She forgot all her reasons for the distance between her and Jesse, and grabbed his arm. She looked about for Mikey. Saw he squatted away from the road, watching something.

Jesse tucked her close to his side. "Howdy, Terence." He called to the man.

"How do, sheriff." The man and horse sauntered by.

"It's okay," Jesse said. "He's from around here."

She kept her attention on Mikey who followed a worm along the edge of the road. She despised her weakness. Ahead of them, the street widened to a square with trees and flowers. Benches stood at all four corners, inviting residents to sit and visit or simply enjoying watching people go about their business. She drew back when she saw the number of wagons and horses lining the street and the people clustered about.

Jesse stayed at her side, quietly offering encouragement. "It's Saturday, so a busy day in town."

"I don't think I want to confront so many people yet."

He studied her face and must have seen how unsettled she felt. "Maybe it is too soon. I'll take you to visit Annie. Would you like that?"

"I honestly don't know what I'd like. I feel rudderless."

He caught her hand. "Come on. I know something you might enjoy."

His idea of enjoyment might not be the same as hers. But her pulse quickened at his eagerness and she allowed him to tug her along, Mikey holding her other hand. He turned down the alley.

"The church." He pointed. "The manse where Annie and Hugh live, and Hugh's son, Evan."

"Hugh's son?"

"Yes, Annie started by looking after Evan and she and Hugh ended up married." He stopped them past the churchyard. "You can see my office and the jail through here." He held her shoulders and turned her the right way. "If you ever need me for anything you'll find me there. Except..."

"Except where you're out hunting bad guys or rescuing helpless maidens."

He grinned at her. "I doubt very much that you are helpless." He looked at Mikey, who ran back and forth trying to catch a butterfly. "Any woman who has traveled the country from..." He shrugged. "From somewhere with an energetic little boy with her is far from helpless."

She held his gaze for several heartbeats. Was it true? Was she normally strong and self-sufficient? It was nice to think so. "Thank you for saying that."

"Come on, let's keep going before Annie sees us." He pulled her to his side and they hurried onward.

"What would Annie do?"

"Let me tell you about Annie. Her mother died when she was fourteen, maybe fifteen, I don't rightly remember. She took over running the household which, at that time, consisted of three older brothers, her father, her grandfather—"

"That's the Grandfather Marshall that you told me about?"

"That's right. Most people see the Marshall men as—how do I say this without sounding harsh—"

"Big, tall?" She'd seen how tall Annie was and guessed her brothers might be as well.

He shrugged. "It's more than their size. They're—"

"Wait. Let me guess."

He grabbed Mikey's hand as they crossed a side street, ducking out of the way of a wagon. Jesse waved in response to the greeting of the occupants but hurried on, drawing to a halt behind a shed sheltered by a tree. "You want to guess? Go ahead." He leaned back, grinning as he watched her.

"They're strong?"

He nodded.

"Both physically and in their attitude?"

"Yes, they have strong opinions."

She considered the little bit of information she had learned about the Marshall family. Grandfather had not only started the town, but kept it organized according to his directives. "I'd guess they were used to being in control. Having things done their way."

He chuckled. "That they are." Side by side they sauntered down the alley, letting Mikey explore every nook and cranny. "You'd think Annie would be ordered about by all those men folk. Nope. She is the only one I know who can tell her grandfather what to do and he does it."

"She's bossy? I might feel sorry for Hugh and Evan." Though she'd seemed like a kind person when she brought clothes over for Emily.

"No, you won't. She's good and kind but not the least bit intimidated by the men in her family."

"Good to know." Why did she feel a personal victory in Annie's behavior? Had she been forced to deal with strong men? Cruel men? Why would the word *cruel* come to mind? Jesse had said nothing to indicate such. In fact, he seemed genuinely fond of the Marshall family and respectful of them. Cruelty did not earn respect. Her insides twisted at the idea.

She needed to change the direction of her thoughts. "Where are we going?" Emily asked.

Again, he stopped and pointed. "See that line of trees?"

"Yes, what about them?"

"They are beside the river. Mining Creek."

"Is it a river or a creek?"

"What's the difference?" He waited a moment and when she couldn't answer, he continued. "It flows into Mineral River so maybe it's really a creek. I don't know."

They crossed a grassy field.

"We had a fair here last summer." He chuckled. "Grandfather Marshall ordered Conner and Kate to put it on." He laughed again. "Grandfather is somewhat of a matchmaker. I suppose it helps him pass the time."

"From what I know, it seems to me that men on ranches have plenty to keep them occupied."

He stopped and came round to face her. "You're from a ranch?"

She considered it a moment then shook her head. "I don't know."

"Never mind." He took her hand. His work-roughened palm promised strength and protection, and she shoved away her struggle to remember. Hadn't the doctor warned her she must not try and make it come?

Jesse enjoyed the way Emily quickly recovered from her frequent pauses as something touched a memory but failed to bring it all back. He could tell she had an agile mind.

He held her hand as they went down the narrow path through the trees toward the river.

Mikey pulled away and raced ahead, but Jesse knew it wasn't safe to let the boy go. "Mikey, wait."

Jesse dropped Emily's hand and ran after the boy, scooping him into his arms. "You must not go near the water. It's dangerous."

"'Kay."

Emily caught up to them and rubbed Mikey's back. "We wouldn't want anything to happen to you." The look she gave Jesse, worry and affection for Mikey interwoven, made him forget any idea of caution. He wanted only to ease the worry and receive some of the affection. And if the notion seemed at odds with the way he normally viewed his life, he credited it to the unusual circumstances.

He put the boy down, staying close at hand as Mikey picked up one stone after another and presented it to Emily.

"Nice," he said with each.

"Thank you." She pocketed them.

After a dozen or so, Jesse started to laugh. "You'll soon so heavy you won't be able to walk."

She leaned close to whisper in his ear. "Some are falling to the ground when he's not looking. How high can he count, do you suppose?"

Her breath fanned against his cheek. Knowing he should step away, but unable to remember his vow to be cautious around women, he turned and looked directly into her dark blue eyes—like the water in the deepest, stillest part of the river. Did those two words not describe Emily—deep and still? He did not fear she had a dark secret. As he'd said, he prided himself on being a good judge of character.

What about Agnes? his heart mocked.

Agnes was the one responsible for his guarded judgment.

Except perhaps he was letting Emily's circumstances confuse him. He needed to be more careful of where he let his feelings go.

He made sure to stand between the river and Mikey as he continued to explore Emily's gaze. Jesse felt, as much as he saw, the pleading in her eyes. *Help me find myself.* He vowed he would do so.

Her gaze was long and searching. He made silent promises as her look probed deeper and he hoped she would read them. He was about to give them words when Mikey patted his leg.

"Big."

Jesse looked down and laughed. Mikey held a rock almost as big as his head. "How did you manage to lift that?"

"Big."

"It sure is." Still laughing, Jesse took the rock.

Mikey patted his hands together, pleased with the gift he'd given Jesse.

Jesse brought his gaze back to Emily's and saw admiration as well as amusement. She'd said he was noble and kind. Did she admire him for other qualities, as well? When she got her memory back would she see him differently? Like his mother had? Like Agnes had? He heard the warning in his questions but he could not deny the pleasure in sharing a few moments with her.

Only the need to watch Mikey overruled the call of his heart and he jerked away to follow the boy. They stood on the bank and he showed Mikey how to skip a stone. Mikey grabbed rock after rock and threw them into the water, laughing at the splash they made.

Jesse chuckled, heard Emily laugh, too. She came

to his side, standing close enough that their arms brushed. There was something special about sharing the moment with them. He remained motionless enjoying the warmth of his arm against hers.

She grew quiet, staring toward the trees across the river, her expression serious.

He held his breath, afraid to intrude into her thoughts. Was she remembering?

She sighed and looked at him. Then let her gaze slip past him to Mikey and she grinned. "We better move on before he clears the bank of every last rock."

"I have something special to show you."

"You mean, this isn't it?" Her eyes widened. "It gets better?"

He squinted at her, trying to decide if she teased or not, but he didn't have long to wait as the corners of her mouth crinkled. With a little chuckle, he took her hand. "I can't take any credit for the surprise I have for you. It's all God's creation." He scooped Mikey into his other arm and they walked along the shore.

Mikey babbled away. Occasionally Jesse understood a word or two but not enough to have any idea of what the boy said. He grinned at Emily. "I wish I could speak Mikey. He might be able to tell us lots of things."

"He certainly tries."

The creek turned ahead of them. Rather than following the curve, he drew them toward a little meadow in the crook formed by the bend in the creek. He'd visited a few days ago so knew what to expect.

"This is one of my favorite places."

"Because it's so peaceful?"

He caught the hint of teasing in her voice and

laughed. "Maybe in part, but mostly because there is always something new to see."

She moved away, looking about at the tall grass, the tiny bluebells, and then she saw the flash of brilliant orange. "Wild tiger lilies. They're beautiful. I only recall seeing them once before and that was—" She stared into the distance as she tried to remember.

He waited, silent, hopeful and nervous.

She twitched and let out a sigh, then turned back to admiring the flowers.

She hadn't remembered. Tension slipped from his shoulders—a mixture of relief and disappointment.

"Would you like me to cut a few stems so you can take them home?"

"I don't think so, thanks. There are plenty of flowers in your grandmother's garden. It seems a shame to think of ripping them from where they belong. I'd prefer to leave these here for others to enjoy."

He hadn't thought of ripping them, as she said. Did her words signify something about her past?

They poked about for a bit longer before Mikey came to him.

"Up." He lifted his arms to Jesse.

Jesse picked him up. "Did we tire you out?"

For an answer, Mikey rested his head on Jesse's shoulder and stuck his thumb in his mouth.

"Let's go home." He turned back the way they had come.

She stumbled on the rough ground and caught herself by grabbing his elbow.

"Hold my arm," he said. "The last thing we want is for you to take another tumble."

She clung to him, her breathing rapid, as if she'd been running.

He stopped to look at her. "Are you okay?"

"Yes. I just relived those few seconds when the stagecoach went over the edge." She shivered and her voice fell to a whisper. "It was terrifying."

He shifted Mikey. The little guy protested being disturbed. "Shh. You're okay." He pulled Emily to his side. By rights, she should have died in the accident or been shot like the two men. "God protected you." Somehow he managed to keep his voice steady. But to think he might have found this pair in the same condition as the driver and shotgun rider twisted his stomach into a knot.

"I know, and I'm grateful." She sucked in air, but they only went a few more steps before she pulled away. "I'm fine. I know my life was in God's hands at the time. Just as it is now."

She sounded strong but he knew she must feel uncertainty, given her loss of memory.

They left the shelter of the trees. He glanced about, making certain no danger faced them. They crossed the open meadow. Again they headed for the alley. She might be strong but she wasn't ready to deal with a bunch of strangers, not knowing who to trust and who to be fearful of.

They drew abreast of the manse. Annie flew out the back door and across the yard. "I was hoping to see you."

"For your sake I was hoping to avoid her," Jesse murmured.

"She's safe, isn't she?"

He wondered at her choice of words, but Annie

had reached them and he couldn't ask her about it. "Tomorrow after church we're gathering at the ranch. Jesse, we want you to come, too, and bring Emily and Mikey."

"I don't know," he replied. Emily had made it clear she wasn't keen on meeting others.

Annie wasn't above begging. "Please. It won't be the same without you."

"Emily isn't really up to a lot of socializing."

To his surprise, Emily spoke up. "I don't mind. It might be interesting to meet the Marshalls I've heard so much about."

Annie's eyebrows rose. "What's he been saying?"

Jesse spoke before Emily could answer. "I told her how you boss everyone around and rule the place with an iron rod."

"You said that?" She jammed her fists to her hips.

"I guess you don't so much anymore, now that you're married to the preacher. Seems he's made you straighten out a tad."

"He what?" She looked about ready to explode.

Jesse laughed. "Careful, you're about to prove me right."

She dropped her hands and her expression cleared. "You are such a tease at times." She shifted her gaze to Emily. "I hope he's not giving you a hard time with his teasing."

A hint of pink blossomed in Emily's cheeks. She lowered her eyes then lifted them to Jesse. His heart almost stalled at the warmth in her gaze.

"He's been nothing but a kind gentleman."

Annie rumbled her lips. "Don't be fooled into thinking he's always kind and thoughtful."

Jesse pretended offense. “When have I ever been anything but?”

“Like the time you and Conner locked the outhouse door when Logan was in there.”

“Annie, I was fourteen. Besides, Logan had hidden our knives, so he kind of deserved it.”

“I expect there’s a lot more to the story than that,” Emily said.

There was, but he certainly wasn’t going to admit it to her.

“Say you’ll come tomorrow.”

He turned to Emily. “Do you want to?”

She nodded. “I think so.”

“Then we’ll be there.”

“Thanks for inviting me,” Emily said to Annie.

They resumed their journey home. “You might not be thanking her after tomorrow.”

“Really? Why would that be?”

He couldn’t explain but had to try. “They’re big and rowdy.”

“Uh-huh.”

“Grandfather is a notorious matchmaker. He’ll try it with you, too.”

“He’ll understand that I am not ready for matchmaking. For all I know, I am married with a houseful of children.” She touched Mikey’s back. “Though it pains me to think I might have born children and can’t remember them. My own flesh and blood.”

He needed the reminder of who she might be.

Just as he needed to remember who he was. A man whose mother had been a soiled dove. A man with no knowledge of his father. There was a name for such a person but he refused to think it. He was a man who would never be accepted by women seeking marriage. He'd grown used to the fact, had accepted his unmarried state, but being with Emily had awakened longings he'd considered dead and buried.

He'd once dreamed of a woman who loved him, and of having children of his own to love and nourish. His arm tightened around Mikey and he rested his chin against the blond head of the boy. He would enjoy both of them for a day or two but remember it was only until he could unite them with the Newmans or other family.

Chapter Eight

It was Sunday, and Emily faced herself in the mirror. She wanted to go to church with Jesse and his grandmother. Truly she did. But to face all those people, not knowing who she was…well, she wondered how she would do it.

She squared her shoulders and fixed her hair. She would do it in God's strength, and she'd never let anyone guess how uncomfortable it made her. Well, no one but Jesse. She'd leaned on him emotionally and physically since he'd rescued her.

The mirror over the chest of drawers showed her reflection. Too bad it didn't reveal more about her than the shape of her face and color of her eyes. What she really wanted to see, needed to see, was who she was.

She looked away from the mirror at the sound of Mikey's voice from downstairs. They'd had breakfast, and she'd dressed him in clean clothes and left him with Jesse while she changed into the gray dress that Annie had brought her. Mikey squealed and Jesse laughed—a deep melodious sound. She pictured Jesse chasing the boy, catching him and tossing him up into the air.

With her shoulder against the door frame, she stood there, listening not only to the two downstairs but to the thoughts in her head. Why did she hear the sound of many children laughing? Not hers. She was almost certain of that. Then whose?

And why had Mikey been sent with her?

With a deep sigh, she went down the stairs prepared to ignore her fears and face a church full of people. It wasn't that it mattered they were strangers to her. What mattered more was that she was a stranger to herself.

She stepped into the living room, her presence announced by a bark from Muffin.

Jesse was bent over Mikey, tickling him, but straightened at Muffin's greeting. His glance swept over her and he met her gaze.

"You look very nice."

"Thank you. So do you." His black hair gleamed. His face, cleanly shaven, still revealed the dark shadow of his whiskers. He wore black trousers, a crisp white shirt and a black vest.

"Where's your star?" She'd gotten used to seeing it and feeling safe.

He turned back the lapel of his vest to reveal it pinned to his shirt.

"Good."

He quirked an eyebrow, asking for an explanation.

Heat rose in her cheeks at how much she'd revealed about her dependence on him. "What if you need to be sheriff before we get back?" She turned her attention to the bird. "How are you, Dickie?"

The bird flapped his wings and scolded her.

"Dickie, behave yourself." Gram hurried from the kitchen wearing a hat and carrying gloves.

Emily had neither. She could use the lack as an excuse to miss church. Except she needed to be with other believers and find strength in the worship service.

Gram hurried up the stairs and returned with gloves and a pretty gray bonnet. "I'd like you to use these."

Both grateful and regretful that she would have no reason to stay away from the service, she thanked the woman and went to the kitchen and the little mirror to put on the bonnet.

"It's a very fine bonnet. Looks good on you." Jesse stood in the doorway watching, Mikey perched in his arms, looking as if he belonged there.

A warning bell sounded in her head. The little guy was becoming very fond of Jesse. He was going to be hurt when he had to leave to go wherever he would go now. Presumably back to where they came from and whoever had sent them, and there they would wait for the Newmans to make arrangements.

The sooner she remembered who she was, the better for everyone involved. She stared at the wall where the mirror hung, but she wasn't looking at her reflection. *Remember who you are. Why were you on the stagecoach? Who are your parents? Where are you from? Remember. You must remember.* Her head began to ache. Tension pressed against her heart.

"Are you ready?"

She welcomed Jesse's interruption. "Maybe going to church will bring back my memory."

He nodded and escorted her out the door.

"Where's Gram?"

"She left so she could get there a little early. She likes to sit in the church before it fills up. Says it helps prepare her for the service."

Emily smiled. "That's what my grandmother said, too." She spoke slowly as the memory came. "My grandmother wore her gray hair in a bun and had a jolly laugh." The memory ended. "I can't bring forth a face or a name. What is wrong with me?" The question sounded like a wail.

"You've lost your memory. It's frightening and frustrating. But the doctor was certain it would return." He paused. "If it hasn't come back by tomorrow morning, do you want to see the doctor again?"

"Yes! He might have something that will make it come back."

They reached the church, and any more discussion about her lack of memory would have to wait.

Jesse paused. "I'll introduce you as Miss Emily Smith. Most people will let it go at that. Word is getting around that you were on the stagecoach and had a blow to the head."

Jesse grinned at Mikey. "They will have nothing but admiration for this fine young man."

"Mem, mem, mem," Mikey said.

She and Jesse met each other's eyes and smiled. She squared her shoulders and nodded.

He understood and stepped forward, pausing at the first person they met. "Mrs. Abernathy, this is Miss Emily."

Mrs. Abernathy. The woman Gram was sewing clothes for. Why could she remember that and not her own identity? She greeted the other woman and they moved on.

Jesse introduced her to each person as they made their way toward the steps.Then she saw Annie. She knew immediately that the tall men near her were her brothers and that the older man was her father. The white-haired man leaning on two canes would be her grandfather. He might be crippled, but his bearing and his expression still shouted authority. Like she'd said, these men were used to having their wishes obeyed.

The three women near Annie would be her sisters-in-law and the children were her nieces and nephews.

As Jesse led her toward the group, Emily tilted her chin upward. She had nothing to fear from these people. *Do what's right and good in the sight of the Lord: that it may be well with thee.* A Bible verse from Deuteronomy 6:18. Why, she inwardly bemoaned, could she remember this detail but not who she was?

One by one Jesse introduced the Marshall family. Dawson and his wife, Isabelle and their ten-year-old daughter Mattie. Emily wondered if Isabelle was in the family way.

Then there was Conner and Kate and a little girl, Ellie, who was about a year and a half.

"Conner and I have been best friends for a long time," Jesse said.

Conner planted a playful punch on his shoulder. "We've had some good times together."

The third brother edged his way between them. "I'm Logan and this is my sweet wife, Sadie. Kids, introduce yourselves."

An almost grown girl said her name was Beth. A young boy of eight, if she could remember the details

Jesse had provided, said he was Sammy. A shy little blonde girl with big brown eyes said, "I'm Jeannie. I'm four." She turned to Mikey. "How old are you?"

He tried to hold up three fingers but one kept escaping. "'Most free." He worked hard to get the words out as clearly as possible.

Annie pulled her husband forward. "Hugh, this is Emily that I told you about."

The man gave her a welcoming smile then excused himself. "I have to get to the front of the church."

Annie drew a little boy from behind her. "This is Evan. He's four."

Emily met Bud Marshall, father of the Marshall brood.

The man on canes edged forward. "They leave the best to the last. That's me. Everyone calls me Grandfather. I'd be honored if you'd do the same."

She took the gnarled hand he held out to her. "It would be *my* honor." She held his steady gaze. His blue eyes were as bright as any of his descendants'. He nodded as he studied her and she wondered what he saw.

"You'll do just fine."

"Grandfather!" Annie scolded.

"I'll do for what?" Emily asked.

"Be an addition to our community."

"I don't think—"

Grandfather waved aside Annie's protest. "I can tell you are a good and kind woman. Just the sort we need around here."

Annie mumbled something about him being surrounded by good, kind women but Emily only vaguely heard her. And Annie's grandfather ignored her completely.

"How can you say that?" Emily asked. "You don't even know me."

"At my age, I can look into a person's eyes and know what's in here." He patted his chest.

"Oh, just humor him," Annie said. "He's getting old and crotchety."

Grandfather scowled at his granddaughter. "You've gotten sharp-tongued since you married Hugh. And him a preacher. One would think—"

But whatever he'd been about to say was drowned out by his grandsons' laughter.

Conner sobered enough to explain. "She's always been that way. No need to blame the preacher."

It was time to go inside, and Jesse guided her to a pew. The Marshalls sat ahead, their family taking up several rows.

The grandfather might be old. For all she knew, he said things that were far-fetched, and yet his words that she was a good and kind person encouraged her. Now, if only she could discover who that person was.

Hugh took his place at the pulpit and led them in singing hymns. She knew every word of the songs. Beside her Jesse held Mikey, who snuggled into his arms. It didn't surprise her that Jesse had a good voice. It was a joy to sing with him.

Then Hugh opened his Bible. "Today I want to talk about the one lost sheep. No one is ever lost in God's sight." He proceeded to tell how his son had been lost to him but God had enabled him to find the boy. "Whether you are lost in the woods or lost spiritually, God sees you. Ask Him to help you find your way back to home and Him."

Emily drank in the words. She would trust God. He would bring her to herself.

Preacher Hugh announced the closing hymn—*Amazing Grace.*

Never before had Emily felt the truth of the words so strongly.

I once was lost but now I'm found. Was blind but now I see.

She was lost and blind, but she would trust God no matter what.

After church Jesse went to the livery station to rent a buggy and they were soon on their way to the Marshall Five Ranch. Emily looked about eagerly. There was something about a ranch that pulled at her thoughts. She both feared and anticipated the visit bringing back her memory.

"There it is." Jesse pointed toward an impressive set of buildings—a two-story log-and-timber house with two smaller houses behind. One had the appearance of being newly built or even still under construction. There were also a good-sized barn and several other buildings.

"It's bigger than I expected."

"I told you. The Marshalls are big."

She laughed at the way he said it, as if he resented it, but she heard the affection in his voice and knew he didn't.

They reached the biggest of the houses. Children raced about everywhere. Grandfather sat on the verandah, his eyes bright and eager. His son and grandsons flanked him.

Emily spoke out of the corner of her mouth. "I feel like I'm being stared at."

Then Dawson rushed forward to welcome them. He reached for Mikey. "You want to go play with the other children?"

As soon as Mikey's feet hit the ground, he ran to join the others.

"I can't believe it," Emily said. "I expected him to be shy. Didn't you?" she asked Jesse.

"He certainly isn't shy around children." Jesse looked thoughtful, as if that bit of knowledge meant something.

She let Dawson assist her down. He escorted her to the house and opened the door. "Ladies, Miss Emily is here." He left her standing in the cloakroom.

Annie hurried to her. "Come on in. We're about ready to eat."

The big, homey kitchen buzzed with activity. The women carried the food through to the dining room and the men and children trooped in. It was a crowded table, a noisy bunch and a bountiful meal.

Emily sat next to Jesse and, beneath the conversations around them, murmured, "I'm quite certain I have never been in such an exuberant crowd before."

He leaned close. "I warned you the Marshalls do everything in a big way."

Annie watched them, grinning as if she knew a secret, and then she turned to her grandfather who sat on her left. "I've been praying a woman would come into Jesse's life."

Jesse groaned.

All eyes turned toward them.

She continued gleefully. "So glad to see my prayers being answered."

Emily opened her mouth to protest but nothing

came out. She closed it, swallowed hard, then tried again, this time with success. "If you want to pray for Jesse, you might ask that he be kept safe as he hunts those who robbed the stagecoach."

Several of the Marshalls looked guilty.

She continued, "And while you're at it, you could pray I'll recover my memory. Seems to me that should be a little more important to any would-be matchmakers than seeing an unidentified woman at Jesse's side."

Hugh chuckled. "Well said."

The three Marshall wives clapped.

Grandfather roared with laughter. "She might not be a Marshall, but she sure does know how to stand up for herself."

Emily's face burned. "Forgive me my rudeness. You invite me to share your table and then I act all high and mighty. I am so sorry."

Annie shook her head. "It is I who should apologize. I am so used to teasing Jesse I didn't stop to consider how it affected you. You are absolutely right." She turned to her husband. "Hugh, I think there has been a prayer request. Shouldn't you deal with that?"

He grinned at his wife. "Let us pray."

Emily looked about at the bowed heads.

Jesse smiled at her, then bent his head as Hugh prayed.

Emily closed her eyes and let the blessing of Hugh's words soothe her to the depths of her soul.

The rest of the day flew by as she was enfolded into the family circle.

She listened as the women visited. They toured the yards, checking on the garden and searching for wild flowers on the hills.

Emily straightened with a bluebell in her hand and regarded the men leaning on the corral fence studying some horses.

Jesse looked her direction and their gazes caught over the distance. Their look went on and on, until someone spoke to Jesse and he turned away.

She stayed riveted to the spot. She felt as if he had surrounded her with protection, and for the present, she welcomed—indeed, needed—his strength.

A shiver snaked up her spine. He would soon enough remove both if she turned out to be—

She couldn't think about what or who she might truly be. All she had was the present.

Jesse's hopes and prayers that the trip to the ranch would bring back Emily's memory were dashed. He knew it even before she said it. All afternoon he had watched for signs of it, knew he would be able to tell. Her face gave away her feelings. All he saw was disappointment and frustration.

On the way home, her voice broke as she said, "The preacher said God will lead all His sheep home. I want to find myself and my home. But I can't remember."

Mikey had fallen asleep on her lap so he was unaware of her tears.

Jesse pulled the buggy to a halt and drew Emily to his chest. "Emily, I promise I will not stop searching until I find out who you are. But even if I never learn the facts about your past, you will always have a home right here in Bella Creek." He'd been about to say she'd have a home with him, but he didn't have the right.

She tipped her head to study his face.

He pulled his handkerchief from his back pocket and wiped her tear-stained face.

"Jesse, how old are you?"

"Twenty-five. Why?"

"You are such a good man. I can't help wondering why you aren't married. Surely there have been others besides Agnes. A woman who saw your goodness."

He shifted so she remained in his arms but wasn't looking at him. "Not everyone thinks that." She barely knew him. Her judgment would change as time went on and she understood the truth about his background.

She edged back to study him. "Someone has hurt you. Someone other than your mother. Perhaps Agnes hurt you more than you said."

He didn't answer but knew she saw the truth in his eyes.

"I'm sorry. But don't let it be the controlling factor in your life. You deserve every bit of happiness."

"I'm happy being a sheriff and maintaining law and order. I get satisfaction out of seeing justice prevail."

She left his arms. Her hands bunched at Mikey's sides.

He waited, wondering why she'd had such a strong reaction to his words.

She released a gentle sigh. "I don't know how I know this, but things are not always just and fair."

They regarded each other and he saw something in her eyes. "Something unfair has happened to you."

Pain filled her eyes, then was drowned by tears. "I don't know."

Their attention was diverted by the approach of three riders. He didn't recognize them. Roughly dressed, their horses dusty, he knew before they drew near that these men posed danger.

"Keep your head down and don't look at them." He reached back for his gun belt, took out the pistol and stuck it in the back of his trousers—not visible to invite a reaction but handy should he need it.

Emily pressed closer and her arms tightened around Mikey. "I pray he will stay asleep."

"Amen." He didn't bother urging the horse to move. He'd let the strangers ride past first.

The men spoke to each other but Jesse couldn't hear them. They spread out, and Jesse tensed as he saw they meant to circle the buggy.

One rode to the right, one to the left and the third stopped in front making it impossible to race away.

"What do we have here?" The man beside Jesse leered at Emily.

"You have the sheriff." Jesse tipped open his vest to reveal his star.

"Hey, ain't it more fun to kill a lawman than anybody?" the front man yelled.

"I would suggest you ride along." Jesse pulled his pistol to his lap, letting them know he meant to defend his passengers.

The man to his right wore a hat so dirty he could have scraped crud off with a knife. He reached out a grubby hand and touched Emily's knee.

Emily shivered and pushed hard to Jesse's side.

Jesse's vision momentarily blurred red. He would shoot the man if he did anything to harm her or Mikey. Though he couldn't likely hope to stop all three. No, he had to calm down and think smart.

"Where are you fellows from? Where are you

going? Just so's I know who to contact should you suddenly meet your demise."

"D'mise? What's that?" the guy on the left asked.

"I think he's threatening us. Ain't he?" The front rider asked the man on the right.

"Huh. How's he going to shoot all three of us?"

Jesse cocked his gun and eyed them one after the other. "Who wants to be the one I get?"

The man on his left lunged for Jesse's gun. Jesse drew it back, keeping it trained on the man's forehead. "What do you want me to put on your tomb? Or you satisfied with an X?"

The other two laughed nervously.

"You let him shoot you, Lammie, and I'll shoot him."

Jesse didn't flinch. "I'm pretty sure I can get two of you before you get your guns out."

The big man at the front reached for his sidearm.

Jesse shot just right of his ear.

At the sound, Mikey wakened with a cry. Emily held him tight and murmured for him to be still.

The man jerked. "You almost hit me."

"If I meant to hit you I would have." Jesse jerked his pistol toward the man beside Emily. "I'd suggest you ride away while we're all still alive."

"I got better things to do than fight a sheriff." The man at Emily's right kicked his horse into action and rode away.

Jesse hoped he continued riding that direction.

The other two cursed and followed their partner.

Jesse leaned over to peer behind the buggy and make sure they didn't circle back.

After he was fairly certain they weren't returning,

he put his gun away and opened his arms to Emily and Mikey who both cried quietly. “It’s okay. We’re safe. They won’t bother us again.” *Please, Father God, give them something else to occupy their nasty minds.*

Emily clutched his vest. “I thought they were going to kill you.”

Me, too. But he would die protecting Emily and Mikey, if necessary. “They thought better of it.”

She sniffed back her tears and sat up to look into his face. “You were prepared to die to protect us.”

He nodded.

“But why? For all you know, I’m a wicked person.”

He grinned at the idea. “I might as well say that for all you know, I’m an elephant.”

Her eyes widened and she burst out laughing. It quickly changed to tears and she buried her face against his chest and cried.

He rubbed her back and made what he hoped were soothing noises.

She’d put Mikey down at her feet and he patted her knees. “Mem, mem, mem.” He sounded concerned as Emily continued to cry.

She sucked in a breath and held it, though shudders ran through her body. Air eased past her teeth. “I’m okay now.”

Jesse still had his arms around her and felt her quivering. “I don’t think you are. They’re gone. There’s no more danger.”

“I c-can’t seem to s-stop shivering,” she stammered.

He held her tight and continued to rub her back. After a bit, he grew concerned. “What’s wrong?”

She sat up and stared straight ahead. “I thought it

was the same three men who robbed the stagecoach and—" She glanced toward Mikey and didn't finish.

He knew she would have said *killed two men*. Men such as that wouldn't hesitate to kill again. He thanked God for protecting all of them, then jumped from the buggy and examined the tracks. None of their mounts had had the odd-shaped horseshoe, although that could mean the horse had been swapped out for another. He had not noticed any silver-tipped boots and he certainly would have. For a moment, he stared up and down the road, but he saw nothing to cause him concern and climbed back to the seat.

"Emily, did you see something familiar about them?"

She didn't answer for a moment then gave a sigh. "Only that there were three of them and they looked mean and nasty."

"You're sure there wasn't something about them?"

She considered. "No. It just scared me." She gripped his hand. Gave him a probing look. "Jesse, promise me you will never do that again."

He cupped her shoulder. "Do what?"

"Face down three men."

"Emily, I can't promise you that. It's my job."

"To die protecting others?"

He nodded.

"So you can prove you're a good man?"

Her words cut him. He slowly removed his hands from her shoulders. "I vowed to honor the law and protect my fellow man, and I intend to live up to my vow." He heard the hard tone of his voice but couldn't help it. Seems she wasn't all that different from the other young ladies he'd tried to court who either hated

his profession or, even more strongly, hated his background. What had made him think she might be? Only his misguided dreams. He deserved the wakeup call. Not that he was courting her or had even considered it.

After all, who courts a woman who doesn't know who she is?

"We need to get home." He flicked the reins and they rode the rest of the way in silence. He pulled up in front of the house and jumped down to lift first Mikey and then Emily to the ground.

Mikey looked from one adult to the other then stuck his thumb in his mouth.

Smart little kid to recognize the tension between Jesse and Emily.

"Jesse?"

He waited but she had nothing more to say. "Tell Gram I'm taking the buggy back and then making my rounds. I might be late for supper."

Gram would demand to know what was so important that he missed Sunday supper. He almost hoped for some kind of ruckus to provide him with an excuse to avoid returning home until after dark.

Emily fled into the house.

Was she crying?

He considered following but her assessment of him stung. He didn't protect the citizens of Bella Creek and uphold the law for his own glory and satisfaction. To make himself feel good.

Then why do you do it? The question refused to be silenced.

He did not thank Emily for building a cauldron of uncertainty in his brain.

Chapter Nine

Emily knew from the surprise on Gram's face when she relayed Jesse's message that it was not normal behavior on his part. She regretted throwing doubt on his reasons for being a sheriff. Her only excuse was that to think of him facing such a risk left her mouth desert dry and her bones weak.

Especially on her behalf.

She didn't deserve it. He'd rescued her once, but she had no desire to see him shot to protect her…a woman with no past and no future.

She went through all the right motions of helping serve supper, cleaning up and then preparing Mikey for the night.

When she told the boy it was time for bed, he went to the outer door, leaned his head on it and cried. Muffin whined at his feet, but he ignored the dog.

"Honey, what's the matter?" Emily knelt beside him and tried to pull him into her arms.

He pushed her away and patted the door.

"I'm sorry. I don't know what you mean."

Gram watched. “He wants to know where Jesse is. So do I. Did something happen?”

Emily studied the floor for a moment but she must own up to her actions. “We had a little spat.”

“You and Jesse? About what, if you don’t mind me asking.”

She explained about the three ruffians on the trail and how he had persuaded them to ride on. “I don’t want him to risk his life for me.”

“Exactly what did you say?”

“I accused him of trying to prove he was a good man.” She hung her head. “I know it was wrong. He is a good man and doesn’t need to prove it to anyone.”

“Come sit.” Gram patted the couch beside her and waited until Emily settled. She took one of Emily’s hands. “You may be more right than you know. You struck close to a wound.”

“I didn’t mean to. I’m very sorry for my hasty words.”

“You’ll have to tell him that.”

“I will.” She rolled Gram’s words round in her head. “He told me about his mother and the house of ill repute. Is that what you mean?”

“That’s part of it. He was badly hurt when people learned of her circumstances. They judged him for the way she’d lived her life. It’s made him almost rigid in the way he lives and what he expects of others. To him, life is simply black and white.”

“‘A man is only as good as his word.’ That’s what he said to me.”

“Yes. He does not forgive easily.”

She shivered. “That doesn’t sound promising for my intended apology.”

"You do what you need to do and let him work out his way of dealing with it."

"You're saying he might not forgive me? That will make it awkward for me to stay here." She forced a smile to her wooden lips. "Though I hope by tomorrow I will know who I am and can get on with my life." Surely the doctor could help her recall who she was.

"For your sake, I hope you regain your memory. As to Jesse forgiving you, all I can say is he's dealt with hurtful things in the past and moved on to become the man he is. A strong, noble man with high ideals."

Emily wanted to know what hurtful things, but it didn't feel right to learn his secrets from a source other than him.

She sighed. When had life gotten so complicated?

Long before this. She jolted at the words that came to her. What did her past hold that was complicated?

She smiled. She had Mikey. But he wasn't hers. What was to become of the poor boy while he waited for his adoptive parents?

The little guy stood with his forehead pressed to the door, his eyes closed.

"He's going to fall asleep right there," she whispered.

"Best take him up to bed."

She scooped the boy into her arms. He made a sound of protest then nuzzled into her neck. He didn't even waken as she tucked him into bed.

But she wasn't any better than Mikey. She didn't want to go to sleep until Jesse came home so she returned downstairs, chose a book from the shelf and sat down to read.

* * *

A light glowed from the living room. Jesse stopped in front of the house and looked at the window. Had Gram left the lamp for him or was she waiting up? He moved to the right and then the left in an attempt to see inside the house. Someone sat on the couch. It wasn't Gram.

He rumbled his lips. He had stayed out all evening, had gone down the road and followed the tracks of the men who had stopped them. Far as he could tell, they'd continued northward. He hoped that meant they were only passing through and wouldn't be a bother. Later, he'd taken supper at Miss Daisy's Eatery. Her sister, Miss Dorie, waited on tables. He spent a considerable amount of time deflecting Miss Dorie's questions as to why he chose to eat there when his Gram was two blocks away.

"She's not sick, is she?"

"How can you hope to run a profitable business if you try and dissuade people from eating at your establishment?" He was certain he'd kept the annoyance from his voice, but Miss Dorie sniffed, refilled his coffee cup and marched away to wait on others. Who—if Jesse was honest with himself—offered her more pleasant company.

He didn't mean to be grumpy but Emily's accusation ground in the pit of his stomach. What made her think he needed to prove to anyone, least of all himself, that he was a good man? It didn't even make sense.

But no amount of internal argument had settled the matter for him and now she appeared to be waiting up for him. Not many hours past he would have found the idea appealing.

Now he would have gone to his office and spent the night in the jail cell, but he'd had to sleep there on occasion and found it most uncomfortable. He wanted his own bed. Sucking in air until his lungs could hold no more, he opened the gate and strode to the door. His hand hovered above the knob for two seconds and then he threw back the door and stepped inside.

Emily jumped to her feet. "Thank goodness you're home. I worried you might have run into trouble."

"What sort of trouble did you have in mind?" he asked dismissively.

She faltered then answered him. "Those three men might have turned back looking for revenge for what happened this afternoon."

He hung his hat on the hook by the door and spent several minutes pulling off his boots. Finally, with nothing more to divert him, he straightened. "You don't need to concern yourself with me. I'm careful."

"That's good to hear." She took two steps toward him.

Not about to let her say anything more to hurt him, he crossed his arms over his chest.

She read his signal and stopped. Regret drew lines from the corner of her mouth.

He had only to reach out and touch her face to rub them away. But a wall of resistance kept him from moving, even though his heart cried out to comfort her.

"Jesse, I want to apologize for what I said this afternoon. It was uncalled-for and untrue. I'm so sorry. I never meant to hurt you." She moved closer. "The last thing I want to do is hurt you. You're a good, kind man and you know it as well as I do." She rested her gentle palm on his forearm.

All resistance melted. He covered her hand with his. "The trouble is, there is truth to what you said." He hadn't admitted it to himself until this very moment.

"How is that?"

"I told you about my mother."

She nodded, her eyes never shifting away, even at the awkward topic.

Finding courage in her steady gaze, he continued. "I always thought there was something wrong with me that my mother didn't see any value in spending time with me. I only believed it more strongly when my friends mocked me. Then I met Agnes."

Emily nodded. "You told me about Agnes."

"I didn't tell it all. She lived here with her family for a time. I courted her and thought she cared for me. But when I told her about my mother, she drew back. After that she refused to see me, and her family moved away a short time later. The only place where I knew people would respect me was in my role as sheriff, so you were right. Through my job I am trying to prove that I am good enough."

Both her hands now rested on his arm, warm and steady. Not a bit of shrinking back. Perhaps that would come later. When she realized that he was a man with no known father. He'd often wondered why his mother had used the last name Hill on his birth certificate but she'd never told him.

Emily edged forward until he could smell the

scented soap Annie had given her and the little-boy smell from having held Mikey.

"Who are you proving it to? Not me, despite my unfair words. Not to Gram or the Marshalls. I venture to say that anyone who knows you knows you are a good, noble, kind man. Don't you need to believe it, too?"

He considered her words. "Not everyone would agree with you."

"Do you need everyone's approval?"

"I suppose not." But to have the acceptance of a woman who would take him with his past, his present and his future would be nice. Perhaps a dream he wasn't worthy of.

"Do you forgive me for my unkind words?" she asked.

"Of course. And forgive me for being offended."

She pulled him toward the couch. "I've been reading. You have an excellent selection of titles. Have you read them all?"

"Not that novel by Jane Austen." He pretended to shudder. "Gram reads it at least once a year and sighs repeatedly at the romance."

Emily laughed, picked up the book she'd been reading and showed him the cover. "Guess what I've chosen."

He shook his head as if distressed when he read the title, *Pride and Prejudice*. "Have you been sighing lots?"

She clutched the book to her bosom and sighed, her eyes merry with amusement. "It's so romantic." She grew serious—or, at least, she attempted to appear so—as she held the book toward him. "Jesse, you really ought to read it."

"Would it fix what's wrong with my life?"

"Well, it won't help you find those bad guys who held up the stagecoach, but it will provide a little romance in your life."

Their gazes melded. He wished he could see to the core of her being and know who she was.

He felt her searching just as deeply and held back only a portion of his thoughts. "Do I need romance?" His voice had deepened. He hoped she wouldn't notice.

"I think we all need love and romance." Her eyes held the color of the last blue of the sky just before the light of the sun vanished. He could almost see the flicker of sunlight behind the darkness of her irises.

"Do you need love and romance?" Would she accept it from the likes of him—a man marked and marred by the life his mother had lived?

She blinked and the moment ended. "What I need is to get my memory back and learn who I am."

How had he forgotten that he didn't know who she was? For all he knew, she might be married. By not taking into account a woman's marital status, he acknowledged he wasn't all that different from his mother. He would apologize to Emily, but she had no idea of the direction his thoughts had gone and he feared to say something that would only make Emily uncomfortable.

She laid the book aside. "I will say good-night now."

"Sleep well."

"I will, now that you have forgiven me." Her smile filled him with warmth.

He listened to her footsteps on the stairs and as

she walked down the hall. Her door closed with a faint click. He picked up the book and stared at the title. *Pride and Prejudice.* How fitting. It was the latter that marred his life. He'd developed the former to protect his heart.

His gaze drifted to the window. She'd been worried about his safety. Concerned that her words had hurt him. Apart from his grandmother and the Marshalls, who were like family to him, he'd never known that kind of caring from anyone else.

Tomorrow he would go with her to the doctor, if she would allow it, and hopefully learn how to help her regain her memory. Would knowing who she was make things easier or more complicated?

The truth shall set you free. He nodded as he recalled the scripture. It would set her free to resume her life. What would it do for him? It would surely make it possible for him to resume his life, as well. A sheriff who did his duty and guarded his heart.

He put the book on the side table and turned out the lamp. For some reason, he felt compelled to make sure the doors were firmly latched. Gram had left open one window in the kitchen to let in the cool night air and he closed it. She would complain in the morning, but Emily was right. There were men out there who would not hesitate to harm others. He couldn't be looking for them and guarding Emily at the same time. In the morning, he would deputize Clarence and send him out to look for a man wearing silver-toed boots and a horse with an odd-shaped shoe. And anything else that might lead them to the murdering trio.

"Do you want me to go with you?" Jesse asked the next morning, as Emily nervously prepared to leave the house to visit the doctor. At his words, he watched the tension drain from her.

"I would appreciate it, but don't you have a job to attend to?"

"I'll look around as we go there and thus do my job at the same time." As soon as he got the verdict from the doctor he would find Clarence and then take care of the paperwork that dogged his heels. He liked being a sheriff but didn't much care for being his own secretary. It was part of the job, though, so he did it to the best of his ability. There were often letters from other sheriffs asking him to keep an eye out for someone. Or asking about a family that they searched for. Today he was more anxious than normal to open his mail, hoping there would be something about a missing young woman and child. Except no one would know of their circumstances. The Newmans had moved on. Whoever had sent her would think she was with them. But, sooner or later, some information would surface.

Emily turned to Gram. "Are you sure you don't mind watching Mikey?"

Gram chuckled at the little boy and the dog playing in the backyard. "It's a pleasure to see Muffin enjoying Mikey's company. You two run along. We'll do just fine together."

Jesse steered Emily down the step to the sidewalk. "Don't look so regretful."

"I know she has sewing to do and I'm keeping her from it. Just as I know I am keeping you from your work."

He tucked her arm around his elbow, liking the feeling of taking care of her. He told her about some of the letters he'd received. "So, you see, it's my job to find lost individuals, as well."

She increased the pressure of her hand on his forearm. "Well I'm glad I am giving you meaningful work." Her laugh lacked mirth. "I welcome your company. I confess I am afraid."

"Of what? Of not getting your memory back? Surely the doctor can fix that."

"I'm as afraid of what I'll learn about myself when my memory returns as I am that my memory won't return."

"You told me to believe I am a good man. I'm asking you to believe you are also a good person."

"I'm trying. Truly I am."

He noticed how nervously she glanced about as they crossed the street. Did she have a reason other than her loss of memory to be fearful? He hated the doubts arising within him, and yet his job and his life had taught him to be cautious.

They reached the doctor's house and entered the office door. A young man and an older woman were already there. Jesse knew them both and they exchanged greetings.

Emily sat on a bench waiting for the doctor to call her. Her hands twisted together so tightly that her knuckles turned white. If they'd been alone he would have taken her hands between his and told her not to be afraid.

Instead, he remained standing, her tension reverberating along his nerves. He tried to imagine how it would feel not to know who he was. No doubt he, too, would wonder what sort of person he'd been. Maybe the hurtful comments others had sent his way would feel true. That must be how it was for Emily.

Doc saw the waiting woman. A few minutes later she emerged, then the doctor saw the young man.

Jesse sat at Emily's side. "Whatever happens, you have friends here. Don't forget that."

She darted a glance his way. "I'm hoping they will still be my friends if I learn something awful about myself."

"I can't imagine there would be anything like that."

The doctor opened the door. "Which of you is the patient?"

Emily jerked to her feet. "Me. But I want Jesse to come in, too."

"Very well."

They followed Doc into the examining room. Jesse looked around. Where was Albert Stevens, the young man who had become Doc's assistant when Doc's daughter, Kate, married Conner?

Doc saw his curiosity. "Young Stevens has gone to check on Mrs. Adams and her new baby. Now, what can I do for you, Miss Emily?"

Emily perched on the edge of the hard chair. "My memory hasn't returned. What can you do to help?"

Jesse knew his hat would be permanently crooked if he didn't quit twisting it, but he couldn't make himself stop.

Doc leaned forward. "Are you having headaches?"

Emily shook her head. "I feel fine. I just need to remember who I am."

Jesse wondered if Doc heard the way her voice trembled.

"My dear, sometimes our brain blocks something

fearful or hurtful and doesn't let us remember until we feel the danger has passed. I suspect that might be what is happening with you." He studied her a moment, his face swathed in sympathy. "Do you experience fear or perhaps sorrow?"

She blinked rapidly as if keeping tears back.

Jesse wanted nothing so much as to take her hands and comfort her.

Her voice crackled as she answered the doctor. "I worry I might not like who I am. I wonder if I've done something awful. I feel nameless fears."

Doc considered her answer for a moment. "Unfortunately, I can't give you anything to help you remember but I can suggest a few things you can do."

Jesse caught his breath, heard Emily do the same as they waited for Doc's recommendations.

"First, realize your fears might be false. Our brain can do strange things to us. So can our hearts. The Bible says 'The heart is deceitful above all thing*s*, and desperately wicked.' In part, that means what we tell ourselves is not always true. Second, stop trying to remember. Go out, visit people, do fun things. Live as normal a life as you can. I believe doing so will make your brain relax. And last, but by far not least, trust the good Lord." He came around the desk and patted Emily's shoulder. "He has good things planned for you."

Emily nodded. "I feel like that man in the Bible who said, 'I do believe; help my unbelief.'"

"Keep praying that and you'll do just fine."

"Will my memory ever return?" she asked.

"I can't say. But I know you can't wish it back or force it back." He patted her shoulder again.

She slowly got to her feet. "Thank you, Doctor."

"I wish I could be of more help."

Jesse led the way out of the doctor's office. They fell in side by side. He guessed she was as unsettled by the doctor's words as he. Trusting God wasn't always easy. And relaxing when it was the last thing one wanted to do was nigh unto impossible. He decided right then and there that it was up to him to help her do both.

"Do you want to see my office?" he asked, suspecting she wasn't ready to return to the house.

"I'd like that." They passed the schoolhouse, now silent as the children spent the summer with their parents, helping with farmwork and gardening and tending younger siblings. They reached the town square.

"It was Grandfather Marshall's idea to have a little park in the center of town, a place that invited friends and neighbors to exchange greetings and visit for a bit." The benches and flowers added to the inviting atmosphere.

Emily glanced about. "It's a nice place."

He understood her distraction. They angled across the street to his office, which was next to one corner of the park. He occasionally sat a spell on the bench closest to his office to watch the activities of the town. From his open window he could enjoy the scent of the flowers.

He held the door and let her precede him into his domain.

She circled the small room, paused to examine the likenesses on the wanted posters. "I wish I'd seen their faces."

He knew she meant the men who had held up the stagecoach.

She continued on to the small cell. “This get used often?”

“*Often* is a relative term. It would suit me fine if it never got used.”

She looked at the rifles racked on the wall and came full circle to face him.

He leaned on the front of the desk. “What do you want to do for fun?”

The way she blinked, he knew she hadn’t taken the doctor’s orders to heart. A teasing light flashed through her eyes.

“Perhaps I could challenge someone to a horse race.”

He eyed her. “Do you ride?”

She shrugged. “If I don’t, there’s no time like the present to learn.” The teasing ended abruptly. “I hoped he could fix me.” She flung away to press her forehead against the front window.

While she sorted her thoughts, he went through the unopened mail on his desk looking for anything concerning Emily and Mikey. He found nothing and shoved aside the mail to deal with later.

“Would you like to come with me to find Clarence? I have an errand for him.”

She looked ready to say yes, then shook her head. “Do you mind if I stay here a few minutes? I need to think what I’m going to do.”

He didn’t like to leave her and certainly didn’t want her wandering about on her own. “On the condition you stay here until I get back.”

For a moment he thought she would argue, then she shrugged. “I’ll wait here for you.”

He trotted down the street, found Clarence helping

his father at the feed store and sent him to look for the culprits. The three men who had bothered Jesse and Emily yesterday plus other men—one riding a horse with an oddly shaped horseshoe and one with silver-tipped boots. They could all be members of the same gang or two different groups of men. He hoped it was the latter and the three that had confronted him on Sunday had continued riding away from the area.

That task done, he headed back to his office. He took a little longer returning as he considered his options.

Doc had given no timetable for Emily's recovering her memory. He hadn't even given assurances that it would return. It was up to Jesse to discover her identity and to guard her until he did, but he couldn't stay at her side continuously.

He reached his office. Emily sat on the wooden armchair, leaning over her knees. His throat tightened at her despair and he knelt by her side.

She looked at him.

"Emily, let me take you around town so you know where the different businesses are."

"I suppose it won't do me any good to sit here trying to remember who I am."

"Nope. You need to follow the doctor's orders." He pulled her to her feet and led her outside and past the town square. He wanted her to relax and stop worrying, but he also wanted her to feel confident enough to move about freely.

They passed the hotel and Miss Daisy's Eatery. "Miss Daisy does the cooking, and her sister Dorie does the serving. It's a friendly place. Don't hesitate to stop in."

"I'll take your word for it."

He didn't push her to consider going in. She had much to think about and deal with.

"This is Marshall's Mercantile."

"Grandfather Marshall's other son? I met him and his wife on Sunday but I have to admit I barely remember them." She chuckled rather mirthlessly. "Big tall man with fading blond hair."

He led her into the store. No other customers were present, which would make it easier for Emily to relax. "George has about anything you'll need and if he doesn't, he'll order it."

George hurried forward. "Nice to see you again, Miss Emily. Feel free to look around."

She thanked him and headed for the yard goods to finger several pieces of fabric.

Jesse watched her. Did she wish for more clothes? No, he understood she wished for her own clothes and hoped something in the many bolts of cloth would trigger her memory.

She turned away, disappointment darkening her eyes. "You have a very nice store," she told George as she headed for the door.

Jesse followed her outside. They continued down the street. "The assay office. Across the street is the barber and then Mr. Eugene's office. He's the local lawyer." He pointed out several more businesses that they could see from the corner. "Behind the assay office is the boardinghouse."

She studied it, a serious look on her face. "Perhaps I should move in there until—"

"That's not necessary, and Mikey wouldn't have

the freedom to run about and make as much noise as he'd like."

Her countenance brightened and she laughed. "He can be rather noisy at times."

Relieved to see her more cheerful, he grinned. "Especially when he's playing with Muffin."

A horse and rider thundered down the street toward them. Jesse stepped out to wave him down and warn him to slow down in town. He recognized Ernest Davis, a small-time rancher from east of town. Normally a cautious man. Jesse's nerves twitched.

Ernest reined up hard. "Sheriff, just the man I want to see."

"What's the problem?" He kept his voice calm, and his thoughts composed, even though he knew he was about to learn of trouble.

"The supply wagon has been robbed."

Jesse's heart sank. "Bo?" Had the driver been killed?

"Shot but still alive." Ernest gave a snort of amusement. "He's madder than a cornered badger. Took four of us to get him into a wagon." He glanced back down the street. "They'll be going a lot slower than I did, but they should be along shortly."

"I'll wait and talk to him before I ride out to the scene." He thanked the man for all he'd done then looked at Emily for the first time since he'd intercepted the rider.

Her eyes were dark as a midnight sky, her lips set in a hard line. "It could be the same men."

"Maybe. Maybe not. I want to hear what Bo has to say. In the meantime, I need to get you home." Despite his hope that she would feel free to move about town, he wasn't prepared to leave her wandering around, especially with robbers in the area, and they made their way back to the house.

He paused with her at the front door. "I wish I didn't have to rush away."

Her smile was wide but her eyes were still dark, indicating troubled thoughts. "Thanks for taking care of me. But you needn't worry. I'll get myself sorted out."

That didn't sounded much positive as resigned. But he couldn't stay and help her, even if he'd thought he could be of help. "I'll be back as soon as possible." He squeezed her shoulder and hurried away.

Even though Gram was there, he felt as if he had abandoned her. He stopped at the manse and asked Annie to pay Emily a visit. "She's rather discouraged after Doc told her he could do nothing."

"Evan has been asking to play with Mikey, so I don't mind going to see her."

With that he had to be satisfied for now.

A wagon stood in front of Doc's house and Jesse hurried in. Before he opened the door, he heard Bo roaring. He went into the examining room where Doc prepared to remove a bullet from Bo's arm.

"They meant to kill me," Bo yelled. He saw Jesse. "You go catch them. Bring them to me. I'll learn 'em not to mess with me."

Jesse ignored Bo's anger. "Can you tell me anything about them? How many were there? Did you see their faces?"

"Three men. They kept their faces covered. After they shot me and left me for dead, they rifled through my goods and scattered them all over." He half sat. "Doc, I gotta get my supplies."

Doc pushed him back to the table. “Lie down. You’re not going any place until I get the bullet out. Hang on now, son. I have to dig a little.”

“I’ll make arrangements for your things,” Jesse said, and he slipped away as Bo roared like an angry bull.

He arranged for a couple of men to ride east and take care of the supply wagon, then he got his horse. “Come on, Rocky. We got work to do.” It took twenty minutes to reach the wagon. He arrived before those coming with another wagon to get Bo’s things. Jesse shook his head at the senseless way the goods had been scattered about and bags of flour and oats torn open. He dismounted a few feet away and left Rocky waiting. Studying the ground for clues, he circled the area.

And what he saw turned his stomach sour. The same misshapen horseshoe. The same trio who had robbed the stage and killed the driver and his guard.

Jesse straightened and stared down the road. He needed to ride after the robbers before he lost the trail, but what if they made their way to town? Would they recognize Emily and see her as a threat?

They’d left her for dead. Had no reason to suspect she’d lived. Likely they hadn’t even looked at her, so they wouldn’t recognize her. He was worrying needlessly.

He returned to Rocky and followed the tracks of the robbers.

But all the while his gut complained, warning him that Emily could be in danger. After all, how long would a person have to be in town before they heard about the woman who had been rescued from the stagecoach robbery?

Chapter Ten

Emily went out to the backyard where Mikey played. The boy ran to her arms and she held him tight, finding comfort in his hugs. The doctor couldn't help her. She might never regain her memory.

Gram straightened from cutting flowers. "Where's Jesse?"

She let Mikey resume his play then explained about the robbery. "What if it's the same men?" Her limbs were brittle as glass at the thought.

Gram moved closer. "Is there any reason to think it might be?"

"I suppose not." She didn't think the three who stopped them on Sunday were the same as the ones who robbed the stagecoach but wasn't sure why she thought that. Was it something about the way they rode or spoke? She couldn't be certain. But there were too many bad men around and it made her nervous. "I'm overreacting."

"What did Dr. Baker say about your memory?"

Emily relayed the information in a shaking voice.

"What will become of me if I never get my memory back?"

"Someone will be looking for you. When they find you, I suppose you'll have to make a choice as to whether or not to return to the life you don't remember or start a new one here. And that, my dear, will depend on who is looking for you."

"I'm almost certain I'm not married." Except how could she be so sure when she didn't know who she was?

The conversation ended with Annie coming around the house with Evan in tow. The two little boys began to play together.

"I'll leave you young ladies to visit and enjoy the sunshine. I have things to take care of." Gram went inside.

"I should help," Emily said, but she didn't follow.

"Like she said, let's enjoy the sunshine." Annie went to the bench Emily had shared with Jesse and patted the spot beside her. "Jesse told me about your visit to the doctor. I'm sorry there wasn't better news."

All the turmoil and uncertainty escaped in a rush of words. Finally, she slowed. "It's so unsettling."

"I can't imagine. Jesse said the doctor told you not to dwell on it, so let's talk about something else."

Emily gave a weak grin. "I have little else to talk about, seeing as I don't remember my past."

Annie chuckled. "That's okay. I can talk enough for the two of us." She proceeded to do so, regaling Emily with stories of growing up with three older brothers, the pain of losing her mother and then the fun of watching her brothers court the women they married. "My best friend, Carly, recently married, too."

"And so did you." Emily laughed. "Maybe they should change the name of the town to Wedded Bliss."

Annie chuckled and got to her feet. "It's time for me to leave."

"Thanks for visiting. I needed to talk."

She grinned. "Seems you mostly listened." She collected Evan and they departed.

Emily took Mikey and the dog inside. "Gram, I need to be busy. What can I do?"

Gram studied her a moment. "Very well, right after dinner I am going to my sewing room. There are things there you can do."

So after they'd eaten, Gram led the way. "I don't know if anyone told you, but I am one of the seamstresses in Bella Creek. In fact, I am the best. I have as much work as I can handle and often turn down requests."

"And I've been keeping you from your work."

"Not at all. I did some work while you were out." She pointed out the projects she had going. "I don't know how good you are, so I'll start you out on easy things. Here are the buttons for this shirt. Can you sew them on?"

Emily sat and took up the task. It felt familiar. Of course, she would have sewn on buttons before. But as she cut the thread and attached them, she knew it was more than that.

She willed the memory to return but she found nothing but black emptiness.

"These are done. What else do you have I can do?"

Gram examined the buttons. "Very neat. How do you feel about hemming a skirt?"

"I can do that." She spent the next hour doing so and Gram looked at the finished project.

"I couldn't have done better myself. Let's see if you can set the sleeves in this shirtwaist."

"I know I can." They spent the rest of the afternoon sewing, taking the work out to the yard so they could supervise Mikey playing.

"That's enough for the day." Gram folded up the dress she was making and waited for Emily to do the same.

Emily returned the garment to the sewing room and paused to look out the windows. When would Jesse return? What news would he bring?

Gram joined her. "He might not be back for supper. If he's on their trail, he'll stay on it until he finds them or can no longer track them."

"Don't you worry about him?"

"I try not to. He's smart and careful, and when I get to fussing, I remember God can see him and is better able to take care of him than I."

They ate supper without him returning. Emily put Mikey to bed, but he went under protest because he wanted Jesse. She stayed up an hour after Gram had bid her goodnight but finally accepted that Jesse wouldn't be coming before she fell asleep, and she went to her bed.

She had waited only because she wanted to be sure he was safe and wondered if he'd apprehended the bad guys. Not, she insisted to herself, because she missed him or because she felt empty inside with him gone.

Jesse had not returned the next morning. It required a great deal of effort on Emily's part to pretend everything was normal, and maybe she didn't quite succeed for Gram hugged her.

"I've gotten used to him being gone overnight. It isn't anything to worry about. He'll be back when he's finished his business."

They went to the garden and picked peas and baby carrots then sat side by side against the house and shelled peas while Mikey played with Muffin. The morning hours dragged but it was soon time for dinner. Gram tried to engage Emily in conversation but Emily kept losing track of what Gram said.

"Do you want to help with the sewing again?" Gram asked as they did dishes.

"I'd love to." Something about the activity seemed familiar. Perhaps it would trigger her memory. She asked to work on a bodice with tiny pin tucks. "I can do this."

Gram looked uncertain. "It's very detailed."

"I've done it before. I don't know where or when, but I have."

"Very well. Do a little then show me your work."

Emily did so.

"I'm impressed," Gram said. "Perhaps you were a seamstress."

Emily nodded. "I wonder. It seems so familiar." But still no details came.

It took a couple of hours to complete the bodice. Gram declared herself pleased.

"Maybe you can help me with this." Gram opened a closet to reveal a beautiful wedding gown. "It's for Amelia Strong. Her family owns a ranch some distance from here. They seldom come to town, but she'd heard I was the best seamstress around and wanted me to make her gown. We chose the style together but I didn't realize how difficult it would be to get the lace inserts perfect. My eyes don't work well enough. Would you have a look at it?"

Leaving the dress on the padded hanger, Emily examined the lacy parts Gram indicated. She saw how Gram had caught a thread of the lace. That was all it took to keep it from lying perfectly.

"I can fix this if you like."

"I'd be most grateful. I promised to have it done in three weeks. I'm running out of time."

Emily checked the rest of the gown. There were more lace gores to be sewn into the skirt, sleeves yet to be set in, buttons to attach and button loops to make. After that would come the final fitting before the hem could be done. "It won't take long to finish." Though she hoped she would be back with family and loved ones before the three weeks ended. She closed her eyes against the fear that she had no family and no one who cared about her.

She carefully took the dress down, spread a clean white sheet over her lap and work area, and painstakingly set about removing a few stitches, straightening the material and, with tiny, precise stitches, putting it correctly in place.

She'd worked on such a gown before. She knew it with certainty. A rush of emotions flooded her. But was it anger or sorrow she felt? Happiness or sadness?

A tear dropped to the back of her hand. She dashed it away, thankful it hadn't fallen on the dress. Hurriedly, she pulled the sheet over the fine silk. Why was she crying?

* * *

Jesse stomped the dirt off his boots and strode into the house. Mikey greeted him at the door and Jesse swung him into the air and rubbed his whiskered face on the boy's cheeks, careful not to rub hard enough to give him a burn.

The door to the sewing room stood open and he crossed toward it.

He ground to a halt at the sight before him and his heart stalled. He put Mikey on the floor and eased forward.

Emily sat, her hands entangled in a white sheet and tears flowing unchecked down her cheeks in twin silver tracks.

He took a step toward her before remembering he had two days' worth of trail dust on him. Gram would have his hide nailed to the wall if he soiled any of her work.

"Gram," he said softly.

She'd been so engrossed in her work that she hadn't paid any attention to his entrance, likely thinking he would head straight for the kitchen and a cup of cold water. She jerked toward him at his call.

He tipped his head toward Emily. "Can you take away the sewing?"

"Oh, my. I didn't realize." She set aside her own project.

Emily didn't give any indication she was aware of the movement.

Gram carefully laid the dress and sheet on the table. "I'll take care of Mikey." She hurried out of the room and closed the door.

Jesse hunkered down in front of Emily, uncertain

how to proceed. If she was regaining her memory he didn't want to do something that would interfere with that.

"Emily?" He spoke softly, afraid to startle her.

She appeared not to notice.

"Emily." He spoke louder. Touched her shoulder.

She jerked, blinked and sobbed.

He did the only thing he could think of. He stood up and pulled her into his arms, letting her cry.

When her crying had subsided into shuddering breaths, he tipped her face up and wiped it with his handkerchief and let her blow her nose.

"Tell me what happened." His throat still tight, his voice grated. When he'd seen her in such a state, he'd thought he wouldn't ever be able to breathe right again.

"I know it sounds silly, but nothing."

He wasn't accepting that answer. "Something made you cry."

"I was working on that wedding dress." She tipped her head toward the table where the garment rested. "And I was overwhelmed with emotions."

"It made you sad?"

"Maybe. But there was happiness and excitement, too. I really don't know what I felt. I didn't even know I was crying until a tear dropped on my hand." A short-lived sob escaped.

"What was there about the dress? Can you remember?"

She shook her head.

He knew he shouldn't push but he wanted to help her regain her past. "Was it your dress? A friend's? Were you making it for someone special?"

She shook her head. "All I remember is a dress."

It wasn't very helpful. But what he'd discovered was not very helpful, either. He put his arm about her shoulders and led her from the room. They passed through the kitchen. "We're going for a little walk, Gram."

Gram nodded. "Mikey is helping me." Mikey had a piece of biscuit dough and was shaping it into a ball.

Jesse chuckled at how gray the dough had become in the little boy's hands.

He led Emily out of the room, and sensing her restlessness he guided her out the back gate to walk along the alley. "What have you done since I last saw you?"

"Annie came to visit. I helped Gram with her sewing. She says I'm very good. Maybe I was a seamstress."

They stopped in the shade of a willow tree.

She faced him. "Did you find the robbers?"

"'Fraid not. They're good at hiding their tracks. They went into a herd of cows. There was no way I could follow them after that."

"But you know the direction they went."

"Unless they circled back, I suspect they have disappeared into the mountains. A man could hide there for months and not be found."

"That's not good."

"I'll find them eventually, or they'll do something foolish and get caught."

"Is there any evidence they might be the same three who robbed the stage?"

He didn't immediately answer, fearing the truth would upset her. She had more than enough to deal with without worrying about the thieves.

She tipped her head back to see him better. "What aren't you telling me?"

Her gaze demanded honesty. She deserved it. So he told her about the oddly shaped horseshoe he'd seen at the stagecoach. "I saw it at the supply wagon, too."

She stared at his shirtfront. "If they know I'm alive..." A shudder snaked through her. "They won't know that I can't identify them."

"You were face down. I doubt they would know you if you stood ten feet away and stared directly at them."

"You can't be sure they wouldn't know me." Her eyes held his, demanding nothing but honesty.

"I can't be completely sure, no. But you're safe in town. They'd be crazy to do anything with any number of people ready to protect you." He wanted her to believe it and feel safe. He wished he could believe it, too.

"Who would?"

"Besides me?" He tried to sound strong, but his lungs would barely work at the knowledge she might be in danger. "I spoke to George at the store, Hugh and Annie, Doc, everyone along Mineral Avenue and Silver Street." That took care of the major streets. "I also spoke to a dozen or more people along the side streets." He would stay at her side all day, every day, but it would be better if he apprehended the men responsible for her fear.

She shivered as if a cold wind had blasted down the alley and glanced around nervously. "I'd feel better if we went back to the house."

"It's time for supper. But I don't want to see you living in fear." He said it for her sake, because he had half a notion to lock her inside until all of this was over.

They returned to the house and a hot meal.

After supper was done and the kitchen cleaned, Mikey brought some children's books Gram had found. He handed them to Gram, wanting her to read to him.

She sat on the couch and pulled Mikey to her side. Smiling, she looked at Jesse. "Why don't you two run along while Mikey and I entertain each other?"

He hadn't told Gram of his fears, but he would when Mikey wasn't around to hear. Assuring himself there was no danger for Emily outside, he guided her toward the door, ignoring her reluctance.

"Let's go visit Sadie and Logan." This was one time he was particularly glad to have one of the Marshall brothers living in town, though as soon as the house on the ranch was completed, they would be out there. He strapped on his gun belt as they left the house.

She waited until they were outside to voice her objection. "What if those men see me?"

"First of all, they aren't likely to show their faces around here after having committed a crime. Secondly, I'm ready for them."

"Three against one. I don't like those odds."

He went on as if she hadn't spoken. "Most importantly, it's doctor's orders."

"How's that?"

"He said to relax and have fun. Hence the visit to Sadie and Logan's."

She gave a prolonged sigh.

He chuckled. "You'll thank me later."

That brought a grin to her face. "We'll see about that."

They crossed several streets. Children laughed

and chased each other up and down the dusty lanes. Somewhere a piano was being played. A young couple walked by hand in hand.

Jesse smiled at Emily. “It’s an evening to enjoy.”

Her steps slowed, her face grew serious. “I might be able to enjoy it if I knew who I am and what kind of enjoyment I should allow myself.”

Her words sobered him. He had no right to be escorting her about town. She might be a married woman, though he had convinced himself she wasn’t. Until he had proof, one way or the other, he must treat her as if she was, and he put several inches between them.

They reached the house where Sadie and Logan and the kids lived just as the family exited.

Emily drew back. “They’ve got plans.”

Logan saw them. “You’re just in time to join us.”

Emily refused to move so Jesse asked, “For what?”

“Some fun. Not It.” He dashed away to the open area by their house.

“Not It.” Sadie followed.

One by one they ran off, leaving Jesse and Emily to decide what to do. While he was waiting for her to indicate what she wanted, she said, “Not It,” and joined the others.

“Not fair,” he called after her. “I didn’t know if you wanted to play or not.”

“Didn’t I hear you say I was going to have fun?” She danced about on her tiptoes in a clearly challenging way.

“Can’t get me, Uncle Jesse,” Sammy called as he darted by.

Jesse shook his head in sad resignation. “Seems I

have no choice." He took after Sammy, zigged as he neared Emily.

But she sensed his intent, picked up her skirt and ran away. He shifted direction again and tagged Beth.

They played until dusk then returned to the house.

Jesse had succeeded in not chasing Emily, knowing he came too close to wanting to hold her for no particular reason. There wasn't even the excuse of tears to wipe or fears to soothe away.

Likewise, she had always chased one of the others as if she felt the same way. Or perhaps, on her part, she wouldn't feel anything until she knew who she was.

Tomorrow he would redouble his efforts to find the men responsible for the robberies and murders. He would do his job as sheriff and keep his thoughts and feelings under a tight rein.

He knew the chances were good that once she knew who she was and didn't need him to help her she would also see him as others did, a man with a soiled background, a man with nothing to offer but his heart.

His heart had never been enough.

Chapter Eleven

Day after day, Emily worked on the wedding dress. Every stitch jabbed at her emotions. But her brain remained impervious to her feelings. All she knew was she had done this before. And so she ignored the way her heart twisted and protested, and continued to sew the lace inserts and the gores, hoping it would cause her memory to return.

Jesse had been gone for three days. Before he left he'd said he wouldn't be back until he found those responsible for the robberies and murders.

Emily had quit looking out the window at the sound of an approaching horse or men's boots. She stopped setting the table for four.

Midway through the afternoon, Mikey was racing about the house. He knocked over a vase of flowers.

Emily set aside the white silk dress and rushed to mop up the water. "He's restless," she said to Gram. "I think I should take him outside for a while."

"You go right ahead. Don't feel you have to spend all your time sewing, though if you decide to stay in Bella Creek for some reason, I am prepared to offer you a partnership in my business." Gram almost looked like she wanted that to happen.

Stay? It sounded tempting. But Emily could decide nothing until she discovered who she was. She'd named states and towns in the hopes of triggering something, but none of them sounded like home to her.

"Thanks. It's a most generous offer and one I will consider, but I'm hoping..." She didn't finish. People must be growing tired of hearing her complain that she didn't know who she was.

"I understand. Now run along and enjoy the afternoon."

Emily opened the front door, and with a whoop, Mikey dashed outside. Usually when they walked he dawdled, examining every rock, bug and blade of grass. This time, he ran as fast as his short legs would carry him.

"Don't go too far," she called, and he immediately switched directions and raced back to her.

She laughed and bent to hug him. "You are such a good boy."

"'Kay." And away he went again.

They reached the intersection and she paused, wondering which way to go. She wasn't as fearful as she'd first been, now that she had met many of the town's residents. At least every person wasn't a stranger who filled her with fear.

"Hello."

Emily turned toward the sound. "Annie, hi."

"Going shopping?"

She had no money. And she wasn't about to put something on Jesse's bill. He'd already gone above and beyond the call of duty. "Just out for a walk."

"Me, as well. Mind if I join you?"

"Not at all." It was better than being alone with her endlessly circling thoughts.

With Evan trotting along, Annie fell in at Emily's side. The two boys chased each other up and down the street.

"Let's go over to the school yard and let them play."

Annie's suggestion sounded good, so the four of them crossed the street. Annie and Emily sat in the shade on one of the benches and let the little boys race about.

Annie spoke. "I want to ask how you're doing, but you must get sick of it."

"I get sick of not knowing who I am. Sometimes I feel like I can almost remember, and then a black fog clouds my mind."

"I'm truly sorry. I wish there was something I could do...anyone could do."

"Every day I beseech God to fix my brain. So far, He has chosen not to do so."

"It's hard to trust God in some circumstances."

"True." For a moment, Emily thought about trust. "More and more I am learning how dependent my trust is on things going well, but if we only trust when we can see the future, we aren't really trusting." She embedded the thought in her brain. This situation required she trust God completely—for her past and her future and for her memory to return. Though she thought more and more about what she'd do if it she never got it back. Each time she hit a roadblock. She couldn't plan anything until she knew who she was. "Jesse's out looking for the robbers. He said he wouldn't come back until he found them." She chuckled. “We might never see him again.” Without warning, her voice broke.

“Emily, what’s wrong?”

She swallowed hard. “What if he doesn’t come back?”

Annie laughed at the idea. “He’ll be back. This is his home and Gram is here.”

Emily tried to find encouragement in the words. “It doesn’t make sense, but his presence makes me feel safe. His was the first face I saw when I came to out there. I immediately knew I was safe with him.” She gave a shrug and attempted a laugh. “I’m being silly, aren’t I?”

Annie considered her a moment before she answered. “I can’t begin to know what you are going through, but I understand why you feel safe with Jesse around. He has a very strong code of conduct that guides his every action. He would never compromise his ideals. I think that comes across to anyone who meets him. So I’m not at all surprised that you feel that way.” She paused to let the words sink in. “I wouldn’t want to see Jesse hurt.”

“I’m not going to hurt him.” But the warning was timely. She’d leaned on him too much, looked to him for assurance and comfort. She’d be more cautious around him in the future. Not turn to him so much. But it was Annie’s words about Jesse’s high ideals that worried her. Just as she knew sewing meant more to her than one would expect, she knew she had reason to fear what her past would reveal.

Nevertheless, she wanted to know who she was. She would face whatever she learned and move forward.

A rider passed on the street and Emily turned. It

wasn't Jesse. She told herself she hadn't expected it to be. Tried to make herself believe her eagerness to see him stemmed only from the hope he would bring the murdering robbers to justice.

Mikey fell and banged his arm. He came running to Emily and she pulled him onto her lap and rubbed his back. He stuck his thumb in his mouth and rested against her a moment, then he squirmed down and trotted back to Evan.

"Those two little guys are so much alike," Annie observed.

"I don't see it. Evan is dark like his father and Mikey is as blond as any Marshall."

Annie laughed. "Not in looks but both are sparing with their words and bursting with energy."

"They are that." The two women chuckled as the boys ran in circles until they fell down.

"I love seeing Evan run about and enjoy life. When I first saw him, he was locked inside himself." She related a story about Hugh finding his son neglected and treated like an animal and told how he'd advertised for someone to care for his boy. "He'd planned on a marriage of convenience with an older, sedate woman." Annie chuckled. "Hugh didn't think I could deal with Evan, but something clicked between us from the start."

"Locked inside himself? Sounds like me."

"Then be encouraged by what you see Evan to be now."

Emily studied the boy. "Nothing is too hard for God, is it?"

"No, it isn't." Annie squeezed Emily around the shoulders. "Keep trusting."

Emily gave a dry chuckle. "Seems I have little choice but to do so."

They talked about their faith, Annie's family and the town. Every bit of information contributed to Emily feeling less and less like she lacked a life.

"It's time I got back," Annie said. "I like to be at home when Hugh leaves his office."

Emily grinned at the pink stain in Annie's cheeks. "I keep forgetting that you with a four-year-old have been married such a short time."

"God has supplied the family I needed and the love I secretly wanted." Annie's face glowed with joy. "I pray God will supply all your needs."

"Thank you. I think Gram is hoping to convince me to stay here. She thinks the whole town is ready to embrace the lost and lonely." Those hadn't been her exact words, but Emily got the feeling that's what she meant. "And who is more lost than I?"

Annie squeezed her hands. "But not lonely, I hope."

"How could I be lonely with so many kind people around?" But she was, and would be, until she knew what her past contained.

They called the boys and made their way back home. Annie turned in at the manse and Emily continued onward.

She and Gram had fallen into a routine of sorts. Gram made dinner, Emily made supper. Cooking came easily to her, though she had to be careful not to cook too much. Gram said it indicated she was used to preparing meals for a big family.

She went into the kitchen and started the meal. If she'd cooked for a large family, shouldn't she have some recollection of them? Were those people siblings or children, or had she run an eating establishment? She must have been extremely busy if she was a seamstress, as well. "Why can't I remember?" she murmured.

"Talking to yourself now?" Jesse leaned in the open doorway.

She ordered her heart back into place. "I didn't hear you. When did you get back?"

"This very moment." He stepped into the kitchen.

Mikey yelled a greeting and raced across the room into Jesse's arms. He babbled and waved his arms.

"I think he's telling you about his day."

Jesse grinned at the boy. "It sounds like you had fun."

Mikey nodded.

With a heart light as sunshine, Emily set the table for four and served the meal.

Jesse was back and all was right in her world for the moment…until she had to deal with reality again.

Jesse waited until Mikey was asleep in bed before he told Gram and Emily he'd failed to find the culprits. It wasn't for lack of trying. "I scoured the country, hoping to find their trail, but they know how to hide their tracks."

"You did your best," Gram said. "No one can ask more of you. Not even you."

"Yes, Gram." He grinned at her. It was a message she gave him often. And he needed to hear it often.

"I'm off to bed," she said and climbed the stairs, leaving Jesse and Emily alone.

"What have you been doing?" He wanted to hear about every moment of every day, just as he'd thought of her every moment of the days he looked for the criminals. Not only did he want to do his job and bring them to justice, he knew Emily would never be totally safe as long as they were at large.

"I'm still working on the wedding dress." A troubled look crossed her face, though he guessed she tried to hide it. "I've helped Gram weed the garden, and I had a nice visit with Annie." She told him of taking the boys to the school yard to play.

Emily's eyes clouded, but before he could ask for an explanation she reached for her Bible on the nearby shelf. "I've been reading, searching, really, hoping to find something about myself." She opened the Bible and slowly turned the pages. Her hands grew still and she seemed not to breathe.

"Emily, what is it?"

Tears glistened and she pointed to the page before her.

He turned the Bible so he could read the words. She had underlined a verse in Isaiah chapter forty-three. *When thou passest through the waters, I will be with thee; and through the rivers, they shall not overflow thee: when thou walkest through the fire, thou shalt not be burned; neither shall the flame kindle upon thee.* In the margin she had written *Even in this.* And a date. *February 1, 1887.* Four years ago. What had happened on that date?

She pressed her hand to her chest, made little rubbing movements as if trying to ease a pain.

He watched her warily, prepared to rush her to the doctor if she showed any sign of fainting.

"I remember," she whispered.

He waited, not moving or making a sound, afraid that doing would stop the recovery of her past.

"I don't know what happened, but it almost destroyed me. I felt like I was drowning, like my life was consumed by flames." She rocked back and forth. "I was so hurt. I think I must have done something and paid a heavy price. But I only remember the pain, nothing else." She bent over her knees, as if in agony.

He longed to pull her into his arms and comfort her, but she seemed too fragile to even touch. He knew the chapter she had marked and ran his gaze down to the verses he sought. *Remember ye not the former things, neither consider the things of old. Behold, I will do a new thing.* He read the verse to her.

She nodded but did not seem to get any comfort from the words.

He wanted her to know that she could start over without ever recovering her memory, but he didn't wish that for her, knowing she could not be whole, could not be free until she knew who she was. What could she have done that frightened her so much?

She straightened, wiped her eyes. "What can I do but trust God to bring me the answers I need?"

He watched her, wishing he could ease her worries. Instead, he sat beside her without moving. His ultimate goal was to help her regain her memory and remember her past, see the possibilities of her future. He would not acknowledge that he wondered if there might exist some anticipation of her seeing him in the picture.

No, he reminded himself that he had decided to guard his heart against destruction, and that meant not pinning any hope of a young woman seeing him as enough. But his job meant helping her remember, and the doctor had said her memory might return when she least expected it…perhaps when she was happily doing something else. "Would you like to visit the falls?" He hadn't planned to say that but it would fulfill the doctor's orders to do something besides think about regaining her memory.

Her eyes lit. "Falls? Really?"

"Libby Falls. They're very spectacular."

She smiled. "I can hardly say no to that, can I?"

"We'll go tomorrow, then."

"Okay."

His heart captured Emily's laugh. It would forever hold a special place in his memories. "What about Mikey?" Emily asked.

"The trail isn't suitable for someone his age. Maybe Annie will keep him. I'll ask her."

Emily could not deny her excitement at the prospect of visiting the falls. Jesse had taken Mikey to stay with Annie, saying he would be back in half an hour to get her. She needed to conceal her anticipation from Gram, so she filled the time with tidying a kitchen cupboard.

"The falls are a lovely place, though I've not been in years," Gram said.

"Would you like to come with us?"

Gram laughed merrily. "Oh, no. I have no intention of interfering with your outing. Besides, it's not the sort of outing an old lady like me could enjoy." She chuckled again. "But it was sweet of you to ask."

Sweet? Her? Was she? Emily considered the idea. She wanted to be sweet. Wanted others to see her that way. Wanted to feel that way within herself. But maybe she was something else.

She chased away the troublesome doubts. Today she would simply enjoy being Miss Emily Smith.

A conveyance stopped at the front of the house. Emily stilled her urge to run to the other room and see if Jesse had returned. She waited, her excitement growing as his footsteps thudded on the steps and the door opened.

"I believe your ride has arrived," Gram said with a degree of amusement.

Jesse entered the kitchen. "All set."

Emily hoped no one noticed the slight trembling of her hands as she placed a borrowed bonnet on her head and tied the ribbons.

He held out his elbow. "Shall we go?"

She took his offered arm.

"Have a good time," Gram said.

They stepped out into the bright summer sunshine. Jesse had rented a buggy pulled by a black horse with four white stockings. From a nearby tree, a robin sang. Surely it meant they were going to have a wonderful day.

Her heart as light as the air around her, she took Jesse's hand and held it firmly as he helped her into the seat, his other hand light upon her waist.

He climbed up beside her and smiled. "Let's go have a good day." His dark eyes held hers, promising her so much more than she could accept.

But today she would take whatever came her way with a full heart. Tomorrow she would deal with the facts of her life.

He flicked the reins and they drove away from

town. Soon they were alone on the trail. They turned to the west. Pink, orange, purple and blue flowers dotted the grassy slopes. The trail climbed and trees grew more abundantly…dark green spruce and pine among the deciduous trees.

She leaned back and let the peace of her surroundings ease through her. Except for one nagging thought. "If I get my memory back, will I forget all this?" She meant far more than the passing scenery. Would she remember the days she had spent at Bella Creek? Would she remember Jesse and his grandmother?

Jesse didn't immediately answer. He stared over the horse's head.

"I don't want to forget." Her voice grated from her tight throat.

He brought his gaze to her, his eyes dark and, if she read correctly, troubled. "I know it's a possibility. All I can say is—let's make the memory as bright and happy as we can, so you will recall the feeling even if you can't recall the event."

"That makes sense." Just as she could now recall the emotions of her past but not the events. "I like that."

He squeezed her hand. "Me, too."

Their gazes held for several more turns of the wheels, silently promising each other a good day with no regrets. And if a little voice whispered a warning in the back of her mind, Emily simply ignored it.

The trail grew steeper and more narrow. A breeze blew in their faces. She turned her head toward a deep rumbling sound. "Do I hear the waterfalls?"

He chuckled. "I believe you do. It's not far now." They continued to a small clearing where he stopped.

She looked about. She could hear the roar of the falls but couldn't see them.

He set the brake and jumped down, coming round to help her to the ground.

The sound of rushing water echoed in her heart, stirring unfamiliar longings. She wanted to know who she was so she could move forward.

She willingly forgot her inner turmoil as Jesse took her hand and led her up a rocky incline. Through the trees she saw foaming water and leaned forward hoping for a glimpse of the falls. One foot slipped.

"Emily." Jesse pulled her back, his eyes wide. "Are you trying to give me a heart attack?"

Pleased at his concern, she grinned. "I can always count on you to rescue me."

He drew in a deep breath. "I prefer it not become a habit." He led her back toward the buggy. "We'll follow that trail." He pointed out a barely there path through the trees, so narrow they must go singly. But he reached back and took her hand as the path grew rocky.

The thunder of the water grew louder. The roar within her increased. She struggled to breathe and tugged Jesse's hand to get him to stop.

He turned, must have seen her turmoil in her face for he caught her by the shoulders. "What's wrong?"

"I don't know. You know that Bible verse about deep calling to deep?"

He blinked.

She understood his confusion. Her question didn't make sense.

Then he nodded. "Yes, I know the one you mean. It's a Psalm."

"That's how I feel hearing the roar of the waters." She pressed a hand to her chest. "There's a roaring inside me and I don't know what it is."

He closed his arms about her and she leaned against him. Her turmoil eased.

"Do you want to turn back?" he asked, his voice so gentle it was a mere whisper.

She tipped her head up. He was such a good man. One who deserved nothing but the best. But before the troubled thought could take root that she might not be what a man like him deserved, she dismissed it. "I would not forgive myself if I came this far and didn't see the falls. Besides, I'm feeling much better now." Thanks to his strength and comfort.

"You're sure?"

"Completely sure."

He held her hand more firmly than he had before, and they continued navigating the rough trail. Rocks made it hard to keep her footing and she gratefully clung to his hand. They stepped to a granite embankment. Jesse drew her to his side and pointed to the right. Not just one waterfall but a series of them rushed into each other as if falling down a stone stairway.

The powerful display washed away every fear of her past, every worry about her future. God, who made the mighty waters roar, was more than strong enough to take care of her small needs.

"We can get closer." Jesse spoke in her ear.

She hadn't realized she'd leaned back against him. Nor did she feel any need to bring the moment to an end.

"Soon," she said. A Bible verse filled her mind.

"'God is our refuge and strength, a very present help in trouble. Therefore will not we fear, though the earth be removed, and though the mountains be carried into the midst of the sea; Though the waters thereof roar and be troubled, though the mountains shake with the swelling thereof.'" Such joy filled her she didn't know if she could contain it. She turned to face Jesse.

His eyes widened and then darkened as he read her expression. "I don't know what just took place but I like it." He wiped her cheeks, drying moisture from her face.

"Nothing matters but this moment." That wasn't exactly what she meant. "Rather, I can enjoy this moment, knowing my times are safe in God's hands."

"Then I say let's enjoy the time we have." His gaze lingered on her face, rested on her lips.

For a heartbeat she thought he might want to kiss her and she leaned closer.

But his gaze returned to her eyes. "Wait until you see the waterfalls up close." He took her hand and they continued along the rocky shore.

She wasn't disappointed. Only the overwhelming joy of anticipation made her wish he had kissed her, as she'd expected. Except, of course, she didn't *expect* it. That was nonsense.

They reached a spot close to the falls and stood mesmerized by the rushing waters, the mighty roar and the rising mist.

After a bit, she sighed. "Thank you for bringing me here."

"No need to hurry away." He indicated a natural granite bench and they sat on the sun-warmed rock.

She lifted her face, the spray of the water dampening her skin. If only she could stay here and enjoy this peaceful feeling forever. Or, at least until she got her memory back.

"There's more." He got to his feet and pulled her up to his side. Keeping her hand in his, he led the way back along the river. But they passed the trail and continued downstream.

She didn't ask their destination because it didn't matter where they went, only that he seemed to want to prolong this afternoon as much as she.

Ferns grew in the shade of the trees. Ahead were bushes with palm-shaped leaves and red berries.

He picked several berries and handed them to her. "Thimbleberries."

"I've never seen these before. Well, not that I recall." She popped one into her mouth and sucked it.

He watched her, his eyes dark and…

She shifted her gaze past him at the claiming look in his eyes that made her wish for things that were impossible at the moment. "Delicious. Both sweet and tart."

For a few minutes, they picked and ate berries.

The breeze rustled the leaves, the river gurgled behind them and bird song rang through the air. Again, peace filled her.

Ahead, a crow squawked as it tried to pull something from among the rocks. They laughed at his antics. He heard them and abandoned his task.

"Let's see what he was after." Jesse said.

At the spot they discovered a red ribbon stuck among the stones.

"I heard they liked bright things," Jesse said as

he yanked it free. "Someone lost a hair ribbon." He handed it to her.

"It's past saving," she said. She fingered the ribbon. Why did it tug at her memory? Like so many times she'd recalled a feeling but not an event. She tossed the ribbon aside in disgust but didn't know if it was frustration from something in the past or because of her inability to remember. Perhaps it was both.

Jesse had not noticed her momentary lapse and reached for her hand and they walked along the edge of the river.

She gladly pushed aside the feelings stirred by the hair ribbon. Today was for making better memories than the ones that half surfaced from her past.

He jumped down a three-foot step and reached up to help her. The rocks were uneven, their surfaces smooth. Her foot slipped and she fell into his arms.

Air whooshed from his lungs and he staggered back.

She gasped as she saw the ground disappear behind him. They were about to tumble off the rocks into the rushing water. She tried to right herself but could find no footing and closed her eyes, waiting for the thud.

He scrambled, fighting to get control before they went over the edge.

Just when she knew there was no way of preventing the fall, he jerked forward. They teetered on the rocks. She kept her arms about his waist and backed away until they reached the safety of the tree line. Her knees weakened and she leaned against the solidness of a trunk.

He rested his elbows on either side of her head

and his forehead against hers. "That was too close for comfort."

"I thought we were going over. I don't know how you managed to stop it."

"I prayed. There's no other explanation." His breathing was still ragged.

She tightened her arms about his waist. "You're shaking."

"Maybe because I'm shaken."

She laughed at his play on words, but the sound ended on a moan.

"We're both safe. That's all that matters." He caught her chin with his finger and tipped her face toward his. "I couldn't bear the thought of you being hurt." His gaze went to her lips.

She saw his intention of kissing her, knew this time she wasn't mistaken, and leaned forward.

He caught her mouth with his damp, cool lips. She closed her eyes and lost track of everything but the sweetness of the moment. He was so lean and strong. His shirt warm. How had her hands moved from his waist to pressing on his back?

He eased away. "I'm sorry."

"I'm not."

He grinned. "Truthfully, I'm not either. Whatever happens, we'll have this afternoon to remember."

"I know." She trailed her fingertip along his jawline, enjoying the raspy sound. Tomorrow could well bring a new chapter in her life. Or perhaps a return to the old one. But she would not let the future or lack of a past rob her of enjoying the present.

Jesse had never felt such fear as he had when he realized he was about to go over the edge. The relief when he'd found solid footing had left his knees weak. If anything happened to her—

He couldn't finish the thought.

Kissing her seemed the best way to assure himself she was okay. He shouldn't have done it, knowing she would move on once she remembered who she was, and even if she didn't, she would eventually realize he was only a sheriff and it would begin to dawn on her what it meant that he was a man whose mother had lived a sordid life. No one cared about that in a sheriff. But to a man, especially a man who longed for a wife and children of his own, it had proven to be a hindrance. But they had agreed to put aside the reality of their lives and make this a day to remember.

He knew he wouldn't ever forget one detail of the afternoon.

Neither of them seemed ready to leave this spot and they sank to the ground beneath the trees, their shoulders pressing together. She told him of the outing with Mikey. "He's such a special boy. I hate to think of him having to wait months to join his adoptive family."

"Me, too. I've grown very fond of him." Jesse would hurt when the boy left. His house would seem empty. Would Mikey return to wherever he'd come from to wait for the Newmans? Would they cross the mountains again to get him or would they change their mind about adoption? Then what would happen to him? Would Emily leave, too, to go with Mikey? Or would she remember a family she would return to? His heart echoed with loneliness.

A sad silence filled his heart and then he realized she, too, had grown quiet. Was she feeling the same as he? He shifted to face her.

"I wish we would hear from the Newmans. I can't see myself going to Oregon with Mikey, but they'll know who Aunt Hilda is and where she lives. Once I know, it seems to me the best thing to do is go there. She'll know who I am. I'll be able to pick up the pieces of my life."

"That makes sense. And if you don't like the life you discover, you can always come back here."

She studied her folded hands.

He had to ask. "Don't you think you could have a good life here?"

Her gaze came to his, full of longing and uncertainty. "If I couldn't remember the feelings of the past, I expect I could be very happy here. But something troubles me, and until I can learn what it is, I can never feel free to belong anywhere."

He took her hands between his. "Then I hope and pray you will get your memory back and learn your fears are groundless." Even if remembering made her forget him. Her peace of mind was far more important.

A sharp crack jolted them both to look around.

"What was that?" she asked.

He knew the sound. "Someone is shooting nearby."

She started to scramble to her feet.

He pulled her down. "Don't move. Stay low." He studied their surroundings, his thoughts racing. He couldn't see any wild animals being hunted nor any puff of smoke to indicate the shooter. Were he and Emily targets? His first thought was of the three men responsible for robberies and murder.

If he and Emily edged back into the trees…

He signaled her to follow him and stay low. They crept deeper into the shadows. When he deemed they would be impossible for anyone at a distance to see, he signaled her to stop and pulled her close to protect her.

"Who would be shooting at us?" she whispered.

"I don't know that they are, but it's better to be overcautious." Than dead. But he wouldn't share that concern.

They sat in strained silence. He heard a sound far to his right. Couldn't tell if someone moved through the trees. It could be an animal. Or just the wind. But at least it wasn't between them and the buggy.

"I don't think we're in any danger," he said after a few more minutes, and he got to his feet, keeping Emily close. He had no intention of leaving her vulnerable.

He stood several seconds and when nothing happened, slowly made his way to the edge of the trees. They would be in the open until he reached the trail through the woods. Why had he gone so far downstream?

She clung to him and perhaps wondered why he didn't go faster, but he had no desire to risk going over the edge because of haste. She chuckled softly. "I feel like we're stuck between a rock and a hard place, only it's truly rocks and trees."

There'd been no more shooting, no movement through the trees that he could detect. His tension eased marginally. "I think someone must be out hunting."

"So long as they're not hunting us."

He smiled. "Nice to know you can joke about it."

"Like your Gram says, you have to choose whether to laugh or cry, and laughing is better if you can do it."

"Yup, I've heard that a time or two."

They reached the cover of the trees and he relaxed. Now all they had to do was get to the buggy and get back to town. At least in the buggy he would have his gun. He'd chosen not to wear it on their outing. Perhaps a foolish decision, but he'd wanted her to see him as something other than the sheriff.

He set a leisurely pace going back through the woods, and wanting her to remember the good parts of the afternoon, he talked about the waterfall, the river and the crow.

The clearing lay ahead of them and he paused with Emily behind him to scan the area. His breath eased out as he saw nothing to cause him concern. He turned to her and smiled. "Are you ready to go back?" He didn't expect any answer but yes.

She slipped by him and went to the spot where she could see the waterfalls below them. "Thank you for bringing me here. I hope I always remember this day, no matter what happens."

He gave a wry chuckle. "You'll have lots to remember."

She faced him, her eyes soft.

He'd heard others say their heart skipped a beat and had silently mocked the notion, but now he understood as his own heart did exactly that at the look in her eyes.

"I will cherish every moment, one in particular."

He understood she meant their kiss. He touched her cheek. "I'm glad. I will, too."

He helped her to the buggy, and if his hands held her a moment longer than was necessary, there was no one to notice. They made their way back to town in companionable silence, content to be sitting close together thinking of each special moment of the day.

Even falling on the rocks had had its good side. It had given them a reason to kiss, and hearing a gunshot had made it necessary to hold each other. He could ask for nothing better to clutch to his heart when she left.

They reached town and he slowed the horse as they passed a house on the outskirts. A nice house with a picket fence. The yard was overgrown now. Grandfather Marshall owned the house. A young couple had lived there until two months ago when the wife had developed a health condition and they'd moved to Great Falls so she could get regular medical attention. He'd often looked at the house and thought it would make someone a nice home.

Always, before, he'd thought of another young couple moving into it. Now he hoped no one would.

He shook his head. Did he really think he might be the one to move in? And not alone? The damp air at the falls must have affected his brain.

He would not be living there with Emily as his wife. He knew that. But he meant to enjoy every day he was able to share with her.

After that, he was back to being Jesse, the sheriff. A man who lived with his Gram and had no interest in courting young ladies.

Maybe he'd get a big dog to keep him company.

He refused to admit his heart hurt at the thought.

Chapter Twelve

Sunday morning, Emily brushed the skirt of her dress. It was a lovely dress and it was so kind of Annie to lend it, but Emily wished she had clothes of her own, if only because they might provide a clue to her past. She went to the mirror, rolled her hair into place around her head and secured it with hairpins. At least the pins belonged to her. The Bible that was hers sat on the bedside table, and she opened it to the page on which she had written *Even in this*. She drew in a deep breath. *Yes, Lord, even in this, I will trust you.*

Her thoughts drifted to the previous day. She would hold the special memories close to her heart the rest of her life. Even if she couldn't remember the event, she was sure she'd never forget the feeling. Her throat tightened. She didn't want to lose the memory of these days at Bella Creek but she wanted to know her past. Dr. Baker had given no assurances she could have both.

She touched her lips, remembering the sweet, tender kiss. Yes, she would take unforgettable memories with her from yesterday. And, God willing, more of the same today. She blushed at her choice of words. She didn't mean another kiss but simply more time with Jesse.

She heard Gram descend the stairs, and the outer door open and close, and knew she had left for church. It was time for Emily to join Jesse and Mikey and follow.

Jesse waited in the living room, hat in hand. His smile warmed her insides. He held the door for her and crooked his elbow. She willingly placed her hand on his arm as they made their way to church, Mikey running circles ahead of them.

"It's to be hoped he wears off some energy before we get there," she said, with a chuckle.

"He'll do his best to sit quietly. He's a good boy." Jesse's voice deepened and she glanced at him.

"I'll miss him," he said.

"Me, too." A bit of the anticipated joy disappeared. Perhaps tomorrow Jesse would receive a letter providing information about her. So many things would change when she learned who she was. Everything but God's faithfulness, and she clung to that fact.

The Marshall family had already gathered at the church and Annie rushed forward to greet her. "He hasn't guessed what's going on," she whispered. Annie had invited them to join them at the ranch for a surprise celebration of Grandfather's seventieth birthday. "Just family," she'd said.

"I'm not family," Emily had pointed out.

Annie had laughed. "Jesse is practically a brother. Gram was my grandmother's closest friend, so that makes them family. Besides, you're my friend, so that makes you family."

Emily had enjoyed a good laugh at her reasoning, but being included warmed her. If only she could belong here in the future.

Grandfather Marshall eyed them as they whispered together in front of the church. "What are you scheming?"

Annie shrugged. "When have I ever schemed anything?"

Grandfather grunted. "I lost track by the time you were ten."

Annie grinned and took Evan's hand as the family moved inside.

Emily took Mikey's hand and they followed. She and Jesse sat with Mikey between them.

Hugh announced the first hymn and they shared a hymnal. They joined their voices together with the congregation. Shared words. Shared love of the child pressed to both their knees. Shared special moments. But not shared worlds. Hers was unknown. His clearly known and understood by all. Jesse was a man of principle. His past, the truth about his mother, had created in him an uncompromising view of right and wrong. Which was as it should be, especially for a sheriff, but she shivered to think what it meant for her if her past was sullied in any way.

It didn't matter. Today was for enjoying and remembering, and she focused her attention on the sermon Hugh delivered.

"'This is the day which the Lord hath made; we will rejoice and be glad in it.' Let's not waste one minute of God's gracious gift with regrets or worries." Thus he began.

Emily drank in every word of God's provision of

her daily needs. In His strength, she would face today, tomorrow and all her tomorrows—whether with her memory restored or not.

The service ended and the congregation exited.

"Wait here," Jesse said to Gram and Emily as the others left. "I'll bring a democrat from the livery barn."

By the time he returned, the Marshall family had all left. He helped Gram into the back seat, and Mikey and Emily into the front, then climbed up beside them. "Everyone ready?" He smiled at Gram and Mikey, and lastly at Emily, and the look in his eyes promised a day to hold forever in her memories.

Ahead of them on the trail, they saw the dust from the Marshalls returning home.

By the time they arrived, the others had entered the house, all except for Grandfather Marshall who waited at the door of the ranch house as they drove up. He hobbled toward them.

Jesse rushed around and helped Gram down. She turned to Grandfather, rested her hand on his and they smiled warmly at each other.

Jesse helped Emily to the ground and lifted Mikey from the democrat. The boy's feet were going before they even hit solid ground and he ran to join Evan and the other children.

"It's nice of you to grace us with your presence," Grandfather said to Gram.

"It's nice to be invited."

Grandfather made a disapproving sound. "You can come anytime without an invitation. In fact, you could move right in."

Gram colored like a summer rose.

Emily gave Jesse a questioning look.

Jesse leaned close to whisper. "Old friends, that's all."

Emily guessed it was a whole lot more than that. She'd seen the spark in Grandfather's eyes and the longing in Gram's face that she likely thought she'd hidden.

They followed the older pair into the house. The women were in the kitchen helping with the meal.

Conner pulled Jesse aside. "Did I tell you—?" The rest of his question was lost as Conner drew Jesse to the dining room.

Jesse glanced over his shoulder to Emily and shrugged as if to say he had no choice but to go with his friend.

Emily shrugged back and with a contented smile turned to help the others with the meal.

The door opened and a petite young woman entered along with a man of medium build. A girl of eight or ten accompanied them and an older gentleman followed.

Annie drew Emily forward. "This is my best friend, Carly Gallagher and her new husband, Sawyer. This lovely young lady is his sister, Jill."

Emily wondered at the way Jill wrinkled her nose at Annie before she greeted Emily.

"And Mr. Morrison, Carly's father."

Mr. Morrison greeted her with a strong Scottish accent.

Hellos were exchanged with the others, and then the men went through to the sitting room to join the other male members of the group. Jill ducked outside to join the children and Carly helped with getting the meal ready to serve.

A few minutes later the food was organized, the children called in and the women were carrying heaping dishes into the dining room. The table had been stretched out as far as it would go and still another table had been shoved to one end. Family and friends gathered round.

Grandfather asked the blessing then looked around. "It's nice to share the meal with so many old friends." He smiled at Gram at his side and Mr. Morrison halfway down the table. "And new friends." He smiled at Emily and Mikey. "And family." His gaze went round the table, pausing at his two sons, Bud and George, and then each of his grandchildren. It lingered at each of the great-grandchildren. "It's a surprise to have you all be here at the same time."

"It's for your birthday," Sammy said, then clamped his hand over his mouth. "I wasn't supposed to say."

Grandfather scowled in Kate's direction. "I said I didn't want any fuss."

"You're the only one making a fuss," she said.

He sputtered.

Gram patted his arm. "Don't pretend you aren't pleased. You've always enjoyed extra attention."

All the adults chuckled at her words. Grandfather looked ready to argue then laughed. "Maybe I won't invite you to live out here. I'm afraid you'd reveal all my secrets."

Gram again blushed and Grandfather looked pleased.

In the general hubbub that followed, as food was passed from hand to hand and news exchanged, Emily leaned over to whisper in Jesse's ear. "Do I sense a romance between those two?"

He looked startled. "I never noticed before."

She quirked an eyebrow. "Either you've been blind or things have changed."

"Things have certainly changed." He studied the older pair and shook his head. "Hard to think of Gram and Grandfather Marshall..." He shook his head again and Emily chuckled.

She turned her attention to Carly, who entertained them with a story about a wild horse she had captured. That got Conner's attention and they discussed preferred ways of breaking the horse. Soon a heated argument ensued.

Annie's father, Bud, leaned forward. "You're both right. To each his own."

His children quieted and concentrated on eating.

As soon as the main course was over, Kate and Annie took away the dishes and carried in a big cake.

"Chocolate?" Grandfather asked, as they put it in front of him.

"Would we dare serve anything else?"

At Annie's signal, they all shouted, "Happy Birthday."

Grandfather was presented with the first piece of cake. "Seventy years old? Where has the time gone?" He glanced around the table. "The lot of you have kept me too busy to notice the passing of time."

His family laughed.

The children finished their cake and were excused to go outside and play, lowering the noise level by several decibels.

"I saw Collins yesterday. He had a deer he'd just

shot. He said his son is doing well." Dawson explained that the boy had been injured falling from the loft.

"Good to hear," Jesse said. "Where did you see him?"

"Where the trail to the falls forks."

Jesse laughed. "That must have been what we heard." He told them of the incident yesterday. "I wondered if someone was shooting at me."

"Who would be shooting at you?" Sadie's voice conveyed disbelief.

"Seems nobody was," Jesse said. "But there are three men running around robbing people and not minding if they kill someone in the process. Emily survived one incident. We also met some ruffians on the trail. Wouldn't care to meet them again."

Emily and Jesse had discussed the trio and she had told him she was certain they weren't the same ones who robbed the stagecoach. Which meant there was more than one set of unsavory characters to be concerned about, though Jesse believed the three who stopped them on the trial had left the area.

"You haven't captured them yet?" Grandfather demanded of Jesse.

"I lost their trail in the mountains."

"I thought you could track over rock or ice."

Jesse laughed. "I never claimed that."

Grandfather studied him a moment. "I assume you will continue to look for them."

"Certainly. You don't need to ask."

Emily squirmed. "It's my fault he isn't out there." She hung her head to think she was keeping him from his work.

"Part of my job is to protect Emily."

All eyes shifted to her. Mr. Morrison spoke, perhaps for them all, "Aye, lassie, and are you in danger from these scoundrels?"

"I don't know. I didn't see any of their faces, but perhaps they don't know that. I'm waiting until I hear from the Newmans regarding Mikey before I make any plans." And then what? She would go home, except she didn't know where home was.

Annie sat back, disappointment in her eyes and her words. "I had hoped you'd stay here."

Grandfather turned to Emily. "You're a single woman. You couldn't do better than to settle here in Bella Creek. We need more young ladies like you."

Gram flicked her fingers at him. "Allan, you old scoundrel. What would Annabelle say to your interfering?"

He looked about the table. "See these fine young families? They can all thank me for interfering. Except for Carly and Sawyer, but they had her father to interfere on her behalf. I think Annabelle would be pleased with what I've accomplished."

Gram shook her head. "You're incorrigible."

"If that means I'm successful in what I do, I have to agree." He laughed at the scolding look on Gram's face.

Emily kept her attention on the top of the table, hoping Grandfather would not return to his suggestion that she should stay in Bella Creek.

More and more she longed to do so.

Many days had passed since Emily wrote to the Newmans. She knew it would take time for the letter to cross the mountains and reach them, and then for a reply to come. In the meantime, she kept busy, finding solace in work. She helped Gram with her sewing. She made supper. She spent time in the garden and she played with Mikey. Her love for the child grew. It would be a terrible wrench when the Newmans came for him.

Today she had left Mikey to play with Evan and headed to the store to buy Gram more pink thread. The warm sun shone in a sky as blue as the bluebells she'd admired on their trip to find the Newmans. The air carried the scent of flowers and trees and the songs of happy birds. Dogs barked as she passed their yards. Peaceful town life.

The sound of a horse approaching from behind her brought her to a standstill and she pressed to the side of the road. For the most part, she'd gotten over her wariness of strangers. She was learning to recognize more and more people and that helped. Still, she was cautious until she could identify folks.

The rider wore dusty clothes, as if he'd been on the trail a long time or was simply careless about his appearance. The man looked at her with bold eyes. She drew in her breath. Had she seen him before? If so, where and when? She searched her brain and could not come up with an answer.

The man's dark eyes remained on her as he passed. Something about those eyes—

Horse and rider continued down the street.

She remained frozen at the side of the road.

Those dark eyes—

With a frantic cry she lifted her skirts and rushed past the church, and without looking either way she crossed the street and flung open the door to the sheriff's office.

Jesse sat at his desk looking through his mail. When he saw her expression, he bolted to his feet and came to her side.

"Emily, what's wrong?"

"I saw—" She gulped. "I saw a man. I don't know who he is but—" She wobbled her hand indicating she didn't know anything. "I have this awful feeling."

"Describe him."

"Dirty. Very dark eyes. A bold stare." She shivered.

"His horse?"

"Black with a narrow white blaze."

"Was he one of the stagecoach robbers?"

"I can't say for certain, but there was something about those eyes." She couldn't stop shivering.

He drew her away from the windows and hugged her briefly then pulled the hard-backed chair to her side. "Sit here. Stay away from the windows. Don't open the door. I'm going to look around."

He slapped his hat on and hurried out, pausing to lock the door behind him.

She rocked back and forth over her knees. Why was she so frightened by a stranger? She closed her eyes and let the sight of those bold, black eyes fill her thoughts.

Had she seen him before she lost consciousness at the stagecoach accident?

Or was it simply an overreaction to her strange situation? Not knowing when and of whom she should be afraid.

Jesse returned a short time later. "He must have left town right after you saw him. There is no sign of him in Bella Creek and he didn't stop at the store." He pulled her to her feet and wrapped his arms about her.

She welcomed the shelter of his arms, a place where she felt safe. And perhaps more. She felt valued.

"I'll see you home."

With no concern for who might see them and wonder at her behavior, she clung to his hand as they hurried home.

Gram took one look at her and exclaimed. "Are you ill?"

"She's had a fright," Jesse explained before he released her and stepped back to observe her. "Are you going to be okay if I leave you?"

She sucked in air and straightened her shoulders. "I'm fine. Don't worry about me. I overreacted again. It is becoming the theme of my life. I'm sorry." She gave her bravest smile, hoping it would convince him she was over her silly behavior. "You go back to whatever you were doing. I'll slip out and get Mikey in an hour." How she managed to say those words without shivering she didn't know.

"You stay here until I'm certain you're safe. I'll bring Mikey back with me."

"That's not necessary. I was frightened but I'm over it now and I realize there was no cause for concern."

He grew fierce. "Promise me you will stay here and let me get Mikey."

They had a brief, silent argument. She felt the weight of his determination and hoped he felt her determination, as well. She'd spent too many days being afraid of going out and had grown to despise her weakness. She had no intention of becoming a prisoner.

"Emily, promise me. Your reaction was very real, and I can't help thinking either he's someone from your past that you have reason to fear or he's one of the murdering robbers."

Gram gasped. "I'll make sure she stays put."

Jesse and Emily looked at each other. She started to smile and so did he. Then they both laughed.

"I don't see what's so funny," Gram said with a hint of exasperation.

Jesse grinned at her. "It's just the idea that you could stop her. You're smaller and, well, older."

She huffed. "I got a lot more grit in these old bones than you give me credit for."

Jesse and Emily grinned at each other.

"I'll stay here until you bring Mikey back," Emily said. "I have no desire to have Gram tackle me to the ground and chain me to the kitchen table."

Gram shook her head. "I wouldn't go that far…unless, of course, I had to."

The three of them laughed together, recognizing the humor of the situation.

Jesse went to the door. "I have a few things to take care of. I'll get Mikey when I come home for supper. And you will be here?"

She held up her hand as if making a vow and said most solemnly. "I will be here."

He left and with him went all her bravado. The man on the black horse had frightened her. Thankfully, he had left town. Or, at least, appeared to have. She shivered and hoped Gram wouldn't notice.

Needing a diversion, she turned her attention to making supper. "Do you mind if I make a raspberry dessert?"

"Child, you make whatever you want. I have to finish a shirt this afternoon."

Emily went outside and picked enough berries for the dessert she had in mind. She knew the recipe in her head. Had she learned it from her mother or someone else? She straightened, closed her eyes and thought of a mother who didn't know where her daughter was. Or was Emily even missed?

She needed to stop feeling sorry for herself, to stop wondering why no one had come looking for her. It was foolish and a waste of time. Besides, if they expected her to stay to get Mikey settled, no one would realize she was missing…in her own mind.

The dessert was ready and cooling on the counter, the meat, potatoes and gravy done. There was an abundance of fresh vegetables from the garden. She had chosen green beans and beet greens.

Mikey and Jesse came in through the back door and Mikey ran to her. She bent over to receive his hug.

"Did you have a good time playing with Evan?"

"Me did. Me catched ball."

Either he was speaking more clearly or she was understanding him better.

Mikey ran to greet the dog and Emily met Jesse's eyes. She stilled at his seriousness. "What is it?"

"Remember I sent inquiries down the line trying to learn where you started your journey?"

She nodded.

He pulled a letter from his pocket.

Her heart froze. "You got a reply?" she whispered.

He unfolded the page. "It seems a Miss Emily Smith and a young boy boarded the train in Alliance, Nebraska. There is little information apart from that.

But I took the liberty to write back and ask if there was an orphanage nearby and did he know who Aunt Hilda might be. I wondered if Mikey was from an orphan's home."

She stared at him. "May I?" She held out her hand for the letter.

He gave it to her and she read the words. They said nothing more than what he'd told her, but she read them over and over, hoping something would trigger her mind to remember. Finally, sighing, she gave the letter back to him. "It's a start, I suppose."

"I'd say so. First real information we've had yet. We should hear back in a week."

A week. How long was she to keep treading water, wondering who she was?

Chapter Thirteen

Jesse stared at the trail ahead as he rode toward home and considered the events of the last few days.

The hours had passed slowly as they waited for a reply from Alliance. Alternately, they flew by as Jesse thought of how the news would likely take Emily and Mikey from Bella Creek. He spent as much time with them as he could, but his determination to find the crooks took him away for long spells. In the past two weeks, despite his best efforts, he'd found nothing new. He'd scoured the area again and again, hoping for some careless indication of where they'd gone… a dropped cigarette butt, a dislodged rock, a broken branch. Even fresh horse droppings. But he found nothing. Either they were very smart or incredibly fortunate.

Today was Saturday. He turned toward home. He'd decided to put aside his job as sheriff and his hunt for bad guys and just be Jesse Hill, a man with dreams and wishes. Yes, he knew that his parentage, the reputation bestowed on him by his mother's choices, made those dreams impossible, but for one day he would forget all that. Just as he hoped he could help Emily forget her concerns.

He'd had plenty of time to consider what they might do but dismissed everything he thought of. A picnic, a buggy ride, even an afternoon at the river that ran by town put her out in the open, and since she'd seen the dark-eyed man who unsettled her, he'd been concerned. Taking her away from town would, in his estimation, constitute an unnecessary risk.

Instead, he planned a quiet day close to home. He would whisper in Gram's ear that he'd like some time alone. She'd understand.

He reached town. Rode the streets to make sure all was well, unsaddled Rocky, gave him a good rubdown and an extra ration of oats then turned him free in the little pasture. The horse raced about the perimeter fence, as if knowing he was going to enjoy a day or two of rest.

Jesse's next stop was his office.

Clarence bolted from the chair behind the desk. "Howdy, boss."

"You're welcome to the chair. How's things?"

"Quiet. No important letters or anything. Oh yeah, I broke up a fight between two young fellas." He laughed and told of two boys about ten getting a little too involved in a tussle.

Jesse chuckled. "Good to know that's as bad as things get in Bella Creek. No sign of a man with dark eyes and a black horse with a blaze?"

"I've been on the watch, as you said, but I've seen nothing."

Jesse considered his dusty, trail-soiled clothes. He needed a bath and clean clothes, so he headed for the store where he purchased new duds, then he went to the hotel and ordered up a bath. "Lots of hot water." He did not want to appear at home in this state.

Mr. Hawkins looked at the dirty cowboy before him. If he hadn't known Jesse, he might have refused. "It will take twenty minutes to heat enough water." He went to the back, muttering about the way some men let themselves get so dirty.

Jesse stood at the windows, studying the town. Quiet. But somewhere were three men ready and willing to change that. He had to find them.

Mr. Hawkins returned. "Your bath is ready. Want me to do something with those clothes?"

"Thanks but I'll take them home."

Sometime later he headed down the street, knowing he smelled like lye soap. His new clothes were a little uncomfortable, but he'd soon break them in.

As he approached the house, he heard Mikey in the backyard and went there. Mikey saw Jesse and ran to him. He caught the boy and tossed him in the air.

Gram and Emily sat by the house, shelling peas.

He saw the question in each set of eyes and shifted Mikey over his shoulder. "I didn't find them."

Emily sighed and looked away.

He'd failed her. "Sooner or later they'll surface and I'll be ready."

Emily rose. "I'll make some coffee for you."

He let her go only so he could speak to Gram. "I thought you'd like to take Mikey to visit Sadie."

She chuckled. "I could do that for you." She grew serious. "Jesse, be careful. I don't want to see either one of you hurt. She's a sweet girl but what do we know about her?"

"And she doesn't realize what my past means." He tried to keep his tone light but perhaps failed, for Gram squeezed his hand.

"Jesse, you're a good man and don't you forget it. What your mother did was her choice, not yours."

"I know." But it made little difference to most people. If he hadn't had the support of the Marshall family, he probably wouldn't be sheriff. He'd once harbored the hope he could run from his heritage but soon learned it dogged his heels. Ironic that he would like to forget his past while Emily wanted so desperately to remember hers.

"Do you want coffee outside?" Emily asked from the doorway.

Gram got to her feet and called Mikey. "You two will have to drink your coffee without us. We're going for a walk." And Gram left out the back gate.

"That was strange," Emily said. "She hadn't mentioned any plan to leave."

Jesse didn't say anything about that. "Let's have coffee out here." The setting was pleasant and quiet.

Emily carried a tray with two cups of coffee, a generous slice of cake on one plate and a much smaller one on a second plate.

He grabbed a stool and brought it close for her to put the tray on.

They sipped coffee and ate the rich spice cake. He suspected she had made it. "Good cake."

"Thanks. I like baking." She chuckled. "I've wondered if I ran a restaurant or was I a seamstress. Doesn't seem I could be both."

She could be anything she chose to be, but he kept

his thoughts to himself. He understood well enough that saying it didn't make it happen.

"Gram has overcome a lot in her lifetime. She told me how difficult it was when your mother chose the sort of life she did. Gram said she agonized in prayer for her daughter to repent." She shifted so she could look at Jesse as she spoke. "She said the only good to come from that situation was you."

"So she says." It hurt to think of his mother's wasted ways.

"Gram says getting you away from her gave her a new lease on things." She studied Jesse, her blue eyes intense.

He wondered what she saw—a man who didn't know who his father was, a man from a sordid background, or a man who wanted nothing more than to be accepted as part of proper society?

"You've been a real blessing to her." Emily's eyes darkened with emotion.

He leaned closer, wanting to know if that emotion was approval of him or of Gram. "Not everyone sees me as a blessing."

"You mean people like Agnes? How long will you continue to let her opinion shape yours?"

He sat back. "I don't. I'm not. Others share her opinion."

"I suppose they do, but not everyone does. My question is, do you listen to the nay voices or the yea ones?"

He stared at her.

She continued. "Maybe it's time you forgave your mother."

Forgive her? Never. He looked into the distance,

startled at the words that rushed to his mind. He had long since stopped thinking of her, being disappointed in her, wishing she had cared for him enough to make some changes in her life. He thought he'd forgiven her. But his automatic response indicated otherwise. Could he forgive? Did he want to?

Emily touched his arm. "I'm sorry. I spoke without thinking. I had no right to say that. To judge you."

Others had judged him, but this was different because of the truth in her words. He tried to think how to respond. Someone banged on the front door and the sound of a horse racing away jerked him to his feet. "I have to see what that was all about."

She followed him through the house. He opened the door. No one was there. He looked up and down the street. Because it was Saturday, there was much activity in the center of town but nothing to suggest any sort of emergency.

Emily gave a cry and fell to her knees. She reached past him to something on the step, pulled a soiled white rag toward her chest and rocked back and forth, crying quietly.

He knelt beside her. "Emily, what is it?"

Emily recognized the shirtwaist as soon as she saw it. A scream filled her head but she choked it back. She could not, however, keep back the sobs that consumed her body. Ignoring the blood and dirt on the fabric, she cradled it to her face.

Jesse was at her side, his hands warm on her shoulders. "Emily, what's wrong?" He asked the question several times before she understood him.

"It's mine," she managed between snuffles.

He glanced up and down the street and then urged her to her feet. "Come inside."

She let him guide her to the couch and, at his gentle pressure, she sat.

"Can I look at it?" He held his hand toward the bit of cloth, no doubt wondering why it had triggered such a response.

Her arms held it tighter. "It's my favorite shirtwaist. Mama made it for me." Moaning, she leaned over her knees and braced herself against the storm of emotions rushing toward her. "I can picture Mama standing in the kitchen, smiling as she talked to me while she stirred a pot. She loved me." Her rocking grew frantic.

Jesse rubbed her back, keeping silent, as if knowing she had gone deep into her thoughts, trying to capture more of what her mother looked like, what her name was, where she lived...anything.

She sat up and leaned against Jesse's shoulder needing his strength and support.

Would he accept her if her past was sullied? She knew he wouldn't, but right now she needed the comfort he gave so willingly.

"Can I look at it now? I might find a clue about you or—" He didn't finish. Didn't need to. His main concern was to find the brutes who had destroyed her favorite garment.

She forced her arms to release the shirtwaist to him and watched as he unfolded it. The holes in the fabric were cut, not torn. Deliberate. Blood and dirt soiled it in several areas.

She shuddered. "Is it meant as a warning?"

"It's the only explanation for how it was delivered."

His voice was deep and she shivered. He was angry. His eyes were hard, his mouth a tight line.

"It's my fault."

His expression softened. "I don't see how."

"If I hadn't—I should have—" She couldn't explain the feeling that she'd done something terribly wrong that had put her in this position.

"It's not your fault." He looked deep into her eyes. "What do you remember of your mother?"

"Nothing more than what I said." She closed her eyes tight and tried to find more memories of the woman. "She loved me." Her eyes flew open. "I said loved. Does that mean she's passed away?" Agony gripped her and she groaned. "Who am I?"

Jesse held her and spoke comforting words. Eventually she heard what he said.

"Any day now we will hear from the sheriff in Alliance."

"And then what?" She hadn't meant to say the words aloud.

"Then we can learn who you are and find your family."

She bit back the fear that she wasn't going to like who she was and that her family no longer existed. He'd surely heard enough of her irrational fears. "Could that man I saw have recognized me?" She wanted him to say no. How was it possible? She'd been unconscious, presumably dead. Or had he recognized her from another part of her life? Or heard talk around town about her and realized she might constitute a threat. How could he know or believe she wouldn't be able to identify him?

"Someone has a need to warn you. I can't think

of any other reason than they fear you can recognize them as the murdering thieves."

"I'm afraid," she whispered. "What about Mikey? Is he in danger?"

"They'll know he's too young to be a witness."

The uncertainty in Jesse's voice did nothing to comfort her.

"I need to bring him back." She would never feel he was safe unless he was in her care. But he'd been in her care when this happened. "Perhaps he isn't safe with me."

"You are both safe."

"I wish I could believe you."

He caught her restless hands. "I promise I will do everything in my power to keep you from harm. And when I can't provide you with protection, God will."

The words settled into her soul and she inhaled the first satisfying breath she'd taken since she saw the shirtwaist at her feet.

"I had planned a quiet afternoon with just the two of us." His laugh was rueful.

"I'm sorry to ruin your plans."

"Who says you have?" He pulled her to her feet. "The backyard is sheltered. We can enjoy the sunshine out there without fear." Despite his words, he strapped on his gun belt as they went outside.

She couldn't make herself go farther than the chairs against the house and perched on the seat of one. Every noise sent a shiver through her body.

Jesse couldn't help but notice and held her hand. He talked of many things. She heard his voice but his words did not register.

She had been threatened.

She couldn't remember who she was.

Mikey might be at risk because of her.

Trusting God was a lot harder than the words implied.

It seemed forever until Gram came through the back gate with Mikey at her side.

Emily bolted from her chair and hugged the boy to her.

He patted her cheek and giggled at how she kissed him over and over.

Jesse joined them, his gaze searching their surroundings.

Afraid of being out in the open, she carried Micky indoors, calling over her shoulder, "I'll get supper started."

"What's going on?" Gram asked.

The door closed behind Emily. She wouldn't hear Jesse's answer but she didn't need to.

She half listened to Mikey's chatter as she made supper. Gram and Jesse came inside. Gram set the table. Jesse wandered from kitchen to living room, pausing to look out each window. She noticed he kept his gun belt on, though he normally removed it in the house.

Later that evening, she brought her Bible downstairs and sat on the couch. Jesse had gone out to make his rounds. Gram and Mikey had both gone to bed. She was alone with a bird in his covered cage. Muffin had refused to stay with her and followed Gram up the stairs.

She must find strength and courage to face the future and whatever it held and she read Psalm after Psalm. The seventy-seventh held her attention. Over and over she read the words, *I remember.* Would she ever remember?

The door opened. Her heart slammed into her ribs then settled back to where it belonged as she saw through a haze of tears that it was Jesse.

She hadn't even realized she was crying.

He closed the door and hurried to her in long strides, shedding his gun belt as he came. He sat beside her and pulled her into his arms. "How long have you been sitting here crying?"

"I don't know." Her sad voice was muffled against his shirt. "I've been reading my Bible."

"I see that." He took the open Bible off her lap.

She tapped the Psalm she'd been reading. "Has God forgotten me?"

He studied the verses a moment. "The Psalm closes with a reminder that God leads his people like a flock. He does the same for you."

She leaned into his embrace, willing to believe his explanation.

"It reminds me of a hymn." He began to sing. "All the way my Savior leads me; What have I to ask beside? Can I doubt His tender mercy, Who through life has been my Guide?" He sang several verses, his voice reverberating beneath her ear. Trust replaced worry. A smile replaced her frown.

He stopped singing and tipped her chin up so he could look into her eyes. "Feeling better?"

"Yes, thanks to you."

"Good."

They looked into each other's eyes. His were dark and steady. As if promising her now and forever. As if inviting her into his heart.

If only it could be so. She ached with longing to belong right here next to him.

He lowered his head. She saw his intent and lifted her face to meet his kiss. The kiss was brief and light. A tender caress that ended far too soon.

She sighed softly, hoping he didn't hear her disappointment.

He pulled her to her feet. "Run along to bed now and sleep well."

She paused at the stairs. He put his gun belt and hat back on. "Are you going out again?"

"I'm going to check and make sure everything is locked up." He waited at the door. "I'll stay here until I hear you enter your room."

For a moment, she considered staying in the living room until he returned, but on second thought, realized he wouldn't rest until he'd done this, and he wouldn't do it until she was safely in her room. "Good night." She climbed the stairs and paused to check on Mikey. Gram had let the dog sleep on Mikey's bed, which gave Emily a degree of peace about his safety.

She did not sleep until she heard Jesse tiptoe into his room. By then she had reached a decision and rose the next morning determined to inform Jesse of it.

She waited until they had finished breakfast and Mikey had gone to play with Muffin. "Jesse, I've decided to try and draw out whoever left my shirtwaist here yesterday."

"What does that mean?" There was no mistaking the warning note in his voice.

She ignored it. "I'm not hiding in the house or even in the yard. I'm going to go about town freely and openly. If someone is watching for me, I'm inviting them to come out in the open." Over the weeks since she'd lost her memory, she had gone from shaking with fear to forcing herself to meet strangers who became friends. She wasn't about to revert to the former.

He banged his fists on the table. "That's the dumbest thing I've heard in a long time. I forbid it."

Her eyebrows went upward. "What if I refuse to let you stop me? Are you going to lock me in jail?"

"Don't tempt me."

Gram cleared her throat. "I think Mikey and I will have a look at the flowers before church while you two iron this out."

Neither Jesse nor Emily looked her direction as she took the boy and dog outside.

"It's too dangerous," Jesse growled as the door shut behind them.

"What do I have to lose? I don't know who I am and no one has shown any concern about my disappearance." It had been more than three weeks since she'd lost her memory. Plenty of time for family or friends to make inquiries about her absence.

"I don't know why no one from your past has come to find you, but what about people in your present who care for you?"

"Jesse, the last normal thing I have left in my life is the freedom to come and go as I please. I can't give that up. Don't ask me to."

"Would it make a difference if I did?"

She felt the tension in his words. "I don't want to make you angry, but think about it. I'll let you know where I am at all times. You can keep an eye on me or ask Clarence or someone else to."

"I don't like it."

"I will not be a prisoner."

They did silent battle with their eyes. She guessed her expression was as stubborn and unrelenting as his.

Jesse did not like her suggestion one bit. How could he keep her safe? Locking her in jail, or at least in the house, seemed like a reasonable option. No reason it should sting to have her refuse to change her mind because he asked it. His mother had taught him the futility of having a request granted simply because of an attachment between the two people. He could not deny his fondness for Emily. Was sure she held similar feelings for him. But it wasn't enough for her to heed his concern.

"Please, Jesse. I feel trapped enough as it is with my memory missing."

Had she purposely widened her eyes and looked appealing? How was he to refuse? And what was the point? She had no obligation to obey him. It would be wiser to be involved.

"Will you promise to only go out and about when there is someone to keep an eye on you?" The *someone* would be him. He would not trust anyone else with the task.

"I promise. I have no desire to get into trouble."

"Very well."

Gram cracked open the door. "Is it safe to come in? We need to get ready for church."

Jesse gave what he hoped sounded like a happy chuckle. "It's safe."

The women hustled about, cleaning the kitchen and preparing for church. While they worked, Jesse slipped out and circled the block, looking for anything suspicious. The worst thing he saw was a kitten meowing frantically in a tree and a little girl crying on the ground.

"Can you save my kitty?"

He reached up, scooped the kitten from the branch and handed it to the grateful child. If only he could as easily deal with Emily's problems.

Back at the house, the trio was ready to leave. He was more than half tempted to wear his sidearm to church, but he couldn't bring himself to do so. Instead, he clattered up the stairs and found the older model derringer Sheriff Good had given him and stuffed it into his pocket. It was virtually useless except at close range, but he did not intend to take Emily out in public without some protection.

Gram had already gone when he returned to the living room. His nerves twitched as he stepped out into the open and he drew Emily's arm through his. He would not let her get one step away from him until they were safely inside the church. He insisted Mikey stay close to them.

He hurried them across the churchyard and inside.

"I wanted to speak to Annie," she protested.

"Here she comes now."

Emily furrowed her brow at him. "I'm not a prisoner under escort, either."

He smiled.

Annie overheard her comment. "You're a prisoner?"

"I would be if Jesse had his way."

Several other Marshalls gathered round them as Jesse and Emily vied with each other to explain what was going on.

Annie gasped when she heard about the torn and dirty shirtwaist and again when Emily said she meant to wander about the streets. "Emily, are you sure it's safe to leave the house?" Annie's sisters-in-law murmured agreement.

"It's nice to know I'm not the only one who thinks your plan is foolish." Jesse crossed his arms, feeling triumphant.

Emily ignored him and turned to the women. "Tell me which one of you would be happy as a prisoner in your own home."

The women shook their heads and confessed they wouldn't.

"There you go," Emily said with conviction. "So don't expect me to be." She found Mikey, who played with Evan, took his hand, marched to a pew and sat down.

Jesse followed and let out a long, frustrated sigh. Why must she be so stubborn?

She leaned close. "Aren't you always reminding me to trust God? Perhaps it's time for you to practice what you preach."

"Harrumph."

She laughed softly. "You sound very much like Grandfather Marshall."

He considered her comment. Perhaps if he appealed to Grandfather Marshall, the older man would persuade her to be more reasonable.

Their conversation ended as Hugh stood behind the pulpit. "We'll open with the hymn, 'All the Way the Savior Leads Me.'"

Emily nudged Jesse's side as if to say it was time to do as he said she should do and trust God. But it was easier said than done. By the time the service ended he was more resigned that accepting, more accepting than trusting.

He patted his pocket as they stepped out into the sunlight and stuck close to her. So close that she stepped on his toes every time she turned.

"Jesse, I appreciate your concern, but perhaps a little room to breathe, if you don't mind." She spoke kindly but he didn't misunderstand her meaning that she thought him overprotective. Reluctantly, he put two feet of distance between them.

It was Sunday and he had plans for the afternoon. Plans that would serve both their purposes. If he could get her to agree.

They refused an invitation to go the Marshall Five Ranch, though he could not say her reasons. Surprisingly, Gram agreed to ride to the ranch with Kate and Conner. No one missed the fact that Grandfather Marshall rode in the same wagon but having her away suited Jesse fine.

Jesse stared after them. Had Gram put her life on hold because of him? He hoped not.

Annie and Hugh were preparing to go home. "Can Mikey come with us to play with Evan?" Annie asked.

"That would be fine," Emily said.

Jesse knew by the relieved look in her face that she wanted Mikey out of the way so she could march up and down the street begging for someone to jump out of the bushes and grab her.

Well, he might have something to say about that.

"That leaves us on our own," she said, and took his arm as they headed toward home. "There's enough bread and cheese for sandwiches. Is that okay with you?"

"Sandwiches are fine, but why not put them in a basket? I've got something to show you. We can eat there."

She took a few more steps before she stopped and faced him. "Why do I get the idea you have in mind to keep me out of sight?"

"I had planned this a couple of days ago." And if it suited him even more now, he wasn't about to complain.

"You're sure?"

"Do you doubt me?"

She smiled. "You've never given me reason to do so."

He grinned. "I never will."

Her smile flattened and her eyes got that faraway look in them that he knew signaled she'd remembered something. He kept very still, holding his breath, waiting to see if her memory would come flooding back. And if it would leave him and her time in Bella Creek forgotten.

She blinked and her gaze came back to him, blue and focused. "I thought I remembered something but nope. Nothing."

They continued homeward where he got the basket and gathered together cookies while she made sandwiches. He put a dipper in with the food and covered it all with a cloth.

"Where are we going?" She had asked several different ways but he always gave the same answer.

"You'll see when we get there."

"You're a tease," she said after her fifth attempt to

get him to reveal their destination. She tickled him in the ribs.

Little did she know how ticklish he was. He laughed and pushed her away. Her eyes narrowed and he silently groaned. Now she knew and was determined to use her knowledge to torment him. She chased him and tickled him again before he caught her hands and stopped her.

"No tickling." His voice and words were firm.

"Who says?" She wriggled her fingers but he wouldn't free her.

"I do."

"Are you saying you don't like it?"

He never had, but to have her touch him and make him laugh wasn't so bad. "My mother used to tickle me unmercifully until I was sick."

She moved closer until their clasped hands were pressed to both their chests. "I would never make you miserable. Don't you know that?" She looked up at him with such pure sweetness that he forgot every word of warning about trust that he'd ever scolded himself with, every painful lesson about believing promises, everything but the look on her face.

"I guess I know it."

"*Guess* is not a very strong word." She lifted her head and planted a kiss full on his surprised lips then withdrew before he could think. His reaction came quickly and swiftly, though. He lowered their clasped hands to their sides, closed the few inches separating them and claimed her lips. Found them warm and willing. He lingered over the kiss a moment before he broke away, his joy going clear down to his boots. He turned her toward the cupboard and gave her a little push. “Is that picnic ready to go?”

Then, remembering that he had finished packing it, he grabbed the basket, hung it from his arm, took her hand and they stepped out into the sunshine. He led her in the opposite direction of the town square. They passed several houses and he lifted his fingers in greeting when he saw people in their yards enjoying a quiet Sunday afternoon.

He had plans to do the same.

“Are we almost there?” she asked, looking about, trying to guess where they were going.

“Soon.” They went two more blocks.

“We’re almost out of town.”

“Not quite.” He stopped. “We’re here.”

She took in the house before them, standing alone at the end of the block. “This is where we’re going?”

“Yup.” He opened the front gate for her.

“It looks empty.”

“It is. It’s one of Grandfather Marshall’s houses that he rents out. The latest residents left a short time ago.” He explained about the woman’s illness and the need to be closer to medical care. “Grandfather asked if I would check on it. It has a pretty backyard that I thought would make a nice place for us to have our lunch.”

“Oh, fun. I like exploring. Do we get to see inside the house?”

He lifted a key. “We do.” He opened the front door and they walked into the living room, where all the furniture was gone except for a large bookcase.

The house appeared to be much the same design as Gram’s, except there were two small rooms to the side of the living room. They entered the first. She circled it and opened the closet door. Inside, an object lay on the floor. "It's baby sweater. They must have dropped it in their packing."

"Did they have children?"

"No. How strange."

"Who knows? Perhaps they planned one and prepared for one and her illness prevented it. How sad."

"Indeed."

"So they must have planned to use this room for the nursery." They moved to the next one. A desk had been left behind. "This they must have used for the main bedroom or an office. What did the man do?"

"He was an accountant."

"Well, there you go. He likely worked from home some of the time."

The kitchen was empty, the cupboards bare. A small pantry held a crock and several empty jars.

"Can we go upstairs?"

"It would be remiss of me not to check on the whole house." He checked the windows in the four bedrooms upstairs and closed a closet door.

They returned downstairs and she hurried to the back door. "I'm anxious to see the garden." She waited while he unlocked the door and then stepped aside to let her out.

She clasped her hands in front of her. "A gazebo and a swing and look—" She hurried off the step toward the overgrown garden. "Roses." She bent over to sniff one. "It's a lovely yard."

He brought the picnic basket and they went to the gazebo. Benches built along the inside perimeter provided them seating. He swept the bench clean and waved his hand to indicate she should sit. "My lady," he said in his most formal tone.

"Thank you, kind sir." She curtseyed then swirled her skirts and sat down. The pleasure in her eyes was unmistakable as she took in the neglected flowers growing in wild profusion. "What a shame that they had to leave. It's just right for a young family." Her gaze went to the swing. "I can see Mikey—" She stopped abruptly and her shoulders heaved as she sighed.

Not wanting any regrets to mar the afternoon, he lifted the cloth from the picnic basket, spread it on the bench between them with a flourish and set out the lunch.

He dropped his hat to the floor, reached for her hands and bowed his head. His heart was so full of gratitude, worries and unspoken wishes that he had difficulty thinking where to start. "Heavenly Father, thank You for Your many blessings, for food, for this beautiful picnic spot and for love. Grant, I ask, protection and safety for Emily. In Jesus' name. Amen." The words did not begin to express the fullness of his heart.

"Amen," Emily echoed. "I'm hungry." She took a sandwich. He did the same.

They ate a leisurely lunch then explored the yard more fully. They lingered for hours. It appeared she was no more anxious to return to the reality of their lives than was he. He couldn't have asked for a better, sweeter, more promising afternoon.

A wagon rumbled by but didn't stop. They had walked, so no one would even suspect they were in the backyard.

She returned to admiring the roses. He stood back a few feet, enjoying her. After a few minutes, he took out his knife and cut three stems. He was jabbed by thorns but ignored the minor pain as he handed her the flowers.

"Thank you. I need to get home and put them in water."

"We'll put them in water right here." He'd pumped water from the well for drinking, pleased at how sweet it was. He hurried into the house, found a jar he deemed to be the right size, filled it with water and let her arrange the roses in it.

She saw the blood on his thumb. "You're bleeding." She dampened her hankie with water and dabbed his thumb clean.

He didn't know which felt better. The cold water on his puncture wound or her warm touch to his hand.

Thudding horse hooves sounded from the street. The animal slowed as it came abreast of the house.

His heart stalled. Had someone discovered their location? He patted his vest pocket. The little gun wouldn't stop much. He should have strapped on his gun belt, even if it was Sunday.

He strained toward the sound and let his breath ease out when the horse passed. "We need to get home."

She nodded, her eyes wide. She, too, had heard the horse slow in front of the house.

He pulled her to his chest and rubbed her back. "I'll find those men and lock them up. I promise."

"I wish you could also promise to give me back my memory."

He couldn't do that. A part of him didn't even wish it. He didn't want to be forgotten by her.

Chapter Fourteen

Emily made a point of running errands at various places of business over the next few days, always with Jesse watching from his office or from a nearby post. She made several trips to Marshall's Mercantile, had tea with Annie at Miss Daisy's Eatery and took Mickey to play at the school yard. She went for daily walks, always toward the main street. But no one appeared she didn't know.

She explained her frustration to Jesse. "I need to go away from the heart of town. No one in their right mind is going to do anything in view of so many people."

"I don't like it. It's too dangerous."

"I refuse to live in constant fear." It was unsettling to always wonder if she would encounter danger. The passing horse on Sunday had marred an otherwise perfect day spent in Jesse's company. It was not how she intended to live her life.

Jesse hemmed and hawed a little, then said, "If you let me know where you're going ahead of time, I will position myself where I can see everyone coming and going."

"Fine. Today I am going to visit Sadie."

But days later, after several visits to Sadie, several to see Annie and a walk to the house where they had shared Sunday afternoon, still nothing...or perhaps it would be more correct to say, no one appeared.

"I'm going to the river. What better place to invite trouble."

"Exactly. Why must you invite trouble?"

"I didn't invite it but I'm stuck with it, and I simply refuse to let it control me."

Again, he argued against it but finally gave in—on the condition she give him enough warning so he could be in a place where he could watch her.

The next day she wandered to the river. It was quiet. Eerily quiet except for the sound of water running over rocks and the birds overhead. She didn't know where Jesse was, but she knew he would be nearby should she need him.

If not for the threat hanging over her head she would bask in the cool air coming from the water and the pleasure of watching the ripples on the river.

Crashing came from her right and she suddenly regretted this whole idea. She looked about for Jesse but didn't see him. Had he forgotten? Or worse, had he been discovered by the bad men and tied up, thus leaving her alone? Her knees turned rubbery. She ordered them to stay strong so she could run. A glance over her shoulder showed she had wandered a distance from the path leading back to town, and she edged that way, never taking her gaze from the direction of the sound.

A boy of about ten broke into the open. “Hi,” he called. “Didn’t `spect to see anyone.” He turned and raced away.

Her knees folded and she sank to the ground.

Jesse appeared at her side and he sat down to hold her. “You’re not doing this again. My heart won’t stand the strain.”

“Nor mine.” It was several minutes before she had the strength to stand. When she thought she could walk, he took her hand and held it until he had her safely home.

It was two days before she was brave enough to venture out on her own again.

Jesse spent more time at home than she knew he normally did, but she didn’t mention it. After her scare at the river, she was only too glad to have him nearby.

And there were other reasons she didn’t mind his company. He played with Mikey. The boy adored him. Even that wasn’t the main reason she enjoyed his presence.

Her greatest source of pleasure was when Jesse took her for walks throughout the day, always staying close to home, always keeping her at his side, making her feel safe and protected and valued.

Was being valued something she sought? Needed? She searched her thoughts, willed remembrance, but nothing came. She didn’t know if she needed to feel important to someone or not. Of course she didn’t, she thought with some disgust. Besides, Mikey thought she was important, running to her often for a hug or a word of praise. Gram appreciated her help with the sewing and meal preparation.

And Jesse? Was she more than a responsibility to

him? She harbored a secret hope for it, but until she knew who or what she had been before she ended up in Bella Creek—well, she simply didn't feel like she was worthy of someone like Jesse.

Which, to her disgust, answered her question as to whether or not she needed to be valued.

Would she ever learn who she was?

Did it matter anymore? She wished she could say it didn't, but something nagged at her from the shadows of her past, and until she knew what it was she could never be free of it. Every day she asked Jesse if a letter had arrived from Alliance. But no help came from that direction.

No amount of praying or poring over her Bible seeking clues provided a key to her past. Nothing she saw in her walks did, either.

Jesse had gone to check if any new letters had arrived. She understood that Clarence had taken on many of Jesse's responsibilities so he could spend his time guarding her. It should make her feel guilty but it didn't. She could hardly breathe when he was gone as fear clutched at her lungs.

Between worrying about someone who might wish her harm and wanting to know who she was, Emily found it difficult to sit still and help Gram with the sewing.

Gram noticed her restlessness. "You won't be able to settle until you see if Jesse has any news. Why don't you go see if he has anything to report?"

Emily hesitated. "I feel like I should be doing more to help you." Besides, Jesse had made it clear he didn't want her leaving the house unescorted.

"Nonsense. Your life is like an unfinished seam

at the moment. It makes it a little hard to put your mind to something as mundane as sewing on a button. Run along."

Emily made up her mind. She would be safe enough going to Jesse's office, and it was impossible to relax until she knew if he'd received any message concerning her.

And if going out on her own made one of those horrible men show his face, she considered it well worth it so she folded away the shirtwaist she'd been working on.

"Thank you for being so understanding. I'll take Mikey." At least she could do that much. For several days, she'd left him in Gram's care as she tried to draw out whoever left her shirtwaist on the doorstep. She wasn't ready to think of it as anything but a threat. But it seemed less and less likely that's what it meant. Perhaps it had been left for some other reason, though she could think of none.

Mikey gladly came with her. "See Yesse?" he asked.

"Yes, we'll go to his office. You can play in the jail." They'd visited before, and Mikey had been fascinated by the room with bars for walls.

They reached the little building with the Sheriff sign above the door. Before she reached the handle, Jesse pulled the door open. "Is something wrong? Has someone—" He glanced past her as if expecting to see one of those men pursuing her.

Somewhere deep in her heart a pleasant feeling blossomed. It was nice to know he cared about her safety, though he had done so from the beginning. She was growing to like it more every day. "We're fine. Everything's fine. I just wondered if you'd had any messages today." Even if the mail hadn't arrived, Jesse often got letters hand delivered to him.

He drew her inside, looked up and down the street and closed the door. He caught her arms and pulled her close. "I don't like you wandering about the streets by yourself."

"I expect half a dozen people saw me and would come rushing to my rescue, if need be."

"Maybe so, but until I find whoever is responsible—"

She knew he meant responsible for so many things, not just the ruined shirtwaist. "I'll feel better once you find them, as well, and until you do, I will be cautious. But I won't be a prisoner. Now, to the reason I came. Any messages that I'd be interested in?"

He went to the desk, sat on the corner and picked up two letters. "Neither of these is from Alliance. Sorry."

She plunked down onto the chair in front of the desk, but before she could voice her frustration and disappointment, the sound of pounding horses' hooves drew them both to their feet.

The horses thundered up to the office. "Sheriff. Sheriff."

"Stay here and stay out of sight," Jesse ordered as he bolted for the door and opened it. "What's wrong?"

"They need you at Wolf Hollow. Three ruffians robbed the store. They shot and killed the storekeeper then shot their way out of town."

Emily's heart dropped to her heels. Her eyes felt too wide as she stared at Jesse.

"Give me a few minutes." He closed the door, caught her hand and drew her to the back of the office.

"Is it them?" she whispered.

"I don't know and won't until I ask a few questions. But I have to go. I'll let George know at the store and leave Clarence in charge, but please promise me you won't go out in public."

She shivered. "I will be very careful."

"That isn't what I asked."

"I know you want me to barricade myself in the house."

"You're not going to do that, are you?" His voice deepened with resignation.

"At the moment I'm strongly considering it, but no, I'm not going to be locked up in the house." She pressed her fingers to his lips as he started to protest. "You are in more danger going after them then I am staying here."

He caught her hand and squeezed it. "I don't want anything to happen to you." He drew her close and kissed her so briefly she didn't have time to think or respond. It was his job to care what happened to her. But, she smiled at the notion, it wasn't his job to kiss her.

"Mikey and I will go home and let you do your job."

"I'll see you home."

"There are two men out there waiting for you. I'll be fine." She took Mikey's hand and opened the door. Talking about being safe was easy, but her neck tensed and she gave her surroundings hard study before she left the shadow of the office and stepped into the sunlit street.

She glanced over her shoulder. Jesse stood in the open door.

"I'll watch you until you're out of sight. I'll ride by the house on my way out of town."

She gave a little wave and hurried homeward.

Please, God, let him find those men and bring him back safely.

Two days later, Jesse had not returned and she repeated her prayer over and over. Her nerves twitched with every sound outside the house. She rushed often to the window, hoping to see Jesse and praying she wouldn't see a man with dark, staring eyes.

She picked up the shirtwaist that she seemed unable to finish but pricked her finger with the needle and set the work aside in disgust.

"I'm going for a walk."

"But Jesse said—"

"He said to be careful and I will, but I haven't been out of the house in two days and I need to. I think Mikey needs to get out more, too." He'd been confined to the backyard because of her limited movements, though he seemed happy enough. "Don't worry. I'll be careful."

"Please do so. If something happens to you I will have to answer to Jesse."

Emily chuckled at Gram's sorrowful tone then took Mikey's hand as they left the house. She sucked in a deep breath. The air was heavy with heat from the hot summer sun, but it felt good to be outside and able to stretch her legs. Not that she would do anything foolish. She made her way to the town center. She'd stay within eyesight of those instructed to watch her, and she waved at Clarence at the sheriff's office.

"Would you like a peppermint?" she asked Mikey.

"Candy?"

"Me, too." She stopped at Marshall's Mercantile and bought a few. A stranger watched her. She averted her eyes at his bold stare. There was nothing familiar about him—he didn't have dark eyes or silver-tipped boots. Besides, if he was one of the three, wouldn't he be on the run? Still, his study of her made her nervous and she hurried from the store.

Once outside, her nerves settled and her thoughts drifted to the pleasant times she'd spent in Jesse's company. Her favorite was the afternoon at the empty house. She let herself imagine turning the empty house into a home for herself and Mikey and Jesse. Regret and frustration quenched her dreams. She reached the intersecting street at the end of the block but didn't immediately turn around. Would she ever be free to pursue dreams? Not necessarily that particular one, as it required Jesse's participation, but any dream. Living like this was akin to being stuck in a whirlpool, going nowhere and yet unable to escape.

A man headed toward her from the livery barn. The same man as she'd seen in the store. Before she could turn away, he called out.

"Emily Smith, fancy meeting you here. It's been a long time." His gaze dropped to Mikey and his eyes narrowed.

She stared at him, her mind empty, her heart racing. She managed to force her voice to work. "How do you know my name?" She couldn't imagine George telling a stranger.

"Of course I know your name. After all, we were to be married. I'm sure you haven't forgotten that."

"Married? To you?" She glanced at her left hand. "I don't believe I'm married to anyone."

"Well, things didn't work out. What are you doing so far west? Perhaps taking up a new profession?"

She did not care for the way he leered at her. "I'm sorry, sir. I don't know who you are."

He reached her side and grabbed her elbow. "What kind of game are you playing? Of course you remember me."

She tried to shake free of his grasp but he wouldn't release her.

"I remember nothing. Not even who I am. I had a blow to the head and lost my memory."

"Well, well, well. That's mighty interesting."

"Not for me." He did not release her. Instead, he pressed intimately close, filling her nostrils with an artificial scent that stirred her memories and made her shudder. Whoever he was, she couldn't imagine she'd agreed to marry him.

"You don't remember being engaged to me—Fred Ellesworth?"

No recognition came from hearing his name. "To me, you are a stranger and I'd thank you to remember that." She again tried to shake free of him, but he squeezed her arm hard enough to hurt. The way he looked at her made her skin crawl.

"Maybe this will help you remember." He pressed against her and kissed her.

"How dare you?" She would have slapped him but he held her hands tight. Panic roared through her. Had she been the sort of woman who allowed this kind of familiarity? Was she like Jesse's mother? Nausea rose within her at the thought.

The sound of horses approaching made him take a respectable step back, but he still held to her elbow, hard and cruel, as if he didn't intend to let her go.

Three men, tied at the ankles and wrists, rode horses led by three men. Jesse was one of them. One man wore silver-tipped boots. One looked at her with bold, dark eyes.

"He's captured them." She waved to Jesse.

He rode on without glance. Apparently he hadn't seen her. She pushed aside her disappointment. After all, he had to keep his mind on his business.

Weariness sucked at Jesse's bones after two days of tracking these men and then a gunfight to capture them. Thankfully, no one had been hurt, though the man with the dark eyes had been shot in the arm. A flesh wound only. The three were responsible for robbing the stagecoach. He had all the proof he needed—the misshapen horseshoe, the silver-tipped boots and the man with the dark, staring eyes who had frightened Emily. Apart from that, there were witnesses to the robbery and killing in Wolf Hollow. The judge was due in Bella Creek in a few days. In the meantime, Jesse would keep them in the jail cell. They'd be a little crowded but he couldn't help that. These men would soon receive the justice they deserved.

Jesse had had plenty of time to think in the days he'd been away, even though he'd had to keep his wits about him.

His thoughts had generally harkened back to the afternoon spent at the vacant house. More and more he'd pictured himself living there with Emily as his wife. Upon his return, he'd meant to tell her of his dreams and ask her to consider forgetting her lost memory and starting anew. He knew she would demure because she didn't know what secrets lay behind her, but he'd hoped to make her understand he didn't care about her past and he'd convinced himself she wouldn't care about his. After all, she knew and hadn't been shocked.

Then he'd ridden into town, anxious to lock up the culprits, post a guard and go in search of Emily.

But as it turned out, he hadn't had to look for her. As soon as they'd arrived in town, he'd seen her on the corner, kissing a man in plain view, the two of them pressed intimately close. His insides had filled with disgust, though whether more at her brazen behavior or his own foolishness in letting himself build impossible dreams, he wasn't prepared to say. Seems her past had resurfaced, either because she'd regained her memories or because her experience had told her what to do.

A woman like his mother. A bitter taste filled his mouth.

At least he had his work to do and it demanded his focus. He soon had the culprits locked in the jail cell and Clarence set to do the first watch. He rounded up men to guard the prisoners at night. He went through his messages. Nothing required his immediate attention.

He sat at his desk staring at a Wanted poster but seeing nothing.

"I can manage here," Clarence said. "Go on home and get a good meal and a good night's sleep."

"Sounds like a great idea." With a weary sigh, Jesse pushed to his feet. Sooner or later he had to go home.

Had to speak to Gram. Had to deal with his feelings about Emily. However, he did not rush homeward but took a circuitous route with the excuse to himself that he was only checking on the town.

He ducked into the hotel. “Anything I should know about?” he asked Mr. Hawkins.

“Town’s quiet, as usual, sheriff.”

“No strangers in town?” It was his job to know who came and went, but that wasn’t his reason for asking. He wanted to know who had been with Emily and what his business was.

“A Mr. Ellesworth, who is interested in buying some land around here. He’s been asking a lot of questions, if you ask me.”

“What sort of questions?”

“Wants to know a lot about a lot of people. Who owns certain pieces of land and stuff like that.” Mr. Hawkins leaned closer. “Why would a man be wanting these particular pieces of land unless he’s heard there is a gold vein and he has inside knowledge about the location?”

“I don’t know.” Was it even possible to have that kind of information? He would make some inquiries around town. Perhaps this man had approached others, perhaps revealed his reason for so much interest. “Anything else about him I should know? Did he say where he was from?”

“He mentioned Nebraska.”

“He did, huh?” And Emily had a connection in Nebraska. It seemed more and more suspicious. Had she truly lost her memory, or was she up to something along with this man?

He shook his head. Where had all these doubts

come from? There was only one way to find out what was going on—confront her. Now in a hurry to see her, he headed directly home.

She must have been watching for him as she rushed to open the door before he even reached it. "You got them. You're home safe and sound." She grabbed his arm and pulled him inside.

Mikey launched himself into Jesse's arms and Gram reached out and patted his cheek.

This was the sort of welcome he'd never let himself dream of, and now it seemed built on falsehoods.

Before he could protest or extricate himself, he was pulled into the kitchen and made to sit down.

"Supper is ready," Emily said. "We've been waiting for you."

"Emily has made all your favorites," Gram added.

"I 'elp," Mickey said with such forcefulness that Jesse laughed. His questions would spoil the mood. He'd eat first and then deal with his doubts. "Can I wash up first?"

Emily stepped back to allow him to do so. Mikey clung to his leg, getting a bouncy ride across the kitchen.

Despite the questions crowding his mind, Jesse laughed again.

The meal was, indeed, all his favorites—ham, baked beans, cornbread and baby carrots, followed by thick slices of chocolate cake.

He leaned back and patted his stomach. "That was excellent. Thank you, ladies."

"It was entirely Emily's doing."

"Thank you." He met her gaze and held it. How

could she be so warm and welcoming here and yet kiss a man on the street? "Can we talk?"

He knew by the way her expression changed that she expected he had good news for her.

"You two run along. Mikey and I will do the dishes," Gram said.

Emily was on her feet in a flash, waiting for him to lead the way.

He nodded toward the back door. He didn't want the conversation to take place publicly. Outdoors, he turned toward the bench at the side of the house where he could count on a little privacy. However, he didn't sit.

She remained standing, as well. "You have news?"

He didn't look directly at her. "I saw you this afternoon."

"I saw you, too, and was so relieved to see you back safe and sound and with those three men caught."

"You didn't look like you cared much."

She grew still. "What do you mean?"

"I saw you kissing that man. Who is he?" He looked at her but kept his feelings banked. He would not let her know how hurt he was.

"You're mistaken."

"Are you telling me—?"

She interrupted his question. "I was most certainly not kissing him. He kissed me, as bold as if he had the right." She shuddered. "He says his name is Fred Ellesworth and that we were engaged. I don't remember it and I don't believe it. I would never promise myself to a man of such low moral standards. He treated me like—" Her eyes narrowed and she sucked in a breath. “With utter disregard for my reputation.” She shuddered again and her eyes filled with darkness.

He wanted to believe her. More than that, he wanted to comfort her. Was she telling the truth? “You don’t remember him?”

“No.” she twisted her hands. “Can he really know me from before or is he playing some kind of con game?”

The agony in her voice and the sight of her twisting hands erased all doubt from his mind, and he opened his arms and pulled her to his chest. At least they were sheltered from the public and his actions weren’t jeopardizing her reputation.

“I don’t know who he is nor if he knows you, but I will be keeping a close eye on him.”

She clung to him. “I’m so glad you’re back and have those men behind bars.”

“I’ll be staying close to home until the judge comes.”

“Then what happens to them?” She shifted so she could turn her face up and watch him.

“Then they will likely go to Great Falls and the law will deal with them according to their crimes.”

She was silent a moment. “I’m glad that they won’t be responsible for any more killings.”

They sat on the bench and he told her about following the trio into the mountains. “I knew eventually they would make a mistake and I would find them. This time they left a trail—a broken branch and cigarette butts. They had grown overconfident.”

She studied her hands. “We all missed you.”

“Yeah?”

"Mikey kept going to the door to ask for 'Yesse.' He fussed at bedtime."

Jesse glanced at the sky. The sun had dipped into the west, giving a golden edge to the mountains. "Speaking of which, we better go in and put him to bed. I'll read to him tonight and tuck him in."

"He'll love that."

"No more than I." He paused at the door. "I'm going to miss that little guy when he goes." And Emily, too. Even though he had decided to ask her to consider staying, seeing her with Fred Ellesworth had given him cause to reconsider. He knew she would say he needed to know her past before she could make any plans for her future, and maybe he did. He had no wish to dread people from her former life showing up.

She lowered her head as if something on the ground demanded her attention. "I suppose once I hear from someone at Alliance I will need to go back, if only to find out who I am and what I've done."

He tried to ignore the tremor in her voice, knew his doubts about seeing her with Mr. Ellesworth had triggered her fears that she had a dark cloud of shame in her past. But he couldn't do anything to relieve her concern. He cared about her but intended to guard himself from acting prematurely and unwisely.

They went indoors. He played with Mikey and Muffin then read a little picture book over and over until Mikey couldn't stop yawning.

"He's just delaying," Emily said.

"I know, and I'm going along with it to make up for lost time." And to create moments to cherish in the future. He'd convinced himself he would never marry, but he'd hoped Emily would see him differently. He'd thought she did. But what if she got her memory back and forgot him? Or if her past revealed something he wasn't prepared to deal with? All good reasons to wait.

But the thought left him aching clear through.

"Come on, little cowboy, get on my back and I'll give you a horsey ride to bed."

Mikey eagerly jumped on his back and Jesse trotted upstairs making all the appropriate noises. He helped the boy say his prayers and tucked him under the covers. Mikey insisted on several noisy kisses.

As Jesse tiptoed toward the door, Mikey sat up. "You no go `gain?"

It took a minute for Jesse to realize the little guy was afraid Jesse would go away. He hadn't been much older than Mikey when he began to ask his mother not to go, but she always did, leaving him alone and bereft, and feeling like he didn't matter to her.

He returned to sit on Mikey's bed and hugged him to his side. "If I have to leave I will let you know. Okay? And I will always come back." But who would promise Mikey the same once he left?

He couldn't answer. Couldn't face the pain he felt.

"'Kay." Mikey allowed Jesse to cover him up again and snuggled into his pillow.

Jesse waited a few minutes to make sure he'd settled then went downstairs.

Emily took one look at his face and set aside her book. "Is everything okay?"

"Yes. No. Gram, do you mind listening for him? I need to talk to Emily."

"Go ahead." Emily did not ask what was bothering him, even though it was obvious something was. Her eyes were wary, as if suspecting he meant to pursue her encounter with Mr. Ellesworth.

Wanting to provide a touch of reassurance, he reached for Emily's hand and drew her out the back door. The garden breathed a sweet flower scent. The evening air had cooled and they sat against the house.

"Jesse, what's wrong?"

"I just realized how much Mikey is like me. Oh, I don't mean in looks, but his circumstances." He launched into telling how he'd felt sitting on Mikey's bed. "He wanted to know if he could count on me. Do you know how many times I asked my mother to stay? I wanted to count on her. I suppose, with her occupation, it was a good thing she left me with my grandmother. But to this day I wonder why she didn't care enough to change who she was. Her reputation about ruined my life. It would have, if Grandfather Marshall hadn't stepped in and brought us out here." He couldn't keep the bitterness from his voice. "In my estimation, people should live honorable lives and avoid even the appearance of evil for the sake of those they care about."

She took his hand. "I am so sorry about your past. I can't imagine how much it hurts. I suppose it's what makes you a good sheriff."

"I'm a good sheriff?" He figured he was, but wanted to know why she thought so.

"Yes, you are. You have high ideals and allow no compromise. I suppose you see things as black and white."

"There are no gray areas in my job." He couldn't see himself allowing such in his personal life either.

"I am a gray area."

He stared at her. Did she have something to confess? Had that man—Fred Ellesworth—compromised her in any way? If he had, he would pay for it. "What do you mean by that?"

"I can't remember my past, so I could be anything. Good or bad." Her voice grew so soft he had to lean forward to catch the final words.

He cupped her head with his hand and turned her to face him. "I haven't seen any wanted posters with your likeness on them, so I'll assume you haven't broken the law."

Eyes as dark as the evening sky met his. "There are other way of earning that label."

He thought of his mother and the label she had earned and the one she had left him to bear. "Like being illegitimate?"

She caught his hand as he pulled away from her. "That's not a fair label because it's not one you earned."

For the first time that he could remember, he realized the truth of her words. It had been someone else's actions and choices that gave him the label, not anything he'd done. It was a freeing thought.

"I guess that's so."

"Like I said before, perhaps you ought to forgive your mother."

"Why would I want to do that? Why should I?"

She tipped her head to one side and considered him. "Because until you do, you carry her label with you. It's an unnecessary burden."

"I cannot forgive her for the choices she made and how they affected me. A fallen woman should be punished."

She blinked as if having to force herself to meet his gaze. "I expect she was." Seeing his stubborn disbelief, she continued. "She would be shunned by so-called decent company. She had to leave her son behind in order to give him a decent life."

"You want me to believe she left me for my own good?"

"It's a possibility."

He wanted to refute it. But he couldn't disagree with her when she held his hand and looked at him so intently.

Her gentle smile was his undoing and he pulled her into his arms.

"Think about it," she said.

He promised he would, though he couldn't see what difference it would make. He'd learned to live with his past.

Maybe she could learn to live without a past.

"Would you be able to forgive me if I turn out to be a fallen woman?"

Her question threw back the dark curtain he'd pulled into place when he saw her kissing that man in plain view. He had to answer honestly. "I don't know."

"Fair enough." She slipped into the house, and when he finally forced himself to move and stepped inside, she was gone. He could hear her moving about upstairs.

Was this what she had feared since her arrival?

Why hadn't he guarded his heart more carefully?

Chapter Fifteen

The next day was Sunday and Emily jumped from bed. Jesse was home. Of course, that was not the reason for this bubble of joy inside her heart. Well, maybe in part. She'd again realized how his feelings about his mother had shaped him into the man he was—strong, unbending.

Knowing he saw the world in black and white stopped her eager morning preparations. If her past contained something—anything—unpleasant she would be seen as black. Jesse had made that clear. There would be no welcome for her here.

She shivered. Something about Fred Ellesworth unsettled her. Had she really known such an unsavory man in the past? It didn't speak well for the kind of woman she'd been. She tried to dismiss the thought, but it weighed heavily on her mind as she finished dressing and made her way downstairs.

She'd helped Mikey dress earlier. He and Gram were in the kitchen. Emily had heard Jesse go down the stairs but he wasn't in the room.

Gram answered her puzzled look. "Jesse went to

check on things at the jail. He said he'd be back for breakfast."

Emily's steps were measured as she set the table. Was he avoiding her? Seeing her as an echo of his mother?

When Jesse stepped through the door a smile widened her mouth and then fled as she tried to gauge his feelings. Their gazes connected. He smiled and her insides warmed. If only her life could begin right here. For a moment she considered forgetting any effort to discover who she was.

But then Jesse's smile disappeared and he turned away, but not before she caught the doubt and uncertainty in her eyes.

She helped serve the meal, her joy quenched by the dreadful possibilities of what she might have been.

Soon afterward they left for church. "It's good to be free of the threat of those men," she said. The fear of being recognized by them and in danger was gone. She could go anywhere she wanted now.

So many people greeted them and thanked Jesse for capturing the bad guys that it took longer than usual to get inside the church. When they did, Emily slipped in beside Gram with Mikey between herself and Jesse. She released a satisfied breath. Her peace was short-lived as Fred Ellesworth sat in a pew across the aisle. He looked her way, his gaze demanding before it slipped to Jesse at her side and then rested on Mikey. Something about the way he studied the boy made her grip Mikey's hand.

Hugh approached the pulpit and announced the opening hymn, and Emily ignored the man across the aisle. He meant nothing to her, despite his claims.

Ignoring him proved more difficult than she anticipated, as at the end of the service, he waited for her to step into the aisle then followed her. He leaned close to speak softly. "Your sheriff might be interested in knowing more about you."

She forced herself not to react, though every nerve in her body twitched and she had an incredible urge to slap the man's face.

Jesse was several steps ahead, surrounded by eager people grateful for the work he'd done. As Fred drew closer, Emily noticed that several of those at Jesse's side gave the man a frightened look and scurried away.

What was that all about? Had Jesse noticed? But, of course, he had.

She joined him and couldn't stop herself from resting her hand in the crook of his elbow, even though he stiffened and studied Fred Ellesworth. She needed the strength and courage Jesse's physical closeness provided.

The dark cloud in the back of her mind that had been her company since the stagecoach accident swirled with fears that she could not calm.

The next day she learned she had reason to be fearful. Jesse came home for the noon meal with a troubled look on his face. Her first thought was that the trio in the jail had escaped and her heart raced.

"Emily, can we talk?"

She left Mikey with Gram and followed him outside. They went to the little bench, but somehow she knew this would not be a pleasant interlude like the ones they'd previously shared at this spot. Her knees shook, but he didn't sit so she didn't, either.

He paced away three steps, rubbed the back of his neck then slowly turned. His face was a plane of hard lines and she shivered.

"Did they escape?" It was the worst thing she could think of.

He crossed his arms over his chest. The action made her feel very alone and afraid. "I had a caller this morning."

She nodded. People were eager to heap praise on him and it was well deserved.

"Your Mr. Ellesworth paid me a call."

Her mouth twisted as she thought of the man's boldness. "He's not *my* Mr. Ellesworth."

Jesse went on as if she hadn't voiced a protest. "He told me a story."

Emily stiffened, sensing the story was about her and wasn't anything she wanted to hear.

"He said he knew you in Lincoln, Nebraska. He offered his hand in marriage but withdrew the offer after you spent the night with a man and made no secret about it." The way Jesse's lip curled matched the way her insides reacted.

"He said your reputation was ruined to the point you left town in disgrace. According to him, your aunt arranged for you to join her. I might have had doubt, but he said your aunt lived in Alliance." Jesse turned away, disgust clear in his expression. It seemed he couldn't bear to look at her.

Her insides had grown so brittle she feared her next breath would shatter them into a thousand fragments. Could it be possible? Was she really that sort of woman? Why couldn't she remember?

"One more thing."

She forced herself to remain standing, though she had lost all feeling in her legs.

"Mr. Ellesworth suggests Mikey is your child. The time from when you left Lincoln would indicate it might be so."

She let out a wail and collapsed to the bench, rocking back and forth over her knees. How could it be so? Was she really a fallen woman? "Can it be true?" *Please, God, make it not so.* Was this why she didn't want to remember?

"I didn't want to believe him. But a letter came from Alliance today."

She sat up. "Someone who knows me?" Someone besides the horrible Mr. Ellesworth?

"Why don't I read it to you?"

She nodded.

"It's from a woman who runs the Alliance Home for Children. She signs her letter as Matron Hilda."

"The Aunt Hilda of the letter in my Bible?" She wanted it to be good news, but the look on Jesse's face warned her it might be otherwise. Although he was less than a yard away from her, it felt as if a huge chasm had divided the ground between them.

"It would seem so. She says Miss Emily Smith has worked at the orphanage for four years having being highly recommended by her aunt, Mrs. Martha Morgan. She knows Miss Smith came from Lincoln but has little information apart from that. She says the woman is a great help, wonderful with the children and an asset to the home. The plan was for the boy, Michael, to be delivered to adoptive parents but the adoption has fallen through and the Matron requests that Miss Smith bring him back."

Jesse flipped the paper closed. "Everything confirms what Mr. Ellesworth says." Except that Mikey was Emily's child. He had only her word against Mr. Ellesworth's. If only Mikey's age didn't fit the time Emily went to work at the orphanage.

Emily studied her hands, unable to look at Jesse. A moment later his footsteps faded away, taking with him every hope for her future.

She was a fallen woman. She knew Jesse would never see her as anything but a reflection of his mother. A woman he despised. He would feel the same toward Emily.

One thing she knew without a doubt. Mikey was not her child. She would never have allowed him to be adopted by someone and lose touch with him.

She didn't know how long she sat there, immersed in misery, before she began to think. Her shaky weakness gave way to determination, and she rose and went to the house.

Thankfully Jesse had departed. Her strength might not have lasted if she had to face him.

Gram's face was full of sympathy.

"I can't stay here any longer," Emily said and went upstairs to pack. It was all well and good for this Matron Hilda to say she should take Mikey back to Alliance, but how was she to do that? She was penniless, homeless and a woman with a shameful past.

She folded her few clothes into the basket. Even her clothes were not her own. She did the same for Mikey's clothes, pressing each little garment to her lips. *Oh, Mikey, if you were really mine I would never let you go.*

Gram came upstairs. "You don't have to leave. You will always be welcome here."

"I don't think everyone shares your opinion."

"Jesse can be a little hardheaded at times, but he's got a good heart. He'll come round."

Emily paused at her task and faced the older woman. "He has never forgiven his mother for her choices in life."

Gram nodded. "Like I say, he can be hard."

"He sees me as a copy of his mother. If he can't forgive her, I know he'll never grant me anything but his disdain."

Gram looked so sad that Emily wanted to hug her, but she wasn't sure how people would react after hearing Mr. Ellesworth's story. And she had no way of knowing if it was true or not.

"Where will you go?"

"I intend to throw myself on the mercy of the preacher and his wife."

"At least let me pay you for your help with the sewing."

"Absolutely not. You've given me a home for the past month. It is I who owe you." Her belongings were gathered up, her Bible on the top of her things. At least she had One friend she could count on. Jesus had promised to be with her always. She found comfort and strength in that assurance even as her throat closed off with pain she would not give voice to.

Downstairs she called Mikey to her. The boy took in the packed basket and gave her a surprised look.

"We go?" he asked.

"We're going to stay with Evan and his mama and papa." *If they'll have us.* There was every reason to think they would not. “Or we might find some other place.”

“Yesse go?”

“No, sweetie. Jesse has to stay with Gram and take care of her.”

“Muffin go?” He held onto the little dog’s fur.

“Evan has a dog, remember?”

“Me not go.”

“Don’t you want to play with Evan?”

Mikey looked at Muffin, at Gram and then at Emily. He read the determination in Emily’s face and sighed. “Me go.”

But not with any enthusiasm, Emily thought.

Gram hugged the boy. “Come and visit me often.”

“’Kay.”

Emily eased past Gram, wanting to quickly end this awkward moment.

Gram reached for her and pulled her into a warm embrace. “I know there is more or perhaps less to the story that man told, but how do we find out the truth?”

The tears Emily had been holding back threatened to pour from her eyes, and she turned away, grabbed her bag and headed for the door. *How do we find out the truth?* Why couldn’t Jesse have uttered those words?

Because, as she’d said, her story was too close to his mother’s.

Holding to Mikey’s hand, she went out the back gate and up the alley. Look at her. Hiding from public view because of accusations against her. There was something familiar about that thought. Had she really done what Mr. Ellesworth said? Why would she? It seemed so unlike who she felt she was. Had the blow to her head altered her personality?

What did it matter? She had no way of finding out the truth. There was nothing she could do.

Her feet ground to a halt. That wasn't exactly true. There was something she could do.

She reached the manse and knocked. Annie flung the door open.

"Come on in. What a nice surprise." She saw the basket on Emily's arm. "What's this?"

"You better hear my story before you let me in."

The two little boys ran off to play and Emily repeated the story Jesse had told her. "So I can't stay there."

"You can stay here."

"Are you sure? If people hear, they will judge you for having me."

"I would suggest they hear the words of our Lord, 'He that is without sin among you, let him first cast a stone.'" She pulled Emily into the kitchen. "We have lots of space." Annie led the way down a hall. "Choose your room."

"Thank you. I won't stay long." Just long enough to find a way to leave.

"Stay as long as you like. I'll leave you to get settled, then come and join me for tea." Annie slipped away.

Emily sat on the bed as every ounce of energy drained from her. A few minutes later she went to the kitchen. "There is something I must do. Can I borrow paper and pen to write a letter?"

"You'll find both in the front room. Help yourself."

"Thank you." She sat at the writing desk and composed her letter.

Dear Matron Hilda,
Thank you for the information regarding me. I still do not have my memory back and would like the address for my Aunt Martha so I can write her regarding my family.

I am currently unable to travel, but Mikey is safe with me and I will take good care of him.
Sincerely,
Emily Smith

As she signed her name she felt a touch of familiarity. Was this her customary signature? So many questions.

She sealed the envelope, tucked the letter into her pocket to mail later and returned to the kitchen where Annie shared tea with her.

How long before she couldn't enjoy such pastimes? As she'd once told Jesse, women with a soiled reputation were not welcomed in decent company. She doubted if Jesse would have any cause to repeat the story Mr. Ellesworth had told, but the latter had no reason not to spread it far and wide.

Jesse listened to the man before him. Mr. North had come in to complain about Fred Ellesworth.

"He wants my land so bad he's offering more than it's worth. At the same time, he's uttering vague threats. Says it's in my best interest to sell now while I can. He even went so far as to say that if something happened to my wife or one of my sons I might wish

I had left earlier. Now, I know you might think it was simply idle conversation, but I saw the look in his eyes and the way his mouth turned into an ugly smile as he looked at Johnny. I know a threat when I hear one." The man leaned forward. "Sheriff, there's something odd going on and I think you should find out what."

"I intend to do just that." This was the third man to come in with complaints about Ellesworth. "Let me do some investigating."

"Thanks, sheriff." Mr. North shook Jesse's hand and left.

It was time for Jesse to take a ride to Great Falls and ask a few questions, and he welcomed the excuse to leave town. The trio of murdering robbers had been tried and found guilty. Five days ago, Emily had moved out. It was for the best, Jesse told himself repeatedly. She was not the woman he'd thought her to be. Yes, he'd found her charming and sweet but having had a mother who was a soiled dove, he had no intention of repeating the experience with a courting-aged woman.

If he left town this afternoon, he would be absent from church and not have to endure seeing Emily sitting with Annie, Mikey at her side. His stomach soured to know she'd been willing to let the boy go to strangers or live the rest of his life in an orphanage. At least Jesse's mother had left him with a loving grandmother.

He found Clarence and told him he was in charge while Jesse was gone. "I'll be back when I find out what's going on." He bought some supplies at the store and let George know his intention. Then he saddled his horse and stopped at the house to pick up his bedroll and tell Gram his plans.

"You are misjudging Emily." She'd repeated the same message every time Jesse came home.

"I wish I could believe it, but all the evidence says otherwise." He threw some cookies into a sack.

"You believe that man. I don't care for his shifty eyes."

She might be more right about that man than she knew. "There's also a letter that substantiates his story."

"Jesse, the way I see it, this isn't so much about Emily as it is about your mother."

He stopped rummaging through the cupboards for food to take with him and stared at her. "There are similarities, but this isn't about my mother."

"Those similarities are blinding you to the possibility of other explanations."

"Hogwash." He found a can of peaches and two of beans and added them to his stash. "I'll be back when I find out why Mr. Ellesworth is so interested in certain pieces of land."

"I pray when you get back you will have learned the truth about what's in your own heart."

He knew what was in his heart, and it was caution. Determination not to live the same pain he'd endured as a child—the shame of illegitimacy, the shame of what his mother did and the disappointment of having her choose a life of shame over him.

He left town and rode until dark before he stopped and made a cold camp. After riding so many hours, he should have fallen asleep immediately, but instead, he lay awake, looking up at the stars. How was Emily? Did Mikey miss him? Did she? Who was she?

Scene after scene replayed in his head. The trip to the waterfalls. The visits to the Marshall Five Ranch. The afternoon spend at the house on the edge of town. He folded his hands under his head. He'd been so full of dreams after that day. Dreams that involved her.

Was she like his mother? Was that why Mr. Ellesworth's story had hurt him so badly? All through his childhood, until his mother's death, he'd wanted only for her to stay and make a home with him and Gram. It had cut to the bone when he learned that she chose other men over him.

He sat up as he tried to sort out his tangled thoughts. He hadn't even given Emily the opportunity to explain or the option of choosing a different sort of life. Was he willing to give her a chance? Let her start over? Forget her past? He snorted. She wanted to remember her past and here he was, wanting her to forget it.

But was it that easy?

He lay back, longing for sleep. Eventually it came, but he rose the next morning feeling groggy and he fought to shake off the sluggishness.

He reached Great Falls late in the afternoon. Because it was Sunday, he waited until the next morning to go to the sheriff and present his questions about why Mr. Ellesworth was so interested in certain parcels of land.

"I can't say, but I know someone who might know." They went over to the lawyer's office and learned that he and Mr. Ellesworth were cousins.

The lawyer came out of his chair at Jesse's question about the land. "He vowed he would not take advantage of the information I inadvertently revealed to him." The lawyer went on to explain that one of his clients was on the board of a railway company looking to expand west, and Bella Creek was under consideration to be on the route. "Nothing is certain yet, but he's obviously bent on taking advantage of those folks."

The next morning Jesse started the return trip. He stopped early in the evening, built a fire and made a pot of coffee. So, Mr. Ellesworth was a scoundrel. But did that make his news about Emily any less true? Why would he fabricate a story about her?

Did he fear she would regain her memory and have unfavorable things to say about him? Did he hope, by spreading his story, to discredit anything Emily said?

Jesse could see that as a possibility.

He hunkered down at the fire, watching the flames flicker and dance. He had no idea what to believe.

Both Emily and Gram said he needed to forgive his mother. He knew it to be so. It was easy to talk about forgiveness, but how could he let this lump of anger and disappointment go?

He tossed a stick into the fire and watched it burn until only red coals remained.

The fire had consumed it.

The thought flared within his head. Was forgiveness the same? Could he simply toss it out and watch it be reduced to ashes?

He got to his feet and picked up several sticks. "Father God, all my life I waited for her to change. She never did and still I waited for something to be different. Now I see it's me that needs to change. I need to let go of what was, just like I let go of this stick and let the fire burn it up." He tossed it into the fire. It caught immediately and the flames flared upward. "I let go of what I hoped for and accept what I have. I have a good life, a grandmother who loves me and raised me to do right. I have a job I like and I'm good at." He tossed another stick into the fire and watched the flames lick it up. "And, maybe, I have a chance for the home and love I've always dreamed of." He tossed the rest of the sticks into the fire, letting go of his fears and anger at the same time.

It didn't matter what Mr. Ellesworth said about Emily, he'd seen who she truly was in the way she took care of Mikey, in the way she laughed and cried, in the things she enjoyed, like the roses at the empty house.

Somehow he had to convince her that she was exactly what he wanted in his life. What he'd wanted for many years.

His heart lurched against his ribs.

What if she had left Bella Creek while he was away? Maybe gone to Alliance or even Lincoln? He would have no one but himself to blame. He'd practically told her to leave.

If she had gone, he would go after her. He would go after her and tell her that her past didn't matter. He'd follow her to the ends of the earth if he had to.

One thing he couldn't control—her reaction. Would she forgive him for being so hard-hearted toward her?

Chapter Sixteen

Emily stood in Annie's kitchen. Annie had taken the boys to visit Sadie. She'd invited Emily to accompany her but Emily had refused. She had thinking to do, and with everyone else out of the house, she had the perfect opportunity.

She needed a better plan than sitting around waiting. If she contacted her family they might forward her enough funds to return to Nebraska, but she hesitated to do so. What if they had disowned her? The letter to Matron Hilda crackled in her pocket. She hadn't mailed it yet, though she couldn't say why she was so reluctant to send it on its way. Perhaps she'd learn things about herself she didn't care to know.

She turned from the window and walked the length and breadth of the house trying to decide what she would do.

Gram had several times told her she needed help with her sewing. She said she might even consider retiring if someone would take over her clients. Emily could start up a seamstress business. The idea caught in her thoughts. Had she been a seamstress? Had her business failed? Why else would she be working in the orphanage, apart from the fact she loved children?

She made another circuit of the house. Wouldn't it be wonderful if she could stay in Bella Creek? She could rent the empty house from Grandfather Marshall and support herself with sewing and perhaps laundry.

The possibility made her insides tingle.

If she could support herself and a child, would she be allowed to keep Mikey?

A single woman might be allowed to adopt a child, but a fallen woman? Her excitement died as quickly as it flared.

Round and round went her feet. Round and round went her thoughts.

A loud noise shook the house. She rushed to a window. Thunder. Lightning. And then slashing rain closed the house in darkness.

Just like—

It all came rushing back.

A door somewhere opened. Jesse entered. She stared at him as if seeing him for the first time.

"Annie said I could find you here."

She nodded. "I remember." She swallowed hard. She had hoped for something other than what it was.

He must have read the distress in her face, understood that the way she drew her lips in indicated something unpleasant. He crossed the room and stood very close. "Whatever you remember, it doesn't matter. You can start over fresh here. I'm sorry for judging you. I want you to stay and give me a chance to prove I care about you."

She held out a hand to keep him at a distance. He'd

change his mind once he heard the truth. Jesse was a man who believed in black and white and no compromise.

He caught her hand. "Tell me everything."

"My name is Emily Eileen Smith. I am twenty-two years old. I am from Lincoln, Nebraska. My parents still live there. I was a seamstress. When I was eighteen, I made a wedding dress for my best friend. I needed to hem the dress and decided to take it out to Sharon's place for a final fitting.

"She wasn't there when I arrived. She'd gone to visit a neighbor. Only her brother Rolly was home. I never much cared for him. He often drank too much and carried on. Sort of wild, I guess. He said she would be back any minute, so I decided to wait. He went out to do whatever he was doing and I made myself a cup of tea.

"It was late October, and the weather had been mild but a storm came up as I drank my tea and read a book from their bookshelf. I should have been more careful. Should have watched the sky. Should have left as soon as I realized he was the only one home. But it was too late. The snow came in so fast and so heavy I could never have made it to town. I was stranded there the night.

"Rolly came in and laughed. He said, 'Just you and me now, Emily. What do you suggest we do?'

"I suggested he stay as far away from me as possible and spent the entire night sitting at the table with a poker at my side.

"Several times he looked at me and gave a mocking laugh. Finally, he went to the front room and fell asleep in the easy chair.

"By morning the storm had ended, the roads were passable and I returned to town, praying that would be the end of it." She had to take a breath to ease her lungs. They seemed to be made of wood. If only she had done things differently—but hindsight was of little value except to fuel regrets.

"I take it the story doesn't end there."

Jesse's voice startled her and she resumed her tale. "I should have known Rolly wouldn't let it go. He soon let it be known that I had spent the night with neither Sharon nor their parents present. I couldn't deny it, as several people saw me return at first light and had jumped to their own conclusions. He said we hadn't slept, but his tone conveyed that we had done other things."

She shuddered. "I hoped people would believe the best about me, but they were all too ready to believe the worst. Oh, not everyone. Sharon understood. But my business fell away until I had no orders. Someone draped red ribbons across my door to inform others of their opinion of me. I appealed to my parents. They arranged for me to go to Aunt Martha. Because no one in Alliance knew me, I was able to find work at the orphanage. I loved it. I loved the children."

She faced him squarely, boldly. "Mikey isn't my child, but he arrived shortly after I did and I found solace in taking care of him. It about broke my heart when Matron Hilda said he was being adopted." She drew in air that did nothing to ease the emptiness sucking at her lungs. That was it. Her whole sordid story.

"What about Mr. Ellesworth?"

"Oh, yes, him. He asked me several times to marry

him and I refused. I didn't care for him. I don't know how many times he introduced me as his fiancée. But I denied it just as many times."

"He won't be bothering you anymore. Turns out he is a land speculator. He's already riding away from town."

It was good to know, but it only reinforced her view of Jesse. He would never accept anyone who had been compromised. She was spent. All she wanted to do was cry but she would not allow herself to do so. She would face her future with strength and, Lord willing, a little boy she hoped to adopt. One more thing had to be made clear.

"So you see, the story he related is true. I am a ruined woman. Not fit for decent company. Annie has been kind enough to allow me to stay here, but I can't continue to take advantage of her kindness. Once people hear about me, there will be judgment. Now, I don't want to make the same mistake twice by being alone with a man, so I'm going to have to ask you to leave."

"Emily—"

"Please."

He didn't move but she refused to look at him. It would hurt too much to see disgust in his face. She had done nothing wrong. Yes, she'd been foolish, but she hadn't done anything wrong—yet she wore the same label his mother had worn. He would never see her in any other way.

Finally, without a word, he left the house and she collapsed. But she would not cry. She lifted her head. She would not let her past mistakes control her life forever. She patted the letter in her pocket. No need to mail it now.

Annie and the boys clattered into the house and Emily pushed aside her concerns.

"I see Jesse is back." Annie hung her bonnet on a peg as she talked. "He barely acknowledged me. I wonder what made him so angry."

"I might be responsible."

Annie turned to consider her. "Why would you say that?"

"My memory has returned."

"Wonderful." Annie crossed the floor and hugged Emily.

Emily did not return the embrace. "I wish I could think it was."

Annie stepped back. "Tell me all about it."

"Mr. Ellesworth's story was mostly correct." She quickly related the details of her past. "Jesse cannot associate with someone like me."

Annie squinted at her. "Did he say that?"

Emily shrugged. "He didn't need to. He's a man who makes no compromises."

"There is no need for him to do so. You were in an unfortunate situation but you did nothing wrong."

Emily's tension eased at Annie's kind words. "Not everyone will agree with you."

"I don't care if they don't."

Emily chuckled, but her amusement ended abruptly. "I can't stay here any longer."

"But where will you go?"

"I don't know." She went to the window.

"Do you want to go home?"

The question made her realize what she wanted.

"I'd like to return to Alliance and seek permission to adopt Mikey." But how was she do to it without any funds?

"Go see Grandfather. He'll gladly help you."

She faced Annie. "I couldn't do that." To reveal her disgrace to yet another person was more than she could contemplate.

"You don't have to tell him the details if you don't want. I promise your story will never be repeated by my lips. But even if you did tell him, he would not judge you. And he'd love to help you adopt Mikey. It's just the sort of thing he enjoys doing. He's a match-maker, you know."

Emily had heard many stories about his match-making.

"Helping a child and a woman who loves him become a family would be a joy for him. You'd actually be doing him a favor."

Emily began to nod. Grandfather Marshall might be the one person who could help her. "You're right. Thank you for suggesting it." The short-lived storm had passed over and the sun shone. "I'll go out there this afternoon and speak to him. Can I leave Mikey here?"

"By all means. I will pray things work out for you. I hope you consider staying in the community. I've grown quite fond of you." She hugged Emily again and this time Emily hugged her back.

She went to the livery barn, rented a buggy and drove out to the ranch. Grandfather Marshall was thrilled to be able to help her and she returned some time later feeling—for the first time since her memory returned—that she could make a new life for herself.

With keys in hand, she went to the empty house at the edge of town and walked through it. This was to be her home. She would pay the rent as soon as she had income. One room would serve as her sewing room. Hopefully she would soon have customers.

Grandfather had assured her there was no need to go back to Alliance to seek permanent custody of Mikey.

"You write a letter. I'll write one, as well. My lawyer will take care of the rest."

A wagon rumbled to the front of the house and two cowboys from the ranch jumped down and began to carry in the furniture Grandfather Marshall had said would be part of their rental agreement. She didn't need much—a worktable for her sewing room, a couch for the sitting room, a kitchen table and chairs. Besides that, two beds for the rooms upstairs.

Excitement fluttered in her stomach. She was really going to do this. It felt right in every way but one.

How would she live in the same town as Jesse, see him often and endure the way her heart cracked every time she thought of him?

But changing her location would not make her heart hurt any less, so she might as well stay here where she felt she belonged.

Jesse watched the wagon pull up to the house and unload furniture. Someone was moving in. He couldn't deny a sense of disappointment at the death of his dream.

Emily had not given him a chance to explain that her past didn't matter to him. It seemed to matter to her, though.

He talked to Gram about it. "I don't care what people say about her. She did nothing wrong."

"I agree, but she's right. Not everyone will see it that way." Gram studied him for a moment without speaking. "She doesn't want to hurt you."

"Not letting me tell her how I feel hurts."

"She knows how you feel about your mother. Perhaps she fears you will view her in the same jaded way."

"I've forgiven my mother." He told Gram of his experience.

She hugged him. "Good for you."

"I wanted to tell Emily but she wouldn't let me."

Gram chuckled. "All I can say is that actions speak louder than words."

He squinted at her. "What do you mean?"

"I'll let you figure it out. Now, leave me to do my work." She looked past him. "I do wish Emily would take over my business. I'm getting too old for this."

Her remark took him aback. For some reason, he saw her as timeless, always the same, always there. Of course it wasn't so. He patted her shoulder. "You don't need to keep doing this. I can support us."

"I know. But I hate to leave my customers without an alternative."

"I hope something works out for you." He left the house, swung to Rocky's back and trotted down the street to see who was moving into the empty house.

The front door stood open, allowing him a glimpse of a woman sweeping the floor. He slowed and stared. Emily?

She was staying in town.

His sat back in the saddle and chuckled, knowing

he'd been given a second chance. One he didn't intend to waste.

Gram had said actions spoke louder than words. Starting today, his actions would show how much he cared for and respected her.

He went back home, collected some tools and returned to Emily's house, where he went to the backyard and began to cut down the overgrown weeds. An hour later he was hot, dusty and sweaty. He straightened and looked about. It would take several afternoons to achieve his goal of turning the overgrown yard into the beautiful garden it had once been.

After stretching his back and rubbing his neck, he returned to the task. Several times he glanced toward the house, hoping for a glimpse of Emily, but not once did he see her.

It was almost suppertime when he left the yard. He'd come back tomorrow.

He returned early the next morning, before the day grew too hot. By noon he'd not seen her at the house, and with other things to tend to, he had to leave, disappointed. But he wasn't about to give up.

Saturday morning, he again returned. He'd been there an hour when he heard doors slamming, and he jerked around to watch the house. The back door flew open and Mikey ran to him, yelling, "Yesse," at the top of his lungs.

Jesse caught the boy and swung him overhead then hugged him tight. "I missed you, little cowboy."

Mikey hugged Jesse's neck so hard he could scarcely breathe.

Emily came to the door and watched them cautiously. Then she saw the garden. He'd cleaned out one corner. Her eyes widened and she rushed to the bushes, touching the half-dozen red roses.

"You did this?"

He nodded.

"Did Grandfather Marshall ask you to?"

"No one asked me." He shifted Mikey to one side so he could watch her more closely.

"Then why?"

"Because I saw you moving into the house and knew how much you would enjoy the flowers."

"But why?"

He understood that she meant more than the work he had done. He lowered Mikey to the ground and took a step closer to Emily. "Because actions speak louder than words."

She shook her head. "I don't understand."

"The other day I wanted to tell you something but you didn't give me a chance."

"I'm sorry. I've been struggling to deal with getting my memory back and deciding what I'm going to do. What did you want to tell me?"

He moved closer, close enough to see the blue sky of her eyes. And something he hadn't seen in her gaze before—a sense of purpose, perhaps. "You were right about my need to forgive my mother. And I have."

He told her of how he'd tossed the pieces of wood into the fire. "I let go of my hurt. Something else, too. I realized I was judgmental. I think you saw that in me." He hoped it was, in part, the reason she had asked him to leave rather than give him the opportunity to respond to her confession.

"I'm happy for you. But that doesn't explain this." She waved her hand to indicate the garden.

"I don't care about what happened to you four years ago. You did nothing wrong. And you can be assured Mr. Ellesworth will not bother you again. He should be in jail." He explained how the man had tried to take advantage of the landowners. "I don't see you as a fallen woman, a ruined woman or a woman with a shameful secret."

"How do you see me?"

He caught her hand and drew her into the seclusion of the gazebo. "I see you as a kind, sweet, noble, upright, devoted woman. Do I need to go on?"

She sank to the wooden seat. "Are you sure?"

He sat beside her and took her hands. "Very sure. I'm asking you to give me another chance to show you I care. This is just a start." He indicated the garden, where Mikey had collected twigs and leaves into a pile.

She withdrew her hands. "I rented this house. I'm going to start a seamstress business. Your grandmother said she would welcome me doing so."

"Just the other day she told me she wished she didn't have to continue sewing. Said she was too old."

"I'm glad she won't mind me running a business like hers. But that's not all I've decided to do. I'm going to try and adopt Mikey. Grandfather Marshall offered to help me." She wrapped her arms about her chest. "I'm almost afraid to think a single woman will be allowed to adopt."

He could change her single status, but he feared to rush her and lose her. He'd let his actions speak for him.

It took him four days to get the garden into the shape it should be. There was a section intended for growing vegetables. It was too late in the season to plant most things; however, he marked out rows and planted lettuce, carrots and potatoes. If she watered them regularly she would at least get small vegetables.

The day he finished, he looked at the door. Should he knock and show Emily the garden? Or let her discover it herself?

Actions speak louder than words.

He went out the back gate.

Day by day, he'd grown surer of how he felt. He'd let his actions speak.

Emily looked out the window to the back garden expecting to see Jesse there. He was gone. She'd been doing her best to avoid him despite the longing that drew her often to the window. She sensed he cared for her, but she needed time to sort out who she was. Was she the same Emily who had arrived in Bella Creek without any memory? Or was she the Emily who had been foolish enough to be caught in a compromising situation?

Or was she someone else?

Day by day she was learning more about herself. She was strong, ready to face the challenges of her life. She would do it alone if she must, but as the days passed, she grew aware of an empty spot in her heart that had Jesse's name on it.

But she had to make sure of how she felt, not only for her sake, but for Mikey's. The boy loved Jesse. She didn't want him hurt if her feelings or Jesse's were temporary.

She left the house and went to the garden. Jesse's work had uncovered a row of red rose bushes. Pink and yellow buds revealed the other colors. Other flowers would soon bloom now that they had been set free from the weeds. She reached the fallow part and saw several rows marked out. She'd have to ask what he'd planted.

The gazebo beckoned and she went inside. A bouquet of flowers in a tin can sat on a bench. She sat across from the display and stared at it, her mind and heart opening to the possibilities of love.

Could she be worthy of it? Could she accept it? Would loving Jesse compromise his upright way of life?

"Lord God, guide me the right direction. I don't want to make a mistake." One thing she'd learned was how far-reaching mistakes could be, even honest ones committed with no malice or evil intended.

By Saturday she had made up her mind and walked up the street to Gram and Jesse's house.

Gram welcomed her with open arms and Muffin ran circles around Mikey, yapping happily.

"It's about time you paid me a visit."

"Thank you for all the business you are sending my way."

"I'm happy to. I'm thinking of retiring completely."

Emily wondered at the brightness in Gram's cheeks. "I've come to invite you and Jesse to join me for dinner after church tomorrow."

"Oh, that would be lovely, dear. I'm anxious to see your house."

"You're welcome to visit anytime."

Gram drew her inside and served tea. Later, Emily returned to her house, smiling in anticipation of her plans.

* * *

Sunday morning arrived, and with it a song in her heart and on her lips. She checked the roast in the oven and the rest of the meal preparation. She'd made a beautiful chocolate cake with thick butter frosting plus cookies for later in the afternoon should Jesse linger. And Gram, she added. She hadn't forgotten Gram.

Mikey sat at the table swinging his feet. "Yesse come? Gam come?"

Emily bent over the child to hug him and plant a kiss on his head. "Yes, sweet boy, they are coming after church."

She had loved all the children at the orphanage but none as much as Mikey. As she always did when she thought of her hope to adopt him, she prayed for God to make it possible.

Cooking for the children and staff had been one of the tasks she enjoyed, and it had certainly taught her how to prepare large meals. It was a challenge to remind herself that she only had herself and Mikey to cook for. Today she would double that.

"How about I wash your hands and face, and we leave for church?"

"'Kay."

They were soon on their way. Jesse stepped into the street ahead of them. She had timed it perfectly. He looked both ways and waited when he saw them. Mikey ran headlong into his arms and there he remained, his arm around Jesse's neck.

"Good morning," Jesse said. "I understand we are having dinner at your place."

"That's right." Their gazes caught and held, full of warmth and wonder as she recalled a previous Sunday afternoon spent there. Her hope and prayer was that today would be every bit as memorable.

She hadn't planned to sit beside him. On the other hand, she didn't object as they slid into a pew next to Gram. It was as if nothing had changed.

The thought sobered her. *She* had changed. Now she knew who she was and how she'd been judged for a foolish decision.

Hugh took his place. His gaze found her and he smiled. He'd been so kind and helpful the few days she'd spent at his house. No wonder Annie had fallen in love with him.

The hymns were familiar and joy flooded her being.

Then Hugh announced his text. "Second Corinthians chapter five, verse seventeen: 'Therefore if any man be in Christ, he is a new creature: old things are passed away; behold, all things are become new.'"

She drank in hope and assurance as he spoke of the work Christ had done for His followers. Just like new. Unblemished. She clung to the word. In her mind she saw the scarlet ribbon someone had pinned to her door removed by a loving Hand, the label given her taken away.

She knew she was innocent, but it was even better to know she did not have to carry her past with her.

Grandfather Marshall called her name as they left the church. "How is your new home?"

"Lovely, thank you. I've invited Jesse and Gram to have dinner with me."

"I wouldn't mind seeing how you've fixed up the house." He waggled his bushy brows and darted a look at Gram.

Seems the matchmaker had found his own match. Good for them both. "Would you care to join us?"

"What a generous offer." He winked. "I accept."

She looked at his canes.

He nodded. "I can walk that far. I will just take longer than you young folk. You go ahead. I'll get Grace to keep me company."

"You do that." Emily laughed as she looked for Mikey. He perched in Jesse's arms.

Jesse joined her. "Are you ready to leave?"

"Yes, please."

Jesse looked around as they entered her house. "You've made it very cozy."

"It's through the generosity of the Marshalls and Gram. I have nothing of my own." She hoped he wouldn't think she complained, because she was feeling more than blessed. Already her business was thriving. In time, she would replace the borrowed items with her own things.

"Can I help with the meal?" Jesse asked.

"Can you set the table for me?"

He grinned. "Lady, Gram had taught me to set a proper table by the time I was eight." He reached past her for plates.

She held very still, ignoring the urge to turn into his arms and press her face to his chest.

He moved away. The air between them crackled with tension.

She stirred the gravy with undue vigor.

By the time Grandfather and Gram arrived, the table was set and the meal on the table.

She might have worried that the tension between herself and Jesse would make conversation awkward, but Mikey told a long, involved story about Evan's dog that had them laughing, and Gram and Grandfather told stories of their childhoods.

They finished up with her cake and it earned her lots of praise.

As soon as the dishes were done and the food put away, she turned to Jesse.

"I have something to show you." She glanced at the older couple, not wanting to exclude them.

Gram waved her away. "I'd like to sit, if you don't mind."

"Not at all." Mikey opted to stay with Gram and show her the little booklet he and Emily had made with pictures he drew—with a little help from Emily.

Emily and Jesse went outdoors and stood side by side, admiring the garden. "I haven't thanked you properly for all the work you did for me. Thank you."

"My pleasure."

They reached the gazebo but she paused without going in. "You said actions speak louder than words. I'd like to hear what words you meant." She faced him, wanting to…needing to see his eyes and his mouth as he responded to her request.

He looked down at her, dark eyes inviting her to explore. She opened her thoughts to him, as well, holding nothing back, hoping he would see all that was in her heart.

He lifted his hand and pressed his palm to her jaw. She leaned into his touch.

He cleared his throat. "There are so many words. First, I want to say that I don't in any way brand you as those in your past have. Second, I want to make sure you understand that I think you belong here."

"In Bella Creek?"

He pressed his free hand to his chest. "And here."

Her breath lodged somewhere in her throat.

"If you choose." His voice deepened to a groan.

She couldn't let his uncertainty remain. "I choose."

"Really?" Joy wreathed his face.

"Yes. Come inside."

He followed her inside. She'd cut flowers and greenery to fill jars in each corner. She'd prepared a little picnic basket. "I know you're not hungry, but I thought you might enjoy some fudge."

He caught her hand. "Is this how *your* actions speak louder than words?"

She moved closer. "Flowers and candy are supposed to say something special."

"They're romantic."

She nodded.

"Does it mean what I hope it means?"

"Depends what you hope."

"I hope it means you feel for me like I feel about you."

"And what would that be?"

"Emily, I love you. Forever and always. I know I should take my time, but I can't. I want to share your life. Make a home with you and Mikey. Will you marry me?" He paused, hope and uncertainty in his eyes.

"Jesse Hill, I love you so much my insides feel full of fudge. Yes, I will marry you."

His arms closed about her and he bent his head to give her a sweet, promising kiss. In his embrace she knew exactly who she was. A woman loved by a noble and strong man.

Epilogue

They waited throughout what was left of the summer, enjoying bright days and sweet evenings. They wanted the paperwork on Mikey's adoption to be in order before they married.

The day finally came. Their wedding day.

Emily looked down at her gown. She'd chosen pale pink silk and had sewn the dress herself. Annie was to be her only bridesmaid.

"Are you ready?" her father asked.

She smiled up at him, through tears. "Having you and Mother here is the best gift I could dream of." She had written them to let them know of her location and her plans. They had arrived two days ago.

"Your mother and I are so happy you have found a place where you are accepted as the beautiful, pure young lady you are. Jesse is a good man." He kissed her cheek. "And he's probably tired of waiting."

They followed Annie down the aisle. Emily almost stumbled at the sight of Jesse at the front, dark and handsome in a black suit with Mikey holding his hand.

Three years old already. He wore a black vest,

black trousers and a white shirt, all of which Emily had made.

They went forward. Emily kissed her father and mother then turned to Jesse and repeated the vows as Hugh prompted them. After exchanging rings they stood to the side, beaming with joy as Gram and Grandfather then came to the front and were married. The two couples signed the register. Then the judge set out the adoption papers and they were duly signed.

Hugh stood before the people of Bella Creek. "Folks, I present to you Mr. and Mrs. Allan Marshall."

Gram and Grandfather kissed, then made their way down the aisle to cheering and clapping.

Hugh signaled Jesse and Emily forward. "I present to you Mr. and Mrs. Jesse Hill and their son, Michael Jesse Hill."

"That me?" Mikey asked.

"It is indeed." Jesse lifted him into the crook of one arm. Emily took his other arm and they made their way down the aisle, receiving many words of congratulations.

Later that evening, Mikey went to stay with Annie.

Jesse carried Emily over the threshold of their home. "I often dreamed of a wife and child living in this house."

Still in his arms, she pulled his head down to kiss him. "I am thrilled to help make your dreams come true."

"Dear wife, you are my dream come true." He kissed her again. "Are you happy?"

"Happier than I've ever been before."

He set her on her feet and tipped her head up to claim her lips in a kiss full of so much promise and love she wondered her heart could contain it.

* * * * *

If you enjoyed this story, pick up the previous BIG SKY COUNTRY *books:*

MONTANA COWBOY DADDY
MONTANA COWBOY FAMILY
MONTANA COWBOY'S BABY
MONTANA BRIDE BY CHRISTMAS
MONTANA GROOM OF CONVENIENCE

Available now from Love Inspired Historical!

Dear Reader,

Jesse has been in every one of the Big Sky Country books previous to this, so it was necessary to give him his own story. I have never before written an amnesia story and found it both a challenge and a pleasure. I hope the lessons both Jesse and Emily learned about dealing with their pasts and their futures will help you find the same assurance of God's love and care.

You can learn more about my upcoming books and how to contact me at www.lindaford.org. I love to hear from my readers.

Blessings,

Linda Ford

COMING NEXT MONTH FROM
Love Inspired® Historical

Available May 8, 2018

HIS SUBSTITUTE MAIL-ORDER BRIDE
Return to Cowboy Creek • by Sherri Shackelford

When the bride train arrives in Cowboy Creek, Russ Halloway is shocked to discover his carefully selected mail-order bride is instead his ex-fiancée's little sister—all grown up. Anna Linford's looking for a fresh start—and to keep her secrets hidden from the one man who, should he discover them, could break her heart.

BABY ON HER DOORSTEP
by Rhonda Gibson

To raise the little girl left on her doorstep, schoolteacher Laura Lee's only option is becoming a temporary live-in nanny for rancher Clint Shepard. The arrangement was supposed to be temporary, but soon the single dad's wishing Laura and her baby can become a permanent part of his family.

ACCIDENTAL SWEETHEART
The Bachelors of Aspen Valley • by Lisa Bingham

Lydia Tomlinson will do anything to keep stranded mail-order brides in the Batchwell Bottoms mining camp—even going up against Pinkerton detective Gideon Gault, who watches over the ladies. But when a gang of outlaws threatens the town, Gideon and Lydia must band together to stop the thieves—and to fight any force that would keep them apart.

LAST CHANCE WIFE
by Janette Foreman

Stranded in Deadwood, Dakota Territory, after a failed mail-order match, Winifred Sattler convinces Ewan Burke to give her a job in the general store attached to his gold mine. Busy trying to keep his fledgling operation open, Ewan has no time for distractions—except he can't stop picturing his life with Winifred by his side...forever.

SPECIAL EXCERPT FROM

Love Inspired® HISTORICAL

When widowed Anna Linford comes to Cowboy Creek as a last-minute mail-order bride replacement, she expects to be rejected. After all, her would-be groom, Russ Halloway, is the same man who turned down her sister! But when they learn she's pregnant, a marriage of convenience could lead to new understanding, and unexpected love.

Read on for a sneak preview of
HIS SUBSTITUTE MAIL-ORDER BRIDE,
the heartwarming continuation of the series
***RETURN TO COWBOY CREEK*.**

"I don't want another husband."

Russ grew sober. "You must have loved your husband very much. I didn't mean to sully his memory by suggesting you replace him."

"It's not that." Anna's head throbbed. Telling the truth about her marriage was far too humiliating. "You wouldn't understand."

"Try me sometime, Anna. You might be surprised."

One of them was going to be surprised, that was for certain. Philadelphia was miles away, but not far enough. The truth was bound to catch up with her.

"If you ever change your mind about remarrying," Russ said, "promise you'll tell me. I'll steer you away from the scoundrels."

LIHEXP0418

"I won't change my mind." Unaccountably weary, she perched on the edge of a chair. "I'll be able to repay you for the ticket soon."

"We've gone over this," he said. "You don't have to repay me."

Why did he have to be so kind and accommodating? She hadn't wanted to like him. When she'd taken the letter from Susannah, she'd expected to find the selfish man she'd invented in her head. The man who'd callously tossed her sister aside. His insistent kindness only exacerbated her guilt, and she no longer trusted her own instincts. She'd married the wrong man, and that mistake had cost her dearly. She couldn't afford any more mistakes.

"I don't want to be in your debt," she said.

"All right. Pay your fare. But there's no hurry. Neither of us is going anywhere anytime soon."

She tipped back her head and studied the wrought iron chandelier. She hated disappointing him, but staying in Cowboy Creek was out of the question. Russ wasn't the man she remembered, and she wasn't the naive girl she'd been all those years ago.

LIHEXP0418